Patrick Francis Mullany

Essays educational

Patrick Francis Mullany

Essays educational

ISBN/EAN: 9783337215378

Printed in Europe, USA, Canada, Australia, Japan

Cover: Foto ©Andreas Hilbeck / pixelio.de

More available books at **www.hansebooks.com**

ESSAYS

EDUCATIONAL

BY
BROTHER AZARIAS
Of the Brothers of the Christian Schools

WITH PREFACE BY
HIS EMINENCE CARDINAL GIBBONS

CHICAGO
D. H. MCBRIDE & CO.
1896

PREFACE

$\mathfrak{T}$HIS new edition of the lectures of Brother Azarias, delivered at Plattsburg in July, 1893, is an interesting history of the growth and development of educational institutions under the guiding hand of the Church.

Who that is acquainted with the writings of Brother Azarias need be assured of the treat in store for him in this volume?

In classic style, with an ease and grace that spring from a thorough knowledge of his subject, he sketches with a master's hand the efforts of our forefathers in the attainment of learning and the methods they adopted to accomplish their laudable object.

To many it will be a surprise to learn that the education of the young was a matter of great solicitude to the bishops and priests of the so-called Dark Ages.

Brother Azarias shows that primary schools were established and maintained, not by taxation, but by the self-denying efforts of teachers and the voluntary contributions of the people.

This volume contains a fund of knowledge in detail. It manifests a large reading, a retentive

memory and power of condensation, without, however, the affectation of learning, the cumbersomeness
of erudition, or the indistinctness of a too concise
diction.

The book would prove useful and interesting to
the students and professors in our colleges, seminaries and monasteries, and I hope it will meet the
welcome it deserves.

CONTENTS

CLOISTRAL SCHOOLS

(1)

CLOISTRAL SCHOOLS.[1]

I.

WE name this book only to call attention to the character of its statements. They are many of them wild and misleading, We are told, for instance, that the cause of deficiency in the civilization of the Chinese is to be found in the fact that their whole education was a system of memorizing. This is news indeed. But it is an assertion that is likely to go unchallenged. Few of Mr. Johonnot's readers interest themselves in the complex machinery of Chinese education. Then the author starts off with what he calls the monkish method of memorizing. What that method was, he does not tell us; instead, he lays before us what he considers a toothsome piece of information.

Here is the sweet tid-bit on which our public-school teachers have been chewing for the past ten years:

"The effort of the monkish teachers was as much directed to the exclusion of such knowledge as did not directly suggest their views and authority, as it was to promulgate that of the opposite kind. The school did little or nothing to banish ignorance from the people. Science was interdicted by the

---

[1] *American Ecclesiastical Review.*

"Principles and Practice of Teaching" by James Johonnot. New York, D. Appleton & Co. 1881.

Church as opposed to religion. 'For centuries,' says Hallam, 'to sum up the account of ignorance in a word, it was rare for a layman of whatever rank to know how to sign his name.'"[1]

It is indeed difficult to hold one's soul in peace under the provocation of such reckless writing. Does Mr. Johonnot know that Hallam's assertion has been thoroughly refuted by Maitland in his "Dark Ages"? But it is clear that the light which Maitland has thrown upon this period has shone in vain for Mr. Johonnot.

Now, we have not far to go to find an opposite teaching. Since Hallam wrote and Maitland wrote men are in a position to know better. They can make at the present day no more sweeping assertions concerning the Middle Ages than they can concerning the nineteenth century. We pick up the latest magazine that comes upon our desk, and we read:

"If the fourteenth century village was less ill off than we are apt to imagine it in regard to the medicines of the body, it appears that the training of the mind was less absolutely non-existent in the rural class than it has been our habit to assert. Many of the laborers on the farms of Bonis could sign their names, though probably their science in writing ended there. But every tenant farmer in an age when the accounts of tenant and landlord were peculiarly complicated, was obliged to know a certain amount of bookkeeping; doubtless the steward was often more learned than his lord. Hedge-schools were common; in every considerable village, if not in every hamlet, there was a

---

[1] "Principles and Practice of Teaching," p. 170.

school-master, appointed generally by the patron of the village-living." [1]

This is history; this is truth. It is the outcome of painstaking research. But we dare say, the myth of Hallam's rare layman who could sign his name will continue to pass down upon the tide of prejudice until Macaulay's forthcoming New Zealander shall label it in some future museum with his sketch of the ruins of St. Paul's. But in the meantime we ask ourselves in all earnestness: How comes it that we find disseminated among our public-school teachers, as knowledge, as clear-cut information, statements so reeking with ignorance and prejudice and bigotry? Why is it that the intelligence of this respectable body must be insulted by such gross, unhistorical assertions? Surely, of all men, should educators be familiar with the latest and most accurate word in history, in literature, or in science.

Note how Mr. Johonnot groups all mediæval education under the one heading "monkish," and then brushes it away with a single sweep of his pen. Has it occurred to him — does he know — the number and variety of schools that existed in the early and middle ages? There were rural schools; there were episcopal schools; there were cathedral schools; there were grammar schools; there were cloistral schools; there were the early seminaries, the colleges, the palace school, and the university. Thus do we find the monastic school only one out of many. However,

_____

[1] *The Fortnightly Review*, December, 1890. Art., Rural Life in France in the 14th Century, by A. Mary F. Robinson (Madame James F. Darmstetter).

since the author unwittingly called attention to the
education given by the monks, it may be of interest
to examine the methods followed and the education
imparted in the cloistral schools.

II.

Cloistral schools begin with the establishment of
monastic institutions.　We find them flourishing under Pachomius at Tabenna in the first half of the
fourth century.　The doors of his monastery were
open to children as well as to men.　Lessons were
given three times a day to those whose education was
deficient.　All were required to be familiar with the
Psalter and the New Testament.　Each house contained its own library.　Three times a week did a
brother, set apart for the purpose, explain at length
the truths and mysteries of Faith.　Catechumens
were also instructed at stated times.　The rules enter into such details as give us insight into the educational methods of the East.　Should the aspirant
to religious life not know how to read he shall be
sent to a brother appointed to teach, and standing
before him, he shall learn with all thankfulness.　Afterwards he shall learn to write letters, syllables,
words and names, and he shall be compelled to read
whether he will or no.　None shall be permitted to
remain in the monastery who has not learned to read
and who does not know some of the Scriptures — at
the very least the Book of Psalms and the New Testament.[1]

---

[1] " Regula S. Pachomii," cap. 139, 140.

As on the banks of the Nile, so was it in the monastery at Bethlehem.[1] And in the latter half of the fourth century, St. Basil organized similar schools in Cæsarea. So great was the reputation of this saint as an educator that the magistrates of the town urged him to direct their public school; and when he declined, the people assembled in a body and besought him to comply with their request. But Basil had another field of labor, into which he threw all his energies.[2] In the fifth century, Lerins under St. Honoratus became a nursery of learning and piety. There St. Eucherius had his two sons educated, the oldest being scarcely ten years when, in 410, he entered.[3] There St. Loup kindled the torch that he afterwards brought to Troyes. In the monastery of Our Lady, outside the walls of this city, he established a school that became famous. In like manner does the chivalric and large-hearted St. Martin of Tours establish schools near Poitiers, and at Marmoutier, near Tours.

Then, at the beginning of the sixth century, we come upon a celebrated school of nuns at Arles, under the guidance of St. Césaire. Their rules require that they be instructed, and that they devote not less than two hours daily to reading.[4] There are no less than two hundred of them, and they become renowned for the beautiful workmanship they produce in copying manuscripts both sacred and profane.[5]

---

[1] Mabillon, "Études Monastiques," Paris, 1691, p. 11.
[2] Fleury, "Hist. Eccles.," iii., liv. xiv., p. 545.
[3] "Lerins au Ve Siècle," par Abbé Goux.
[4] "Regula S. Cæsarii," xvii., Ed. Migne, t. 67. col. 1109.
[5] "Vita S. Cæsarii," cap. v. 44.

From the sixth to the eighth century these cloistral schools flourished. But the one who organized them, as he did all monastic life in the west, was St. Benedict.

We will not enter upon an account of his life. It is too well known. Suffice it to say here that to St. Benedict the civilized world owes a debt of gratitude of which it can never be quit. He established a rule that was for his day and generation a marvel of wisdom. In this rule, manual labor seems to predominate; but a glance at the temper and spirit of the times will show how thoughtful this great man was in giving out-door occupation to strong natures but ill-suited to pore over books. As time wore on, and men grew more civilized, and the desire for mental culture became more general, the monks were found equal to the emergency; and so their influence spread from clime to clime, till all lovers of learning hold them as blessed in memory as they are blessed in name.

True it is that the rules of St. Benedict say comparatively little about study, but it were false reasoning to conclude therefrom that all study was proscribed. Within the limitations of the strictest rules there is always freedom of action on many unnamed things according to times and places. And when Benedict recommends his brothers to write in a style brief, simple, and modest,[1] he presupposes that those brothers pursued preliminary studies. And so they did in fact. During his own lifetime Benedict took the young sons of the Roman nobility

---

[1] Rule, chap.

and educated them. These children were trained up to their fifteenth year with the youths whose parents had consecrated them to the service of God. Then they made choice either to remain and enter the novitiate or to withdraw into the world. Already, in the fifth century, we see the effects of this religious grounding upon men living in the world.

Thus Sidonius, singing the praises of Vectius, a distinguished military officer, says :

"He reads frequently in the Holy Scriptures, especially at his meals, thus partaking at the same time of food of the soul and food of the body. He often recites the Psalms, still oftener sings them."[1]

Later, Eginhardt, the biographer of Charlemagne, tells us that that great monarch had some one to read to him during his meals; among the subjects mentioned are ancient history and the works of St. Augustine, especially that saint's masterpiece, "The City of God."

Herein is a new ideal of greatness already established. St. Chrysostom, noting the great benefit of this religious education, thus exhorts parents :

"Do not withdraw your children from the desert before the time. Let the principles of holy discipline be impressed upon their minds, and virtue take root in their hearts. Should it take ten or even twenty years to complete their education in the monasteries, be not troubled on that account. The longer they are exercised in this gymnasium, the more strength they shall acquire. Better still, let there be no fixed time, and let their culture have no other term than the ripening of the fruits thereof."[2]

[1] See Fauriel, " Histoire de Gaule Meridionelle," i., p. 404.
[2] " Adv. Persecut. Monach." lib. iii., cap. 16.

This is a remarkable passage, showing the prevailing custom of the East and also the extensive course of education that must have been given in those monasteries. Indeed, Pope Syricius is so impressed with the order and discipline of the cloistral schools, that he strongly recommends priests to be ordained from candidates chosen almost exclusively from the monasteries.[1]

III.

To understand the rule of Benedict and the writings of the early Fathers as regards literary culture, we must remember that the training of the intellect, as well as the training of the hand, were not for their own sake. They were simply means to an end. It was the disciplining and the developing of the whole man towards something higher. It was the growth of soul towards perfection. All else was made subordinate to this aim. He who enters upon this course must be a willing candidate. "According as one advances in the way of piety and faith, the heart expanding and becoming more generous, one runs in the way of the commandments of the Lord by a sentiment of love and an ineffable meekness."[2]

Therefore, manual labor is not ordained for its own sake; it is simply laid down as an antidote to laziness, and seemingly as a means by which the intellect becomes freshened for study. Thus we are told that, laziness being the enemy of souls, the

---

[1] "Syr. Pap. Ep. i. ad Himerium Tarracon"., Hardouin, p. 857.

[2] Preface of St. Benedict to Rules.

brothers shall give certain times to manual labor, and certain other times to the reading of holy things. They shall labor from the first hour of the day to the fourth, and from the fourth till nearly the sixth they shall devote to the reading of holy things. Ignorance is not only a shame, it is very injurious for religious men. We should not be degenerate children of those Fathers of the Church so illustrious in every species of doctrine.

⋅But discipline and a method simple and easy for all are indispensable in order to acquire science. If anybody is desirous to read in particular, he may do so, provided he incommodes nobody. In winter, having risen from the table, the brothers shall devote the remaining time to reading or learning the Psalms. At the beginning of Lent a book shall be given to each brother, that he may read it from beginning to end. The whole of Sundays shall be passed in reading, except by those having offices and particular occupations. A brother shall be appointed to see that the time assigned for reading and study is so employed, and not otherwise.[1] Even casual visitors to the monastery must not leave without having the bread of life broken to them. And so, one of the points observed in receiving visitors is that a brother shall sit before them and shall first read some passage from Holy Writ, and he shall afterward receive them with all possible graciousness.[2] A beautiful custom this, sowing the seeds of many a rich harvest.

---

[1] Rules, chap. 48.
[2] Ibid., chap. 53.

Such was the intellectual side of the rule of St.
Benedict.   Dom Morel, commenting upon it, says:

"The reading that St. Benedict gives us as a fruitful remedy against laziness, comprises also study; and
of both reading and study, as of manual labor, we
should say that they must needs be of such a nature
as to belong to our state, otherwise they would not
guard us against idleness or loss of time." [1]

It was in this spirit that Benedict insisted that
the brothers should not lose time upon mere works
of the imagination.   He considered sufficient time
spent on them during the period of preparatory study.
Hence the solid character of the work done by those
men from Cassiodorus down to Dom Guéranger and
Cardinal Pitra.   Peter the Venerable has clearly and
beautifully expressed the Benedictine spirit of study
and writing in the following words:

"We cannot always plant or water; we must sometimes abandon the plow for the pen, and instead of
working fields we must turn up the pages of holy
letters.   Scatter upon paper the seeds of the word
of God, which in harvest time, that is, when your
books are finished, shall nourish your famished readers by the abundance of its fruits, and with celestial
bread shall banish the immortal hunger of their souls.
Thus will you become a silent preacher of the holy
word; while your lips shall be mute, from your hand
shall resound a powerful voice among many people,
and after your death the merit of your works shall
be all the greater before God in proportion as their
life shall be the more durable." [2]

---

[1] "Meditations sur le Règle de S. Benoit."   Paris, 1752,
p. 512.

[2] "Acta Ordin. S. Bened." Saec. v., pref. observ. x.   An-
tiquar. labor.

With the advance of civilization the Benedictine studies broadened, and Benedictine labors in the literary field grew apace. Grammar, rhetoric, and philosophy had their respective places in the program of the advanced student. His profane readings he learned to sanctify by prayer and mortification and the practice of obedience. In this lay the secret of the strength and great influence of the Benedictines. It is with permissible pride that the erudite and indefatigable Mabillon could write:

"Almost alone, the order of St. Benedict, for several centuries, maintained and preserved letters in Europe. There were no other masters in our monasteries, and frequently the cathedral schools drew theirs from the same source. It is only towards the end of the tenth and beginning of the eleventh century that secular clerics begin to teach."[1]

The masters were carefully chosen. Benedict laid stress upon three qualifications to be considered in electing a dean; namely, "his person, his wisdom, and his doctrine;"[2] and commentators agree that the word "doctrine" here includes learning. In the Rule as it was in vogue one hundred years after Benedict's day we read: "At hours appointed for reading the young religious shall be instructed by a skilful master."[3] We are told that St. Ferreol dispensed the abbot from all manual labor, that he might have time to study whatever he should teach his religious.[4] It was his duty to see that the master

[1] "Études Monastiques," p. 135.
[2] Rules, chap. 20.
[3] Mabillon "Études Monastiques," p. 18.
[4] Chap. 50.

was equal to his position.   He should devote three hours a day to the school of the professed brothers. He decided what studies each should pursue, according to respective talent, taste, and inclination.

Those teaching in the classes, or pursuing special studies and researches, were exempt from manual labor and the night-offices; but they rose for their devotions at four in the morning.   If it is noticed that a teacher is brutal or incompetent, he is to be removed at once and replaced by another of mature age, who shall be distinguished for his experience, and shall have given proof of certain meekness of character.   From the master let us turn to the schools.

IV.

The primary aim of the monastic school was to prepare candidates for the recruitment of the religious life.   This it was that gave tone and color to studies and discipline.   This was the uppermost idea with St. Basil when he was drafting the rules and regulations of these schools.   In fact, he puts the question:

"Should there be a master to instruct secular children?"

And he answers that under certain conditions secular children may be admitted.

"The Apostle has said: 'And you, fathers, provoke not your children to anger, but bring them up in the discipline and correction of the Lord.' If parents bringing their children here do so in this spirit, and if those receiving the children so offered can rear them in the discipline and correction of the Lord, let us observe the precept contained in these words: 'Suffer little children to come unto me, for of such is the Kingdom of Heaven.' But beyond this end and this hope I deem that it would not be agreeable to God, or convenient for us, or really useful." [1]

Basil received orphans into his schools, and also children from the hands of their parents before witnesses. He must have received girls as well as boys, for the great doctor lays stress on their being kept apart.

Benedict ordained a solemn ceremony to accompany the offering of a child to the service of God. The child's hand, together with the offering accompanying the child and the written promise in which the parents testified that they freely, of their own accord, without coercion of any kind, devoted this child to the service of God as a religious, were all tied together in the altar-cloth or veil.[2] The abbot or one deputed by him received the child as a sacred trust, to guard and protect against all evil and to bring up in the fear and love of God. But, as has already been seen, besides children so consecrated to religious life, and the orphans of which St. Basil speaks, there were children placed within the shadow of the sanctuary to shield them from temptation and confirm them in religious discipline and a knowledge of their religion; these might afterwards honorably return to the world. In this way were St. Maurus and St. Placidius brought up by St. Benedict from their

---

[1] " Regulæ Brevius Tractatæ," Interrog. ccxcii.
[2] Rules, chap. 59.

youth with many other children of the first families of Rome.[1]

These children had a rule of their own. They had their hours for study and play, for rising and retiring ; they sang in the choir and became gradually accustomed to the discipline of religious life. Benedict devotes a chapter to the manner in which old men and children should be treated. The brethren are commanded to have due regard for their feebleness. They must not observe rigorous fasts, and must eat more frequently. But we can best learn the spirit and scope of monastic schools from their great organizer, the large-minded Basil.

Boys are admitted when five or six years old. They should be kept apart from the older members of the community, by whom they should always be edified; "for," he adds, "he who is intellectually a boy is not to be distinguished from him who is a boy in years."[2] He would have their playgrounds so situated that in taking exercise and recreation they could not disturb the older members of the community. Their diet should be substantial and suited to their age and strength. For the daily prayers they were permitted to join the ancients ; but they were exempt from the night-offices.

Basil felt that the touchstone of all education is the formation of character. On this point he enters into details as minute as they are instructive. Does the boy quarrel with his companions? Let him be

---

[1] Mabillon, "Études Monastique," p. 65.

[2] " Regulæ Fusius Tractatæ," Interrog. xv. *Patrol*, Migne, 31, col. 952.

punished properly, and let both then make up. Does he eat or drink out of time? Let him fast the greater portion of the day. Has he lied, or uttered words of pride or vanity, or violated the rules seriously? Let him be chastised by abstention from food and by silence — *et ventre et silentio castigetur.* Has he been eating immoderately or been otherwise unruly at meals? Let him be removed from the table, and notice how the others eat with all the politeness prescribed by the rule. A boy is angry with a companion. Let him apologize to that companion, and even wait upon him for some time, according to the gravity of the fault; "for the continuance of this state of humiliation stifles the last spark of anger in the soul, while, on the contrary, a state of superiority disposes the soul for this vice." The faults of the child should always be corrected with paternal indulgence and with moderate language, and the mode of punishment should be according to the measure of the delinquency. Basil did not permit every master to administer punishment indiscriminately. There was one set apart for that duty, and for all serious faults the child was brought to him. This whole system of discipline tended to self-control.[1]

His rules for study are no less admirable. Indeed, his conception of the youthful intellect is such as would unqualifiedly approve itself to any modern educator. The key to all success lies in controlling the power of attention in the child. In order to repress wandering of the mind, he would have all

[1] Ibid. xv. 2.

F. E.—2

the child's time filled with one occupation or another. And he counsels the master to ask the boys from time to time where their minds are, and of what they are thinking. He likens the mind of the child to soft wax, which may easily be moulded. It must be a constant study of the master to preserve the pupil's mental elasticity. With this view the master should question frequently and give rewards for compositions and exercises in memory, "in order that they may give themselves to study as a recreation of the mind, without fear and without repugnance."

The subjects studied were at first the elements of grammar and rhetoric. At an early age the children were made familiar with Scriptural words and phrases. Instead of poetic fables of pagan times, they were taught "to narrate the admirable facts of sacred history and the sentences of the Book of Proverbs." In these early days, when the lines were sharply drawn between Pagan and Christian, that upon which greatest stress was laid was the religious training of the child. All else was subservient. The public schools of ancient Greece and Rome were disappearing before the light of Christianity ; parents sought a more moral atmosphere for their children, and, knocking at the door of the monasteries, they besought for them the refuge and the religious training that could only be found in those asylums of prayer and study.

What parents desired, and the sentiment with which the Church responded to their desire, may be best expressed in the charge of a bishop of Metz to those ecclesiastics having the care of children :

" Let these children reared or instructed in con-gregations be so well guarded by ecclesiastical discipline that their fragile age, inclined to sin, may not find an outlet for a single fault. Let a brother of irreproachable conduct be given them to watch over them and to instruct them in the spiritual sense of the Scriptures. Let them all be assembled in the same hall, under the authority of a master of age and experience, capable of giving them advanced lessons and good example ; or, in case he does not teach, let him be in position to hold supervision over them." [1]

Jonas, a bishop of Orleans, writes a treatise for the laity, which the Benedictine D'Achery calls a " golden book." It is a practical treatise on the use of the sacraments, on the mutual duties of husband and wife, of parents and children, and on such spiritual topics as death, judgment, and the like. A chapter is devoted to the instruction of children ; but the only point on which the good bishop lays stress is that from their tenderest years children be taught the necessary truths of their religion. [2]

But we must not imagine for a moment that Catechism was at any time the sole subject taught in the cloistral schools. The grammar of those days, for instance, covered a wider field than the mere technicalities now attached to the name. However, we find that St. Basil anticipated modern times in another respect. Much is spoken and written at present concerning manual training and the formation of trades-schools. Now, it so happens that, as a matter

---

[1] " Spicilegium " Acherii, t. i., p. 574.

[2] " Spicilegium ", pp. 258-323. Jonæ Aurelianensis Episcopi Libri tres de Institutione Laicali. Jonas lived in the reign of Charles the Bald.

of course, and as something essential, without which education would be incomplete and monastic life would experience a want, Basil regulated for a certain number of trades to be learned and practised. Children should begin to learn some one or other as soon as they are able. Among those recommended are: weaving and tailoring within certain limitations; architecture, wood-work and brass-work, and above all, agriculture.' Surely, the school training of skilled hands in all these trades is not to be despised.

But even though the regulations are silent, we can elsewhere find indications that the teaching imparted in cloistral schools was both thorough and practical. The student of old books bearing upon history and literature — and what printed volume does not tell an interesting story to him who has the secret of reaching the heart of a book?— is familiar with the book of formulas prepared towards the end of the seventh century by the Monk Marculf, by command of Landi, Bishop of Paris. It contains royal charts and formulas of wills, deeds, transfers, and the like, such as it behooves a practical business man to be familiar with. Now, Marculf is careful to tell us that he wrote these formulas not for the learned, but with a view " of exercising children who are beginners." "I have done," he adds, "as best I could with simplicity and clearness, in order that good will may profit of it."

In the seventh century Irish monks overran the Continent, introducing a taste for Greek and mathe-

---

matics, and initiating the young brothers into their beautiful style of copying and illustrating manuscripts. Moengall brings Irish studies, Irish methods and Irish enthusiasm to the cloistral schools of St. Gall's, and under his direction discussions in grammar and philosophy were carried on with a degree of subtlety that would have rejoiced Dante's own master in the rue de Fouarre.

The course of study in the monastery of St. Hilary of Poitiers extended over seven years. From the lips of St. Achard we learn something of the working of a cloistral school in his day. He was blessed with a master "of such great doctrine and sanctity, that in living with him one had no thought but for wisdom, no action but for justice." Old and young were assembled in the same room. At the beginning, the child was not compelled to learn. He was placed on the front bench, where he listened to the older pupils reciting their lessons. When Achard's teacher, Ansfrid, asked him what he was most desirous of learning, the boy replied: " First, the things pertaining to God; afterwards, I shall learn the elementary branches of study."[1] During the first two years the youth learned only such things as were calculated to open and quicken the intelligence. The master exercised all his ingenuity in giving an elevated and spiritual turn to the most trivial things. The next five years were devoted to the usual courses of trivium and quadrivium. The

---

[1] " De rebus ruralibus,"—what is taught in the rural schools. This is the construction Cardinal Pitra gives to these words. " Vie de S. Leger."

principles of Canon Law were included in the course at Poitiers.[1]

The method was practically the same in the schools attached to all the Benedictine monasteries. The daily routine of school life followed by Ecgberht, brother of the King of Northumbria and Bishop of York, has been handed down to us. No doubt it was that pursued by his old master, Beda. The traditions of Jarrow were transferred to York.

"He rose at daybreak," we are told, "and when not prevented by more important occupations, sitting on his couch, he taught his pupils successively till noon. He then retired to his chapel and celebrated mass. At the time of dinner, he repaired to the common hall, where he ate sparingly, though he was careful that the meat should be of the best kind. During dinner an instructive book was always read. Till the evening, he amused himself with hearing his scholars discuss literary subjects. Then he repeated with them the service of Complin, after which each knelt before him and received his blessing. The students afterwards retired to rest."[2]

Among the pupils so taught was Alcuin. He has left us an account of his studies pursued under the learned Albert. He says:

"The learned Albert gave drink to thirsty minds at the fountain of the sciences. To some he communicated the art and the rules of grammar; for others he caused floods of rhetoric to flow; he knew how to exercise these in the battles of jurisprudence, and those in the songs of Adonia; some learned from him to pipe Castalian airs and with lyric foot to strike the summit of Parnassus; to others he made known

---

[1] Ozanam, "Études Germaniques," ii., p. 541.

[2] "Vita Alcuini," p. 141.

the harmony of the heavens, the courses of the sun and the moon, the five zones of the pole, the seven planets, the laws of the course of the stars, the motions of the sea, earthquakes, the nature of men, and of beasts, and of birds, and of all that inhabit the forest. He unfolded the different qualities and combinations of numbers; he taught how to calculate with certainty the solemn return of Easter-tide, and above all, he explained the mysteries of the Holy Scriptures." [1]

This course Alcuin afterwards carried out when organizing the educational system of Gaul. He made all human knowledge a basis on which to build up Holy Writ.

"Despise not human sciences," wrote he, "but make of them a foundation; so teach children grammar and the doctrines of philosophy, that, ascending the steps of wisdom, they may reach the summit, which is evangelical perfection, and while advancing in years they may also increase the treasures of wisdom." [2]

And in another place he speaks of improving the memory by "exercise in learning, practice in writing, constant energy in thinking, and the avoidance of drunkenness, which is the bane of all serious study and destroys alike the health of the body and the freshness of the mind." [3] In the course of studies

---

[1] De Pontiff. Eborac., 1431-1447.

[2] Ep. 221.

[3] "Alcuini Opera Omnia," p. 1346. Ed. Duchesne, Paris, 1617. There is a fragment of this dialogue between Charlemagne and Alcuin in the Vatican Library (Codex Vat. Lat. 4162), very old and well-thumbed. I have transcribed portions of it containing variations from the printed copy. It might have been part of the very copy that Alcuin had presented to Charles. The fragment is bound up with other fragments, the first beginning with an explanation of the Athanasian Creed.

mapped out by Charlemagne for the episcopal and monastic schools of his dominion are mentioned reading, the study of the Psalter, arithmetic, plain-chant, and writing; and he further ordains that there be placed in the hands of the pupils correct and approved Catholic books. One of Alcuin's chief merits was that he made strenuous efforts to procure correct copies of the various text-books required, and especially of the Holy Scriptures. The Scriptorium which he established and supervised at Tours became world-renowned for the accurate and elegant work done in it.

When he retired from court to the monastery, he organized and directed the studies, and he thus describes the labor of love in which he was engaged:

"I apply myself in serving out to some of my pupils in this house of St. Martin's the honey of Holy Writ; I essay to intoxicate others with the old wine of ancient studies; one class I nourish with the delicate fruits of grammatical science; in the eyes of another I display the order of the stars." [1]

Alcuin's own works are a good criterion of the intellectual level of his day. They comprise treatises on theology, lives of saints, a book on the liberal arts, works on rhetoric, logic, grammar, orthography, arithmetic, and a hand-book of school-method. [2]

An examination of the lives of saints from the fifth to the twelfth century reveals to us the fact that in the cloistral schools youths were taught reading, writing, arithmetic, grammar, logic, the principles of versification, liturgic chant, the Old and the New

---

[1] Ep. xxxviii.

[2] See Duchesne's edition of 1617, or the Migne edition.

Testament, theology, sometimes canon law, and later on Aristotle. There was a difference of opinion as to the extent to which the ancient classic authors should be cultivated. Some, like Alcuin, following in the footsteps of St. Jerome, taught the ancient classics extensively enough ; others, like St. Owen, declared against their introduction beyond what was barely requisite to illustrate grammatical rules.

" Even though the teachings of the Church," says the saint, "should have at their disposal the charm of profane eloquence, they should fly from it, for the Church should speak, not to lazy philosophic sects, but to the whole human race. Of what use are grammarians' disputations, which seem more suitable to throw down than to build up?" [1]

But his reasoning will not hold. Certainly Charlemagne did not agree therewith. He would see every priest and every monk use classic and graceful language, so that all who would hear them, charmed with the science that their reading and singing would reveal, might leave rejoicing and thanking God.[2] Banish all profane learning, and you banish the tools and implements with which to cultivate religious learning. Thereafter it will not be long before the broad joke of Rabelais becomes a literal truth:

" Je n'étudie point de ma part," says Frère Jean. " En nôtre abbaye, nous n'étudions jamais, de peur

---

[1] "Vita S. Eligii," Prologus. Migne Patrol, t. 87, p. 439. See Ozanam, "Études Germaniques," pp. 458 sqq. Ozanam thinks the saint was denouncing the quibbling methods of the Toulouse school of grammarians. But unless the whole is a mere flourish of rhetoric, the saint would also condemn to oblivion all classic authors.

[2] "Capitularies."

des auripeaux.'¹ Nôtre feu abbé disoit que c'est chose monstrueuse voir un moine sçavant."²

But the cloister school had its hours for play and rest as well as its hours for study.   Having examined the methods and the matter taught, let us look at the students in their amusements.   Now it so happens that we have ready at hand a picture of a celebrated cloistral school in the tenth century.   The picture is skillfully drawn, and brings home to us very clearly that those were other days than ours, and they had other manners and customs, that cannot be judged by our standards.   But it brings the period so much nearer to us that I shall not curtail an essential detail.

We are in the celebrated monastery of Saint Gall's.   It is the year 992.   Don't be frightened by that noise, those shouts of joy that you hear.   It is the feast of the Holy Innocents, and the scholars are celebrating the anniversary of a visit made by the Emperor Conrad in 913.   The monarch had on that occasion instituted three days holiday for the younger students.   The door of the recreation hall opens ; a prelate appears ; it is the Abbot Solomon, who has recently been made bishop.   Immediately the more roguish boys put their heads together and concoct a plan ; for there exists a custom that the students can lay hands on every stranger coming to the school, and keep him prisoner till he redeems himself.   It is this custom that the boldest among them wish at present to put into execution.   But a difficulty exists.

¹ Ear-aches.
² "Gargantua," liv. i., chap. xxxix.

The prelate is also the abbot of the monastery, and as abbot he believes himself above molestation. But he has been reckoning without the logic of the young dialectitians. " Let us capture the bishop," say they, "and leave the lord abbot." He yields to their humor. They take him and place him in the professor's chair—*in magistri solium.*

The bishop submitted, and addressing the boys, said : " Since I take the place of your master I have the right to use his privileges; take off your jackets, to be punished." The pupils were amazed, but they obeyed at once, asking, however, that they be permitted to redeem themselves as they were wont to do with their professor. " How is that ?" asked the good abbot. Thereupon, the little ones began to speak to him in Latin as well as they could; the medium ones addressed him in rhythmic language, and the most advanced in verse. Each class defended itself as best it could and so pleased the new bishop. " What evil have we done to you," says the middle class ; "that you should harm us ? We appeal to the king, for we have acted only within our right."[1] The versifiers by the mouth of their poet said : "We did not dream of being punished, since you are a new visitor."[2] The abbot then rose, rejoicing to find that studies which had always flourished at Saint Gall's were still held in honor, and embraced and kissed every child as he was in his shirt—*omnes, ita*

---

[1] Quid tibi fecimus tale ut nobis facias male :
Appellamus regem, quia nostram fecimus legem.

[2] Non nobis pia spes fuerat cum sis novus hospes,
Ut vetus in pejus transvertere tute velis jus.

ut erant in lineis, exsurgens amplexatus et osculatus
— and said : "While I live I shall redeem myself, and
shall reward such assiduity." He added that he had
the chief brothers to assemble before the door, and
he decreed that in future all the scholars and their
successors should have meat on the holidays instituted by the emperor, and that they be served during these days with dishes and wine from the abbot's
own cellar. The chronicle adds that the custom
continued to be faithfully observed long afterwards.[1]

V.

Monastic schools varied in number and in efficiency with different countries and with different
epochs. They flourished greatly from the sixth to
the ninth century. This educational period has
been characterized as the Benedictine period. The
Benedictine monks controlled all the schools. The
smaller monasteries confined themselves to elementary instruction; the larger ones, in addition, taught
the higher branches. The Council of Aix-la-Chapelle
decreed in 817 that those youths aspiring to the
religious life — *oblati* — should be taught in a school
apart from those who were to return to their homes.
But both schools had the same lessons and frequently
the same teachers.[2] In the eighth century Charlemagne gave a new impetus to learning. But wars
and dissensions soon undid the good work.

---

[1] Eckehardus Jun. : "De Casibus Monasterii S. Galli."
Ed. Goldast. t. i.,p. 21.

[2] "Histoire Littéraire de France," t. iv., p. 231.

Already, in 830, the Deacon Florus bewails the decline of learning.

" Formerly," he says, " we saw but one prince and one people ; law and the magistrate ruled every town. . . . Throughout, youths learned the Holy Volume ; the hearts of children expanded beneath the influence of letters and arts. . . . Now is all the boon of peace destroyed by cruel hates."[1]

Not that efforts had not been made both by Louis the Pious and Charles the Bold to encourage schools. The latter, especially, surrounded himself with learned men, and we are told that he was wont to exhort the abbots to consecrate all their efforts to the education of children, and he loved to see the brothers give gratuitous instruction, with the view "to please God and St. Martin."[2] These efforts were of slight avail.

The ninth century set in darkness. The tenth opened up an era of warfare and bloodshed and ravagings, and on the ruins began the building up of a new order of things. It is the beginning of the epoch of feudalism. During the two following centuries there was much ignorance. Here and there, away from the scenes of warfare and depredation, the lamp was kept lighted, and monks labored in silence at the work of writing chronicles and preserving and copying manuscripts. But they are the exception. Synod and Council of that period, especially in France, bewail the darkness. The Council of Troslei, held in 909, in all sadness speaks of Christians who lived to

---

[1] "Carmina de Divisione Imperii," i. Ed. Migne, t. 119, col. 257.

[2] De Chevriers, p. 82.

old age ignorant of their creed and not knowing the
Lord's Prayer. It also tells of abbots, who, when
asked to read, scarcely knowing a word in their abe-
cediary, might reply, *"Nescio literas."* [1] We are elsewhere told of a prelate who gave no time to study,
and who only knew how to count the letters of the
alphabet on his fingers; in other words, who had the
merest rudiments of knowledge.[2] In Italy letters
flourished more extensively. Pope Eugenius II. in
826 confirmed the laws of Charlemagne and Louis,
and gave a new impetus to the study of letters in
this classic land.[3] Ratherius, bishop of Verona — he
was consecrated bishop in 931 — speaks of three orders of schools from which priests may be ordained.
He tells us that he will ordain no young man who
will not have studied letters either in the episcopal
schools, or in some monastery, or under some learned
master.[4] In Spain, also, during this long night, there
were flourishing schools, and science was advancing.

Gerbert (*d.* 1003) studies under the guidance of
his uncle at Vich, and brings back so many new educational improvements that he is regarded by the
ignorant as a dangerous man. He introduced an
abacus that simplified greatly the science of arithmetic. He made important discoveries in astron-

---

[1] Bibliothèque de Cluny, p. 150.

[2] Et studiis quem nec constrinxerit una dierum;
Alphabetum sapiat, digito tantum numerare.
"Adalberonis Carmen ad Robertum Regem
Francorum," v. 49, 50.

[3] See Tiraboschi "Storia della Lett. Ital.," t. vii., lib. iii.,
cap. xvii., xxiii.

[4] "Synodica ad Presbyteros," § 13. Migne, t. 136, col. 564.

omy, and explained the heavens and the earth by
means of globes. He simplified the science of music,
"so that," remarks Odo of Cluny, "children could
learn in three or four days an office that it formerly
took experienced singers years to master."

Fulbert (*d.* 1028) was another light who had many
brilliant disciples. "Ah!" exclaims Adelmann, "with
what moral dignity, and solidity of thought, and
charm of language he explained to us the secrets
of a profound science."

Lanfranc (1005–1089) carried to Bec the learning
of Italy. The torch that he kindled illumined
France. His school was thronged with youths from
all parts of Europe. He taught without fee; such
offerings as were made went to the building up of
the monastery. Before he became known in England
as a great statesman and the counsellor of William
the Conqueror, he had won the esteem of thousands
whose studies he directed. On occasion of his visit
to Rome, Pope Alexander II. rose to meet him,
saying: " I show this mark of deference to Lanfranc,
not because he is archbishop, but because I had sat
under him with his other disciples in the school of
Bec."[1] And the indefatigable Ordericus Vitalis cannot find words in which to express his eulogy of
this great light:

"Forced from the quiet of the cloister by his
sense of obedience, he became a master in whose
teaching a whole library of philosophy and divinity
was displayed. He was a powerful expositor of
difficult questions in both sciences. It was under

---

[1] See William of Malmesbury, " Antiq. Libr.," p. 324.

this master that the Normans received the first rudiments of literature, and from the school of Bec proceeded so many philosophers of distinguished attainments, both in divine and secular learning. . . . His reputation for learning spread throughout all Europe, and many hastened to receive lessons from him out of France, Gascony, Brittany, and Flanders. To understand the admirable genius and erudition of Lanfranc, one ought to be a Herodian in Grammar, an Aristotle in dialectics, a Tully in rhetoric, an Augustine and Jerome and other expositors of the law and grace in Sacred Scriptures."[1]

And of Anselm (1034-1109) the successor of Lanfranc — his successor in the school and successor in the see of Canterbury — the same author is no less eulogistic:

"Learned men of eminence," he says, "both clergy and laity, resorted to hear the sweet words of truth that flowed from his mouth, pleasing to the seekers of righteousness as angels' discourses, . . . all his words were valuable and edified his attached hearers. His attentive pupils committed to writing his letters and typical discourses; so that, being deeply imbued with them, they profited others as well as themselves to no small degree."[2]

Nor was this learning confined to the priors. The same trustworthy witness bears testimony to the general culture of the monks of Bec:

"The monks of Bec," he says, "are thus become so devoted to literary pursuits, and so exercised in raising and solving difficult questions of divinity, and in profitable discussions, that they seem to be almost all philosophers; and those among them who appear

---

[1] "Hist. Eccl.," lib. iv., cap. vii.
[2] Ibid., cap. xi.

to be illiterate, and might be called clowns, derive from their intercourse with the rest the advantage of becoming fluent grammarians." [1]

From this great seat of learning went forth monks into all parts of France and England, to light up the dark ways.

But the simple enumeration of all the cloistral schools that history mentions in the darkest period would take hours. Among others, there was the school of St. Benedict on the Loire, which was frequented by more than five thousand pupils, each one of whom upon withdrawing was required to present the monastery with two manuscripts. [2] There was the monastery of Hildesheim. Under Bernward its school became famous. Bernward himself was one of the most remarkable men of his day. His activity seemed to know no other limit than his power of endurance. He was always questioning, or writing, or engaged in manual labor; never idle. He was skilled in the mechanic arts. An expert joiner and blacksmith, and a good architect, he taught these things to the students of the seminary himself. He also copied and illuminated manuscripts. [3]

Meinwerk, a disciple of Bernward, established a celebrated school at Osnabruck. Idamus (*d.* 1066) inherited his genius, piety and learning, and continued to make the school famous. The course of studies was extensive, and the discipline severe. Even parents were forbidden to visit the students,

---

[1] Ibid., cap. xi.
[2] Chateaubriand, "Études Historiques," t. iii., p. 144.
[3] " Vita S. Bernwardi," § 2, 3, Mabillon, p. 181.
K. E.—3

lest they might distract them in their studies.'   Indeed, throughout all the mediæval schools the discipline was severe.   The birch was considered indispensable as a medium of instruction.   The younger
pupils were subject to the closest vigilance day and
night.   Withal, the students were treated with a
paternal care and tenderness that was not unfre-
quently pathetic.

With the twelfth century dawned a new era.
There is an upward movement of the people.   The
Crusades help to break down the barrier of caste.
There is a general fermentation of thought.   Schools
become secularized.   Men run hither and thither,
devoured by a thirst for knowledge that no known
source seems sufficient to satiate.   The period of
scholasticism has set in.   Men, in their eagerness to
dispute, break down the barriers dividing the diverse
subject-matters they should teach.   Under pretence
of teaching grammar they are found to be indoc-
trinating their pupils in some philosophical subtlety.
These are the men whom Hugh of St. Victor's criti-
cises as indulging in a perverse custom: "When
grammar is their subject, they discuss the nature of
syllogisms; when treating of dialectics they will occupy themselves with the inflection of words."[2]

St Victor's was one of the great centers of learning in the twelfth century.   William of Champeaux
brought thither some of the fires of Bec, and Anselm
of Laon took thence that bright flame that attracted

---

[1] Theiner, "Histoire des Institutions d'Education Ecclési-
astiques," p. 173.

[2] "Eruditionis Didascalicæ," lib. iii., cap. vi.

even the genius of an Abelard. The master-hand of Hugh has sketched for us a beautiful picture of student life in this monastery. It is too valuable to leave unquoted:

"Great is the multitude and various are the ages that I behold—boys, youths, young men, and old men. Various also are the studies. Some exercise their uncultured tongues in pronouncing our letters and in producing sounds that are new. Others learn by listening at first to the inflections of words, their composition and derivation; afterwards they repeat them to one another, and by repetition engrave them on their memory. Others work upon tablets covered with wax. Others trace upon membranes with a skilled hand diverse figures in diverse colors. Others, with a more ardent zeal, seem occupied with the most serious studies. They dispute among themselves, and each endeavors by a thousand plots and artifices to ensnare the other. I see some who are making computations. Others with instruments clearly trace the course and position of stars and the movement of the heavens. Others treat of the nature of plants, the constitution of man, and the quality and virtue of all things." [1]

This represents the kind of work that has been done for centuries in the larger cloistral schools. Hugh's account is almost literally that which we have seen Alcuin give of his own school-days. But as the cloistral school led to the decline of the episcopal school, and in a great measure superseded it, even so did the university lead to the decline of the cloistral school.

---

[1] "De Vanitate Mundi," lib. i., D. col. 707, t. iii., Migne Ed.—Cf. John of Salisbury, "Metalog." lib. ii., cap. x.

THE PALATINE SCHOOL

(37)

THE palatine school is of earlier origin than the day of Charlemagne. There was a palace school in the Merovingian court in which the children of the king and the chiefs were educated.

"From the time of the first race of our kings," says Crevier, "we find traces of a school held in their palace where noble youths were instructed in whatever letters and knowledge their positions required." ("Hist. de l'Université de Paris," t. i., p. 26).

It was an ancient German custom, mentioned by Tacitus ("Germania," xiii.), to have the sons of the various subordinate chiefs recommended at the court of the ruler and brought up with the sons of the king. They were presented and adopted with ceremony. The custom became the source of feudal power. These youths attached themselves to their chief and followed him with unswerving loyalty to battle, to exile, to victory, even to death.

Christianity stepped in, and here, as elsewhere, sanctified the custom. As we have found the school attached to the church and the cloister, even so do we find the palace school become identified with the royal chapel. Indeed, the school is called the chapel, and the chapel gets its name from the *capella* of St. Martin of Tours.

The first chaplain was Aptonius, who lived under Clovis (481–511), and who may be regarded as the father of the palatine chapel. ("Gallia Christiana," t. ii., col. 979). Henceforth this school becomes the centre whence radiates the light of learning in France. The light does not always shine with equal brilliancy. Fifty years elapse before we come across another eminent chaplain, Mrerius, or Mercarius. (Ibid., ocl. 974.)

The names of the great men who Christianized France—all of whom came forth from that palace school — would fill a volume. We mention St. Remy, who baptized Clovis; Waast and Deodatus, his chatechists; Gormer of Toulouse, who learned all the Scriptures in three years; Cesarius of Acles, the learned monk of Lerins, who taught his people how to sing hymns in church in Greek.

The sons of Clovis continued the good work. Under Theodoric, the master, was Saint Gall, granduncle of Gregory of Tours, who charmed Theodoric by his singing, to such an extent that Theodoric could not be separated from him.

Under the fostering care of Childebert and the pious Ultrogotha and her sister, Swegotha, the school flourished. Childebert is known as the first Merovingian king who was familiar with the Latin. Fortunatus calls him "the priest-king, the crowned cleric; another, Melchisedech, victor of peace, glory and rule of pontiffs." This prince gathered learned men from Rome and Constantinople, from England and Ireland. Symposiums were held in the gardens of the court. There those two Bretons, Hermel and Hervanion, sang daily, and their sweet voices made them favorites with the king. Hervanion, or the little Hervé, was learned in many languages, a perfect musician, and composed several ballads and poems. There the young shepherd, Patrocles, displayed his wonderful gifts — Patrocles, who, unknown to his parents, attended the schools, and became such a prodigy of learning that Mummion introduced him to the palatine school. There was the laureate of the court, Venantius Fortunatus, who lifts the veil and permits us to see the school life beneath the clouds of those stormy days.

Gregory of Tours finds learning in decay. But from the time of Clotaire the palace school can be clearly traced. Among the abbots of the palace and the camp; among the chaplains and the arch-chaplains, we can discern the school in which St. Leger and his disciples lived and labored.

There was Betharius of Chartres, — a noble Roman, who after having been nourished in the schools established by Boëthius and Cassidorus became distinguished as an eminent teacher — and Clotaire II. following the advice of Queen Fredegunde named him arch-chaplain of the royal chapel — which position also made him head of the school. ("Acta T. Betharii," Boll. Aug. 2.) He was succeeded by Rusticus, who had acquired in the Roman schools the purest and best traditions of Christian education. Rusticus modeled the school more after the monastic form. His school became a seminary whence emanated venerable bishops and saints to govern the church of France.

Rusticus was succeeded by Sulpitius whose influence upon the youths of the palace was far-reaching. Their lives were passed in the most rigid austerity.

Beneath their rich garments they wore hair shirts, and many of the brightest became clerics or religious — callings, which, up to that time had been considered beneath the profession of arms. You may remember the exclamation of St. Clothilde in regard to her grand-children : " I would rather see them dead than tonsured !"

1. What were the studies pursued ? There were grammar, dialectics, rhetoric ; there were the more special studies of Roman law, national customs and traditions, models of Gallo-Roman eloquence and even of the vernacular Gallo-Frankish idiom. The vernacular tongues were already attracting attention and we find the rhetoricians distinguishing between the artificialness of Greek, the circumspect measure of Latin, the splendors of the Gallic tongue, and the pomp of the English. (Don Pitra, " Vie de S. Leger," pp. 32, 33.) History occupied a large place in the course. Under this head was included a study of the great national epics. (" Vita S. Wandsegisiti," No. 2, S. ii., 13th ed.) Christian dogma and Christian philosophy also found their place. It was the school of superior studies — where privileged youths finished after private studies at home and in the schools of the grammarians — whither they resorted from all parts of Gaul.

Remember that at the period of which we now treat there was no hereditary nobility ; honors were distributed according to merit, and the youth who passed through his course with most satisfaction and had submitted to the rigid discipline of the school was most likely to be honored by the king.

We can easily conceive the great educational influence of this school upon the fierce Germanic nature. It reconciled him to the study of letters; it gave him a taste for the arts of peace ; he became more polished.

Under the long and brilliant reigns of Clotaire and Dagobert, Merovingian royalty becomes Byzantine in its splendor and style. The etiquette of the old courts is introduced. Religious ceremonies are carried out with all possible pomp. Especially magnificent was the celebration of Easter in one or another of the one hundred and fifty Merovingian towns to which the court migrated yearly. (Naudet, "Memoires de l'Institut.," t. viii., p. 404.)

The palatine school had an obscure beginning in the sixth century, grew to be great under Clotaire II., then declined under the management of Varimbert, who busied himself in quarreling with the monks of St. Medard in Soissons ; grew into significance under the illustrious S. Ouen, Bishop of Rouen, who saw three generations pass under his hands.

Then came Léodegar, or Leger, called to court of Queen Bathilde. Under his management and counsels the school became once more thoroughly organized. It flourished under Pepin the Short, and we read of Abelard, cousin of Charlemagne, that he was educated with the pupils of the palace in all human science, and heard the same lessons with the emperor. (Leon Maitre: " Les Écoles Episcopales et Monastiques " I, p. 35.)

Then came the school of Charlemagne. Here we must distinguish. Mention is made of an Academy in which nearly all his court took part — assumed name: Toulouse. This was not the palatine school. That school was distinct, and contained not only the youths as found in the earlier schools, but others who were preparing for holy orders. Thus, the chronicler of San Gall tells how Charles upon returning from an expedition, had all the pupils whom he confided to Clement of Ireland brought before him and classified according to their proficiency and diligence, cautioning the sons of the nobility that unless they studied as well as the poorer youths, they need expect but scant favors at his hands. (D. Bouquet, t. v., p. 107. Mon. Sang. Chron. l. i.)

It has been questioned whether the palace school was permanent, or whether it accompanied the court from place to place. I am of opinion that the school went wherever the court settled. The chaplain was also the custodian of the sacred relics that were an inseparable portion of the royal equipage. When Archbishop Augilran was made arch-chaplain, he was dispensed from diocesan residence by Pope Adrian, which is additional evidence that the school traveled with Charlemagne. Alcuin also complained of his frequent journeyings when he had charge of the school.

Under Charlemagne, the order in which the teachers instructed was somewhat as follows:

1. ALCUIN.— He was the great light of the school under Charlemagne. He brought with him the best literary traditions of England, as handed down from the venerable Bede through Egbert of

York. He was possessed of the best and ripest
scholarship of his day.   At court he not only organized schools, but he aided Charlemagne in his wise
legislation.   Retiring to the monastery of Tours in
his old age, he there established a scriptorium that
became famous for the neatness and accuracy of the
work it sent out.   You will find a fair account of
Alcuin's pedagogical work in the monograph of
Prof. West.   In recommending the book, I feel it
my duty to call your attention to both its merits
and its defects.   His scriptorium — vellum, purple
gold-quaritch.

2. CLEMENT OF IRELAND.— Alcuin found fault
with his theories and his methods.   Even then race
prejudice asserted itself.   Theodolfe, Bishop of
Orleans, was also opposed to him.

3. CLAUDIUS, afterwards Bishop of Turin.

4. ALDRIC, who was a disciple of Alcuin in
Tours, and pupil of Sigulf, and afterwards Archbishop
of Sens.

5. AMALARIUS SYMPHONIUS, also a disciple of
Alcuin, and raised to the archiepiscopal see of
Lyons.

Under Charles the Bold, the palace school became
distinguished about the year 842.   An ancient writer
thus bears witness to its excellence : " His court became a palæstra for all departments of learning.
And so, all the leading men in the kingdom sent
thither their children to be formed in human and
divine science. (See Crevier, "Hist. de l'Univ. de
Paris," t. i., p. 42.)   At the head of the school
was John Scotus Erigena, the translator of the

pseudo Dyonysian writings and whom Roger Bacon praised as a clear-headed commentator of Aristotle. His doctrines were regarded as tainted, and Du Boulay quotes a letter purporting to come from Pope Nicholas I. asking Charles not to allow Erigena to remain at the head of the school in Paris, lest, the bad grain mingling with the good grain, all should be spoiled. ("Hist. Univ. Par.," t. i., p. 184). However, let me add, the authenticity of this letter has been doubted. (*Rev. des Questions Historiques*, Oct., 1892.)

Irish scholars continued to govern the school even after the death of Charles and the disappearance of Scotus Erigena. Thus, under Louis the Pious, Mannon, who afterwards withdrew to the monastery at Condate, raised the tone and standard of the school so well that we find Radbod coming all the way from Utrecht to attend his lessons.

The last master of the school of whom we find mention is St. Remi of Auxene, who died in 908. The palatine school became lost in oblivion thereafter.

MEDIÆVAL UNIVERSITY LIFE

(47)

FATHER Denifle's book on the origins of the universities is epoch-making. The learned Dominican, as sub-archivist of the Vatican library, has utilized to their full extent the rare and exceptional advantages at his disposal. To the extensive materials that lay at his hand he brought to bear vast learning and marvelous patience. No document seems to have escaped him ; he allows nothing in the document that he handles to pass unchallenged. He has an eye for the most minute details. Indeed, it is in grasping the whole meaning of a phrase or sentence that he has been enabled to correct so many illusions in which the historians of all our universities have been living. His method is purely analytical. He leaves very little to inference. He makes no statement that is not based on a docu-

---

[1] *American Catholic Quarterly Review.*

" Die Entstehung der Universitäten des Mittelalters bis 1400." Von P. Heinrich Denifle, aus dem Predigerorden, Unterarchivar des Hl. Stuhles. Berlin. 1885.

" De l'Organisation de l'Enseignement dans l'Université de Paris au Moyen Age." Par Charles Thurot. Paris. 1850.

" Essai sur l'Organisation des Etudes dans l'Ordre des Frères Prêcheurs au XIIIème et au XIVème Siècle " (1216–1342). Par G. Douais. Paris. 1884.

" Monumenta Franciscana. 2 vols. Rolls Series. Vol. i. edited by J. S. Brewer, London, 1858; vol. ii. edited by Richard Howlett, 1882.

ment, or that is not backed up by ample proof. His familiarity with the literature of the subject of universities in all its details enables him to go behind the polish of the sentence and lay finger upon the very text that the author had in mind when stating his propositions. He forthwith discusses and settles the authoritative value of the work drawn from. This is the perfection of critical acumen.

And inasmuch as our historians of universities have been living in a fool's paradise concerning the origin and formation of those institutions, Father Denifle has his hands full in correcting, refuting, rejecting, and discussing the statements of his predecessors. His book in every page bristles with argument. It is a book that shall henceforth be indispensable to the student of history. No man can ignore it and presume to write upon mediæval times. · The three agencies that moulded the Middle Ages into their characteristic shape and gave them life and being were the Papacy, the Holy Roman Empire, and the University of Paris. Each wielded a far-reaching influence, the full extent of which few historians have been able to measure. Therefore do we most cordially thank Father Denifle for the scholarly volume he has given us, and we hope and pray that he be spared the health and strength to finish the other volumes that are to follow.

Prior to Father Denifle's great book the only work that attempted to remove the history of the University of Paris out of the domain of romance in which Du Boulay had placed it was the slender volume of

M. Charles Thurot. Every student of education since 1850 has found the book invaluable in giving him for the first time a correct notion of the organization of the University of Paris. Even the search-light of Father Denifle's acumen, while pointing out a mistake here and there, approves of the main conclusions of the author. When Thurot went astray he was generally misled by placing too great confidence in Du Boulay.

M. l'Abbé Douais did for the Dominicans what Thurot did for the University of Paris. He for the first time mapped out for the general reader the whole complex organization of study under which the Dominicans passed. His book is a valuable contribution to the history of pedagogics. It is largely based upon original documents. The book is timely, for men are now beginning to appreciate the influence of the mendicant orders upon the Middle Ages.

In like manner, the "Monumenta Franciscana" gives us insight into the foundations of the Franciscans in London and Oxford. The first volume includes the chronicle of Thomas Eccleston, the letters of Adam Marsh, and a short register of the Minorites in London. The second volume contains a fragment of Thomas Eccleston's treatise on the advent of the friars, the rule of St. Francis, the statutes of the observant Franciscans, and other valuable records bearing upon the order. Noteworthy is the respectful tone in which the introductions to these volumes are written by the late Professor Brewer and Mr. Richard Howlett. These writers were not Catholic, but no

Catholic could be more zealous in defending the prac-
tises and customs of the friars; none could be more
considerate in making allowance for time and place.

Father Denifle is outspoken in his denunciation
of the synthetic method as applied to history. He
must be analytical or nothing. He is convinced that
naught but unsatisfactory results can be reached by
the synthetic method.[1] But we should distinguish.
For purposes of investigation and verification, the
analytical is the only proper method; but results having been reached, there is always place for the synthetic method. The material having been tested, it
may be safely employed to build up with. Therefore, under leave of Father Denifle, we shall make a
short study of school-life in the mediæval universities, in the course of which we shall attempt to re-
construct that life as contemporaries reveal it, and
as it appears to our view. We shall first consider the
organization of a university.

I.

The oldest mediæval universities of which we
have cognizance are those of Paris and Bologna.
The origin of each is buried in the mists of the past.
Bologna became famous as a school of law;
students flocked thither from all parts; in the
course of time it possessed an autonomy of its own.
Pope and emperor endowed it with certain rights and
privileges, and forthwith it loomed before us as a
great university. So it was with the University of

---

[1] "Einleitung," xxiii.

Paris. For half a century before it became recognized as such, we find it to have been a great intellectual centre, made famous by the brilliant teachings of William of Champeaux, Abelard and Peter Lombard. The masters became organized into a scholastic guild. But the university can be traced to no one school, or no combination of schools as its source.[1] The teachers of that day supplied an educational want; the schools of Paris thus became centers of instruction which grew apace with the concourse of students and teachers.

" They had practical ends," says Laurie ; " their aim was to minister to the immediate needs of society. . . . They simply aimed at critically expounding recognized authorities in the interests of social wants. It was the needs of the human body which originated Salerno ; it was the needs of men as related to each other in a civil organism which originated Bologna ; it was the eternal needs of the human spirit in its relation to the unseen that originated Paris. We may say, then, that it was the improvement of the profession of medicine, law and theology which led to the inception and organization of the first great schools."[2]

To the inception, perhaps, yes ; to the organization, decidedly no. The University of Paris was not organized from the schools of St. Victor's, or St. Genevieve's, or any combination of these with other schools. There is extant no record of a definite act by which one might say, " Here is the charter of incorporation ; here is the decree of organization."

[1] This point has been settled forever by F. Denifle, "Entstehung der Universitäten," pp. 655 seq.

[2] " Rise and Constitution of Universities," pp. 109, 110.

The guild spirit was abroad and permeated all trades and professions. The masters were no exception. When their guild looms into prominence, it receives recognition; but it is only by decree of pope or emperor — and of pope chiefly — that its degrees become entitled to universal respect. Thus, long after the guild of masters in Paris had become recognized, it remained under the jurisdiction of the chancellor of the cathedral of Notre Dame. It was out of the struggle between the chancellor and the masters that the university grew into a corporate existence.

The chancellor of Notre Dame had been an important factor in educational matters up to the beginning of the twelfth century. He held absolute sway over the students of all Paris; he dispensed licenses; he was the students' civil and religious judge; he had the power of excommunication.[1] He became high-handed and abused his power. He exacted exorbitant fines; he had a dungeon of his own, and imprisoned arbitrarily.

The popes and their legates, in order to diminish this power, granted various privileges to students and masters. Thus Innocent III., who had been himself a student in Paris, and had been witness of the chancellor's tyranny and of the long train of evils that followed in its wake, legislated in order to break it down. In 1208 he authorized the teachers to be represented by a syndic; in 1209 he bestowed upon them the right to take oath to observe such rules as they deemed proper and useful to impose

---

[1] Bulæus, "Hist. Univ. Paris.," vol. iii., p. 44.

upon themselves as a body. In 1213, he restricted
the chancellor's judicial powers by forbidding him
to refuse a license to teach, to anybody recommended by the masters. This act is regarded as the
charter of the university.[1] In this manner did His
Holiness constitute masters and students into a
true corporation.

Six years later—in 1219—Pope Honorius III.
forbade the chancellor to excommunicate masters
and students in a body, without the authorization of
the Holy See.[2] The kings of France were no less
generous in the privileges and prerogatives that
they granted the masters and students of Paris.
All this legislation fostered the growth of the university, while it crippled the authority of the chancellor.

But the death-blow was given to that authority
when the masters and students abandoned the
shadow of the cathedral and, flocking to the left
bank of the Seine, found refuge in the depen-
dencies of the abbeys of St. Genevieve and St.
Victor. In 1213 no school belonging to the university stood outside the island of the city.[3] In 1215,
the papal legate, Robert de Courçon, regulated in
regard to the study of theology that no one should
teach it who was not thirty-five years old, who had
not devoted at least eight years to study in the
schools, and who had not in addition attended a

---

[1] Thurot, " De l'Organisation de l'Université," p. 12.

[2] Not *any member* of the University, as Thurot puts it.—
" De l'Organisation," p. 12.

[3] Denifle, " Die Entstehung der Universitäten," p. 662.

theological course of five years.[1] This shows that Paris had already a school of theology, and that dialectics were regarded as simply a preparation for the higher branch.

In 1216, the first year of the papacy of Honorius III., who took an abiding interest in the rising university, a school was opened under the jurisdiction of the chancellor of St. Genevieve's. The chancellor of the cathedral regarded this as an encroachment upon his rights, and refused to regard as valid any license or diploma signed by the chancellor of St. Genevieve's. The quarrel was settled by Pope Honorius III. in a brief to the bishop and chancellor of Paris, in which it was ordered that any licentiate of the chancellor of St. Genevieve's be admitted to teach upon the same footing with a licentiate of the chancellor of Notre Dame. This gave new impetus to the schools on the left bank of the Seine. Students continued to flock thither. Between 1219 and 1222 the largest exodus to Mount St. Genevieve took place.

---

[1] Bulæus, vol. i., p. 82. Thurot mistook the reading of this text in his essay.

UNIVERSITIES.

· *Addenda:* Rome encouraged studies in a more substantial manner than by privileges. Students and professors who held benefits were dispensed from residence, and permitted to enjoy the revenues of such benefits. Du Boulay, "Hist. Univ. Par.," ii., p. 2, 570.

REGENTS.

Addenda: The Regent Master of Arts held a disputation on each of the first forty days after his inception. During that time he was not permitted to wear boots; instead, it was regulated that he wear heelless shoes, known as "pynams," later on, as "slop-shoes." "Mun. Acad.," p. 450. Lyte, "A Hist. of Oxford," p. 218.

About 1227 the schools of theology and law were transferred to the same side. Thenceforth, the abbot of St. Genevieve's assumed a certain amount of jurisdiction over the university, and, finally the chancellor of St. Genevieve's shared the administration with the chancellor of Notre Dame and the rector of the four nations. Thus was the University of Paris — the Latin Quarter — cradled on the island beneath the shadow of Notre Dame. Thus did it grow into a corporate existence out of the struggles of the masters to rid themselves of the thraldom of the chancellor.

Once only did the papacy fail in sustaining the university in this struggle. The incident will throw light upon mediæval university life. About 1221 the university had a seal engraved as the essential attribute of its corporate autonomy. The chapter of Notre Dame took umbrage at this act as a novelty not to be tolerated and brought the case before the papal legate then residing in Paris. The legate placed an injunction upon any further use of the seal until the case should have been properly tried and decided. Before the decision was arrived at, the seal was used, and in 1225 the legate decided in favor of the chapter of Notre Dame, broke the seal and forbade, under penalty of excommunication, the formation of another.

This decision raised a storm. The scholars and masters rose up as one body ; they besieged the house in which the legate dwelt, and caused him to flee to some place of safety. It was only in 1246 that the university afterwards obtained from Pope Innocent

IV. the right of holding and using a seal. In the
meantime the four nations had each its seal, and any
document requiring the sanction of the whole university was stamped with the four seals conjointly.
While examining these seals in the beautiful volume
of Vallet de Viriville we are reminded that the patrons
of the university were the Blessed Virgin, St. Catherine, St. Nicholas and St. Andrew.[1]

Speaking of the four nations reminds us of the
fact that they, no more than the pre-existent schools,
were the elements out of which the university was
directly formed. They came after that formation.
The university grew simply out of the association
of the professors of the four disciplines: theology,
law, medicine, and arts.[2] The four nations were
so many guilds modeled after the Saxon guilds of
an earlier age. The division was more artificial
than spontaneous. It grew out of the peculiar relation of things in the Middle Ages. Youths flocking
to a centre of learning from all parts of the world
found themselves among strangers, exposed to every
kind of imposition. Until it was otherwise legislated
for, and even thereafter, these youths were charged
exorbitant prices for lodging, board, books, service,
and clothing.

True, the university from the hour of its inception undertook to protect the students against the
exactions of the townspeople. Thus, the price of
lodgings was to be fixed by sworn arbitrators, half

---

[1] See the images of those saints on the first seals in "Histoire de l'Instruction Publique en Europe," pp. 129-135.

[2] Denifle, "Entstehung," p. 131.

appointed by the town and half by the city;[1] but there were many other things in regard to which the students required protection, and of which the university could not or would not take cognizance. Hence the necessity of their forming themselves into associations for mutual protection. The natural division was according to nations and provinces.

Oxford had two nations, the North and the South; the students of Bologna were divided into Transalpine and Cisalpine; those of Paris were divided into four nations. The last-named were organized somewhere about 1219. They were composed of all the scholars included in the licentiate, together with the Masters of Arts.[2] The four nations were known as the French, which included the Italian, Spanish and Greek students; the Picardians, which included the students of the northeast and the Netherlands; the Normans and the English, which included those of Ireland, Scotland and Germany. Later on, we find Franciscan students in the university so numerous that for convenience sake they were divided into nations. Such a division was well calculated to bring about a simplification of general management and superintendence. Each of the four nations had its own hall and its own rights and privileges as a corporate body. It had its procurator, and, as has already been remarked, its seal distinct from that of the university, its common purse, its patron saint, and its Masses.[3]

[1] "Story of the University of Edinburgh," by Sir A. Grant, i., p. 5. Gregory IX. obtained this concession from Louis IX. in 1244.

[2] Denifle, "Entstehung," p. 131.

[3] Thurot, "De l'Organisation de l'Enseignement," p. 22.

Members were addressed according to the nation under which they were enrolled. Those of the French nation as *Honoranda Natio Franciæ, Gallorum* or *Gallicana;* those of Picardy as *Fidelissima Picardorum,* or *Picardica;* those of Normandy as *Veneranda Normanorum* or *Normaniæ;* and those of Germany as *Constantissima Germanorum* or *Allemaniæ Natio.*[1] In consequence of the wars between England and France antipathy to England was shown at an early stage of the university by expunging that name and substituting Germany instead. The national spirit waxed strong with the growth of each organization. Party spirit ran high among the nations. Public festivities were frequently occasions for public rioting.

Each nation vied with the others in celebrating the feast day of its patron saints, with the religious solemnities of which were mixed up the most worldly and profane rejoicings. They were made the occasion of illuminations, masqueradings, balls and cavalcades.

As each nation sought to excel in display, members of the other nations endeavored to spoil the celebration. They were attacked while walking in procession. A decree of Oxford University prohibited the nations from going to church or to the public places in a body, dancing or shouting with masks over their faces, or to march anywhere with garlands of leaves or flowers on their heads under penalty of excommunication, and if persisted in, of imprisonment.[2] Not only did each nation seek to rival the

---

[1] Vallet de Viriville: "Histoire de l'Instruction Publique en Europe," p. 134.

[2] "Munimenta Academica," p. 18.

others in pomp and show, but each to a certain degree despised the others, and attached thereto a nickname of opprobrium that was considered characteristic.

The Englishman was a drunkard and a leech ; the Frenchman was proud, effeminate and decked out like a woman ; the German, furious and obscene; the Norman, vain and boastful; the Poitevin, a traitor and a spendthrift ; the Burgundian, stupid and brutal; the Breton, light and changing; the Lombard, miserly, cowardly and avaricious; the Roman, seditious, violent, and quick at blows; the Sicilian, cruel and tyrannical ; the Brabantine, a man of blood, an incendiary, a brigand ; the Fleming, a glutton, a prodigal, and soft as butter.[1] The hurling of such epithets soon led to blows. Even the religious orders became tainted with the race-spirit. We read that the superior of the Dominicans in Oxford objected to the receiving of subjects from other nations in the convent of that place, for which he was deposed in general chapter and subjected to a severe penance for several years.[2]

There was one common enemy in relation to whom all the nations in all the universities were united as one man. That enemy was the town. The students were so protected by papal and royal decrees that they could behave most outrageously with the greatest impunity and escape chastisement.

---

[1] Jacques de Vitry: "Historia Occidentalis," cap. vii., p. 278. Archbishop Vaughan erroneously mentions the Picards in this quotation. Jacques de Vitry does not use the word.

[2] Martene and Durand: "Thesaurus Anecd.," t. iv., 1730, 1731.

The university became the spoiled child of kings and popes. The young men had no respect for person or property. They compelled the passers-by to give up their purses, and spent the booty so acquired in the taverns with the vilest company of men and women. No townsman or townswoman was safe in their hands. No matter how great their crime, if taken into custody by the civil authorities the whole university was up in arms and suspended all lessons till the culprits were released.[1] There was never a peace between town and gown; there was merely an armistice; the feud was only smouldering when it was not open. Affrays not infrequently ended in the plundering of houses, and even in murder.

A characteristic incident that occurred in 1381 in Cambridge, when the country was in a state of intense excitement, is told by Mr. J. Bass Mullinger:

"At Corpus Christi all the books, charters and writings belonging to the society were destroyed. At St. Mary's the university chest was broken open, and the documents which it contained met with a similar fate. The masters and scholars, under intimidation, surrendered all their charters, muniments and ordinances, and a grand conflagration ensued in the market-place, where an ancient beldame was to be seen scattering the ashes in the air, as she exclaimed, 'Thus perish the skill of the clerks!'"[2]

These instances might be multiplied at will.

The nations soon grew beyond the mere purposes of discipline that seemed to have been the

---

[1] For instances see Du Boulay, "Hist. Univ. Paris," t. v., pp. 97, 145, 830; t. vi , p. 490.

[2] "History of the University of Cambridge." " Epochs of Church History," p. 20.

primary object of their formation. The prominence
that they acquired in avenging injuries done any
member of their guild, whether by legal process or
otherwise. gave them a voice in the administration
of the university. Their proctors were received
with the dignity and honor becoming representatives
of bodies so powerful. They elected officers; they
prescribed studies; they were foremost in repelling
every attack made upon the rights and privileges of
the university by chancellor or bishop. They
elected a common head who became known as the
rector. In 1249 they agreed that this election shall
be by means of the four proctors.' The rector was
taken exclusively from the faculty of arts. At first
elected for a month, afterwards for six weeks, he
was by statute of 1278 elected for three months. In
the beginning he was only the common head of the
nations. Denifle says: "If the rector was only
head of the nations, and these were not identical
with the university, it is self-evident that the rector
was not head of the university."[2]

As we have seen, the nations soon became the
most formidable, the most active and the most
aggressive elements in the university. Towards
1300 the faculties of law and medicine were subject
to the rector of the four nations; towards 1350 the
faculty of theology fell under his jurisdiction, and
he then became head of the whole university.[3]
Father Denifle considers the office to have been a

---

[1] Bulæus, "Hist. Univ. Paris," vol. iii., p. 222.

[2] "Entstehung," p. 107.

[3] Denifle, Ibid., p. 132.

superfluous one throughout the whole career of the university.[1]   Be this as it may, the day of the rector's installation was one of great rejoicing.   It was celebrated by a solemn procession, in which the religious orders residing in the Latin quarter joined the members of the university.   His jurisdiction was supreme, extending to all schools, officers and trades under the university.   He was held in great honor and esteem; was frequently called into the councils of the king, and in procession walked side by side with the Bishop of Paris as his peer. He was custodian of the treasury and the archives and controlled the *Près-aux-clercs*.   He gave letters of scholarship to masters and students, conferred on them the privileges of the gown, and received from them in return the oath of perpetual obedience, no matter the dignity to which they might afterwards arrive.[2]   He was addressed in French as *Messire*, or *l'Amplissime;* in Latin as *Amplissime Rector*, or *Vestra Amplitudo.*[3]

The revenue of the rector came out of the sale of parchment which was controlled by the university. The market was permitted only in three places, namely: in a hall of the convent of the Mathurins, at the fair of St. Laurent and at that of St. Denis.   The rector sent out his four sworn dealers in parchment to count and tax the bundles brought in for sale by the outside merchants.   The tax being levied and

---

[1] " Entstehung," p. 693.

[2] Vallet de Viriville, "Histoire de l'Instruction publique en Europe," p. 125.

[3] Ibid., p. 134.

gathered, after the tradesmen by appointment of the king, those of the bishops and the masters and scholars had made their purchases, the merchants were free to sell to whom they would.[1] In 1292 there were nineteen dealers in parchment in Paris, twelve of whom lived on the street then known as *des Écrivains*, now called *de la Parcheminerie*.[2]

The great event in this connection was the fair held at St. Denis. From 1109 it was customary for the people headed by the bishop and many of the clergy of Paris, to go in procession to the open plain of St. Denis in order to venerate a portion of the true Cross.

The relic was exposed, prayers were said, sermons were preached and solemn benediction was given. The exposition of the Holy Cross lasted nine days during which these devotions were repeated. Merchants took occasion of the throngs to expose their wares, and the plain of St. Denis during this season became also a place of chaffer — a fair — *indictum*.[3] As late as 1429 the religious character was still kept up, for we find that June 8th of that year the bishop and clergy went to St. Denis in order to preach a sermon and give benediction of the Holy Cross.[4]

Early in the thirteenth century St. Denis became the chief market for parchments. The rector of the university recognized it as such, and rode in state to the fair, and had his seal impressed upon all the

---

[1] Crevier, "Histoire de l'Université," t. ii., p. 130.

[2] A. Franklin, "La Vie privée d'Autrefois, Écoles et Collèges," p. 94.

[3] Whence l'endit — lendit — *Landit*.

[4] Le Beuf, " Histoire du Diocèse de Paris," t. iii., p. 283.

parchments required during the year.¹ It was the occasion of a general holiday for the university. The students started from St. Genevieve's, and rode in procession to the grounds amid the astonishment of the townsfolk. No sooner had they set foot on the ground than they abandoned themselves to all kinds of disorder. It was a pilgrimage of voluptuousness in which innumerable excesses were committed.² In following the doings of the rector we are getting a further glimpse of mediæval university life. His was a unique position in that life. To attain the goal of his ambition, his nation — and every nation had its own candidate — set on foot intrigues in which they exhausted their ingenuity; there was rivalry open and secret; there were bribings and threatenings; masters and scholars became excited; violence and quarrelling were frequent, ending sometimes in murder.³ Disorder and turmoil preceded the attaining of the office; disorder and turmoil accompanied the celebrations connected with the holding of the office; disorder and turmoil succeeded to the going out of office. This excitement — this constant seething of brain and vibration of nerve — enters into the very life of the university.

It was out of all this turmoil that the university grew into life and being, under the fostering care of church and state. The privileges that both church

---

¹ Le Beuf, *Ibid.*, p. 269.

² Vallet de Viriville, *loc. cit.*, p. 172. A full description — a description that we dare not reproduce — written between 1290 and 1300, has been published in the valuable work of Le Beuf, "Histoire du Diocèse de Paris," p. 259.

³ Thurot, "De l'Organisation," p. 32.

and state conceded were the vital principle of her existence. "A university without privileges," says Du Boulay, "is a body without a soul."[1] Looking back upon her growth, we find her cradled in the sanctuary of Notre Dame, then nourished into full development as an organism, independent of the state, with her own autonomy and with power to make her own laws. She drew her vitality from the Holy See. The same is true of Oxford and Cambridge. It is amusing to note how jealously Oxford watched Paris. Whatever privilege Paris received, Oxford claimed, as being on a par with her sister *Studium*. Nay, if some of the doctors in Paris were given a benefice or made bishops, forthwith Oxford sent a deputation to Rome asking for an equal share in the bounty of the Holy See.

As science is free as truth, even so were these mediæval universities secure from all control. This complete liberty was the secret of their success. Scholars and masters enjoyed immunity from civil jurisdiction, and were answerable for their behavior only to fellow-members. In this respect, the University of Paris stood alone, a power great and unique in the world, ranking in prestige and influence with the Papacy and the Holy Roman Empire. Doctrinal heresies lurked and grew within the precincts of this and other universities; immorality was at times rampant among students and professors, but withal, as children of the Church, encouraged and protected by the popes, they were Catholic in their spirit and

---

[1] " Hist. Univ. Paris," vol. i., p. 95.

in the general tone of their teachings. "Privileged and well-beloved daughters of the Church," says Wimpheling, "they endeavored by their fidelity and attachment to render to their mother all that they owed her."[1] So long as they remained docile to the Church, they flourished; the moment they were secularized and became mere tools in the hands of unscrupulous governments, they fell from their high and exceptional standing. This is their history in a nutshell.

II.

Such was the outward showing of a mediæval university as witnessed in its highest type. Its inner life was more varied and interesting. Let us again confine ourselves to Paris or to its models. The University of Paris was an intellectual center through which passed numerous currents of humanity from every part of Christendom — all devoured by a thirst for knowledge that could scarcely be satisfied. There was scarcely a class or condition of men that was not to be found in a mediæval university. The rich were there, and in their eagerness to acquire knowledge forgot that they were rich, and neglected to surround themselves with the luxuries and comforts that wealth might have purchased. The poor were there, and were not ashamed of their poverty. Prince and peasant, lordly cardinal and struggling clerk, sat on the same floor listening to the same lecture. Boys of twelve were there; a statute had to be passed excluding those under that

---

[1] "De Arte Impressorio," p. 19.

age. Men of thirty were there; "at the age of thirty or forty," says Le Clerc, "the student at the university was still a scholar."[1] Professors in one department of letters were to be seen, after delivering their own lectures, seated in the same hall with their pupils studying the same matter. "This gave to the professorship," says Janssen, "a lively, animated and youthful emulation; to the student a dignity and an influence, traces of which we meet with everywhere in the constitutions of the universities."[2]

Before assisting at a lesson, let us acquire some idea of the attainments of scholars and masters. Students began the university course at an early age. Having learned reading, writing and the elements of Latin grammar, they started to study logic at the age of twelve, and from fourteen upward they were in position to submit to the examinations and carry on the disputations that were requisite before receiving any academic distinction.

The first was that of determinant. In order to receive the distinction of determinant, the student, after his second year's course, applied for examination. This examination was severe. Immediately before Christmas, the candidate sustained, in presence of the school, an argument or dispute on some question of morals against a regent. Finally, there was the crowning test, in which he disputed daily, till the end of Lent, in the school of his nation, rue de Fouarre. Remember that these disputes were

---

[1] "Hist. Litt. de la France au XIVème Siècle," i., p. 269.
[2] "Geschichte," i., p. 74.

carried on by boys not older than fifteen or sixteen years. In 1472 the Lenten disputes were suppressed, and the degree of bachelor was substituted for that of determinant. If successful, the candidate received a certificate showing that he had read the following works:

1. " The Introduction " of Porphyry in the translation of Boëthius. Porphyry wrote the book as an introduction to the " Categories " of Aristotle, a work also translated by Boëthius. It was through this book that the question of Nominalism and Realism assumed such vast proportions during the Middle Ages.

2. " The Categories " of Aristotle.

3. The book on " Interpretation," which was the only part of Aristotle's writings taught before the ninth century in the translation of Boëthius. It is generally known under its Greek title, " Perihermenias."

4. " The Syntax " of Priscian. This contained books xvii. and xviii. of Priscian's Grammar, and was known as the " Priscianus Minor." Priscian (flor. 500) was the standard grammarian of the Middle Ages.

5. An ordinary or an extraordinary course in the " Topics " and " Elenchi " of Aristotle. These books had been translated by James of Venice before 1128.[1]

6. The determinant should, in addition, have followed during two years the course in dogmatics,

---

[1] Am. Jourdain, " Recherches Critiques sur les Traductions d'Aristote," p. 58.

and should have assisted at, and taken part in, the disputations.

The course here given is of the thirteenth century. In the fifteenth century there was a general revolt against the scholastic system, and morals and rhetoric received a more prominent place. In 1452 the rules of versification were made a recognized part of the course, and in 1457 the study of Greek was added. But, looking at the programme of studies here laid down, it must be said that it was heavy work for youths not older than fifteen or sixteen.

It may seem strange to us that boys of that age could carry on such disputes. The precociousness of the youth of those days is a fact that has been frequently commented upon. Tiraboschi called attention to it, and Janssen gives several instances in the fifteenth century, in which extraordinary things are told of studious youths. Adam Potken (1490) read the " Eclogues of Virgil and the Orations of Cicero " to pupils ranging from eleven to twelve years of age. John Eck (b. 1486) completed all the Latin classics from his ninth to his twelfth year. At the age of thirteen he entered Heidelberg, and at fifteen received from Tübingen the degree of Master of Arts. John Muller, the celebrated mathematician, matriculated in the University of Leipzig at the age of twelve, and in his sixteenth year received his Master's degree from the University of Vienna.[1] Multiplicity of subjects and multiplicity of text-books tend to weaken the intellectual grasp of the modern

---

[1] Janssen, "Geschichte," pp. 59, 60.

student. In those mediæval days, when the student had few notes and less books to fall back upon, having listened to his lessons attentively and retained them carefully in memory, he became more self-reliant, and, if possessed of a fair share of talent, could hold his own in disputation.

The determinant had certain privileges and certain duties. He was entitled to wear a cape and to assist at the masses of the nations. Every Friday he was obliged to discuss grammar with the backward boys. He was liable to be called upon as assistant teacher and give special or cursory lessons. This led to abuse; for we find from the statutes of Oxford that determinants, upon receipt of a bribe, were given to neglect the ordinary lessons and devote themselves exclusively to the cursory lessons. He furthermore presided over the disputations of the younger students, reviewed the whole question under discussion, noticed the imperfections or fallacies in the arguments advanced, and then pronounced his decisions or determinations in the scholastic forms.[1] His duty at other times was to dispute logic daily, except Friday, when he disputed grammar, and the first and last day of his determination, when he disputed questions in morals and dogma.

The hours for determining were from 9 to 12 and from 1 to 5.[2] In the meantime, after the first principal test, the determinant continued his studies till he had completed his twenty-first year, when he was

---

[1] Anstey, "Munimenta Academica," i., p. 87.
[2] Ibid., p. 246.

of age to become a licentiate, or one having the inherent right to teach. He should also have made public reading in some school, of a book of Aristotle during a whole year.

For the grand act of inception there was long and severe preparation on the part of the intellectual athlete, and when the event arrived it was accompanied by great excitement and turbulence. The ceremony was held in the hall of the nation under which the aspirant was ranked. The aspirant went from school to school, inviting each master in person.[1] Invitations of most elaborate designs were sent out to distinguished persons, and were frequently accepted. Charles VIII. of France was present in 1485 at the sustaining of a thesis. It was the ambition of every bachelor and his friends to have a brilliant gathering, and they resorted to every means to attain their object. This ambition went to the extent of making it customary to drag in every passer-by, will-he, nill-he, in order to have a large audience. Statutes were enacted forbidding the practice, under pain of excommunication and imprisonment.[2]

The mode of disputation did not vary. The theses had been announced some time before. The conclusions were beautifully inscribed on the invitations that had been sent out. The hour having arrived, let us enter the hall. The master is seated upon a platform, in a large armchair. The candi-

---

[1] Ibid., p. 433.

[2] Vallet de Viriville " Hist. de l'Education Publique," p. 137.

date for inception stands before him. The first
thesis is announced, the young bachelor repeats the
proposition, divides it up into its various headings
and explains each as best he can. It is not permitted to interrupt him, according to the statutes;
but on this point the statutes are frequently broken.
He is not long speaking when an opponent under-
takes to pick flaws in his arguments, formulating
all his objections in the mould of the syllogism.
The defendant takes up the objections, resolves
them into their component parts, discusses separately their affirmative and their negative sense,
throws his argument into the syllogistic form, now
distinguishing in regard to the use of terms, now
denying the major or minor premiss, now calling
attention to the employment of an undistributed
middle term. As the debate grows warm, the
dialectic skill and acumen of each shine forth. The
opponent takes hold of the last distinction made
by the defensor, and actually places him upon the
horns of a dilemma. The audience cheers. The
defensor is staggered; only for a moment, however.
He retorts the dilemma upon his wily objector and
routs him, amid the clamor of the students. Another takes up the cudgels and attacks the thesis
from his point of view. Again, there are distinctions and syllogisms and dilemmas as before.
And so, "amid loud clamor on the part of the
audience, and on the part of the combatants, great
shaking of the head and stamping of the feet, and
extending of the fingers, and waving of the hands,
and contortions of the body as though they were

crazed," [1] the work goes on for hours, during whole days, and even weeks. Be it remembered that a written essay or thesis was in those days something unknown among students. Everything was carried on orally. [2] At last, after a severe struggle, the successful bachelor becomes an inceptor. Here, by the way, is the origin of our word "commencement" as applied to the closing exercises of a college.

The disputation concluded, the newly-made inceptor takes oath to observe the statutes and also that he is provided with a school in which to read. [3] Forthwith the biretta is placed on his head and he gives his inaugural lecture. If it is a candidate who incepts as a master in grammar, the beadle presents him with a birch and a ferule, with which he publicly flogs a boy within the precinct of the school. He pays the beadle for providing the birch and the boy for submitting to the flogging. [4] Then comes the feasting incident to inception, from which none are exempt. Even members of religious orders are obliged to give in money the average cost of a banquet. ("Mun. Acad.," p. 564.) The officers and the invited guests are arranged in order of precedence by the chancellor, or rector, or proctor of the nation. Presents consisting usually of silk or kid gloves, or of a scarlet hood were made to the officers and the distinguished guests.

---

[1] Peter Cantor, "Verbum Abbreviatum," cap. v.,p. 34.
[2] Thurot, "De l'Organ. de l'Université," p. 88.
[3] Mun. Acad., p. 414.
[4] See Mullinger, "History of the University of Cambridge," i., p. 344.

Benificed persons licensed to read " The Sentences" at Oxford were obliged by statute to give robes to the officers just as the bachelors gave them. (" Mun. Acad.," ii., p. 237.) These ceremonies were frequently accompanied by scenes of disorder and even of violence. The statutes of Oxford decreed that on account of such scenes no one on the occasion of the banquet should stop the free ingress and egress of any master or his servants to or from the hall or tent or other place in which the graduating feast is held, and that no one except the servants of the university, or the host, shall enter the said hall or tent until the masters who have been invited shall enter with their servants, and, after they shall have sat down, no one else shall sit down except by the appointment of the chancellor, and each in proper order according to his rank; and furthermore it is decreed that no one shall beat the doors, tables, or roof, or throw stones or other missiles so as to disturb the guests, under penalty of imprisonment, excommunication and a fine of twelve pence.[1] So great became the abuse, that ultimately all these costly rejoicings were abolished.

The inceptor's next step was to apply for the master's degree. This was done as follows: Upon application the inceptor received from the chancellor a book on which he was to be interrogated. After mastering the volume he returned to obtain a day in which he might present himself for examination. Upon the day named he appeared before a jury of several masters presided over by the chancellor, and

---

[1] " Munimenta Academica," i., pp. 308, 309.

after a searching examination he was declared admitted to the honor sought, or was postponed for another year. Furnished with ecclesiastical approbation, he came before the members of his faculty and received at their hands the master's cap. Once made master, the inceptor was required to teach while pursuing his own studies in theology, in medicine, or in civil or canon law.

"The fact," says Mr. J. Bass Mullinger, "that each Master of Arts, in turn, was called upon to take part in the work of instruction is one of the most notable features in the mediæval universities. His remuneration was limited to the fees paid by the scholars who formed his auditory to the bedells, and was often consequently extremely small. When once, however, he had discharged this function, he became competent to lecture in any faculty to which he might turn his attention, and . . . . when studying either the civil or canon law, theology or medicine, might be a lecturer on subjects included in his own course."[1]

Here we leave the master teaching philosophy and pursuing his studies in the professional courses, in order to consider another element that enters into the formation of the university, and though the co-operation of that element was never cordially welcomed, it none the less contributed largely to the university's development and prestige.

III.

Two religious orders that had sprung into existence about the same time with the universities soon became identified with them and exercised

---

[1] "A History of the University of Cambridge," p. 28.

over them a deep and an abiding influence. These were the Franciscans and the Dominicans. Erase from the records of both Paris and Oxford the names of the learned men furnished by these orders, and you extinguish the greatest lights, the most dazzling glories, of mediæval thought. There is a void that nothing can supply. Had these men not lived and labored as they did, the whole trend of modern thought would run differently. The Dominicans were the first religious order admitted to membership in the university of Paris, and with time became the leaders of thought.

The Franciscans, during almost a century, guided the destinies of Oxford. Oxford was the nursery of the order. From the time when Richard Muliner gave the corporation a house and piece of ground for their use, and Brother Agnello, coming up from London, caused to be built a decent school, in which he induced Robert Grosseteste to deliver lectures, and the future eminent Bishop of Lincoln brought that school into high repute—from that time the Gray friars became a power in the university.[1] They made rapid strides in study, in disputation and in teaching. The most eminent men in England considered it an honor to lecture under their auspices. Under the able administration of Adam Marsh, the Gray friars achieved a worldwide reputation for learning. Let one who has made a thorough and a loving study of them speak, though he was not of their visible communion, and

---

[1] "Monumenta Franciscana,"·vol. i., pp. 17, 549.

to all appearances died not a member of their household. Professor Brewer says :

"Lyons, Paris, and Cologne were indebted for their first professors to the English Franciscans in Oxford. Repeated applications were made from Ireland, Denmark, France and Germany for English friars; foreigners were sent to the English school, as superior to all others. It enjoyed a reputation throughout the world for adhering the most conscientiously and strictly to the poverty and severity of the order; and for the first time since its existence as a university, Oxford rose to a position not even second to Paris itself. The three schoolmen of the most profound and original genius, Roger Bacon, Duns Scotus and Occham, were trained within its walls. No other nation of Christendom can show a succession of names at all comparable to the English schoolmen in originality and subtility, in the breadth and variety of their attainments." [1]

This unstinted tribute is not exaggerated.

That the Franciscans should achieve such greatness as a learned body is all the more remarkable, when it is remembered that Francis of Assisi, in making poverty his bride and the chief glory of his Order, had intended that poverty of spirit should extend to deprivation of intellectual food. He dreaded the influence of learned doctors upon his friars. He did not intend to create an order of students; his sole object was to form simple men in the mould of nature's own simplicity, detached from everything in life, and, most of all, from self, burning with love of God and zeal for their neighbor; men

---

[1] "Monumenta Franciscana," i., preface, lxxxi.

of the people, in touch and sympathy with the people, living amongst the poorest upon the fare of the poorest, going into pest-houses and nursing the sick, waiting upon lepers, loving whatever was loathsome in humanity, seeking and cherishing whatever was abandoned or whatever others shrank from ; men free as truth. In moulding such men, he was laying the deepest and most solid foundation on which to build up the noblest intellectual superstructure.

The spirit for study, the craving for knowledge, a spirit and a craving that have never been surpassed, filled the very atmosphere of the thirteenth century. No body of men, with such noble aspirations as those possessed by the disciples of Assisi,[1] could resist the inspiration of the hour, or keep pace with the progress of humanity, without utilizing one of the most God-like gifts bestowed upon man — his intellectual endowments.

As early as 1217, the Franciscans were installed in Paris, and it is not many years before we find them thoroughly equipped for educational purposes. In a short period they grew to be thousands. They provided for their own subjects a school of grammar, a school of rhetoric, a school of logic, and a fourth school for the study of the "Sentences" of Peter Lombard and the "Physics" of Aristotle. The hall for their advanced students was not excelled by any in the university. Their method was that of the university. They held two lectures in the morning — one on dogmatic theology, the other on particular

---

[1] See Luke Wadding, "Annales Minorum," t. i., p. 248.

issues requiring explanation. In the afternoon there was a lecture on Holy Scripture, and from four to five the friars held open disputation, in which any comer was free to join.[1] In their rules of prayer, and missionary labor, and in devoting themselves to healing the ailments of body and soul, they acquired a training and received a special formation that the university could not give.

Their educational influence was many-sided. Mingling with the people, they cultivated the language of the people, and helped to fix the forms of our modern tongues; as nurses of the sick, they compounded medicines and learned the healing properties of plants; as missionaries, they traveled among many peoples, shrewd observers of men and manners and customs;[2] as instructors of the people in the truths of their religion, they organized companies to enact, and enacted themselves, at times, in the ancient miracle-plays, the great truths of our holy religion; as disciples of their saintly founder who loved all things in nature, who called the sun his brother and welcomed death as his sister, they also looked upon bird and beast, flower and tree, with kindly and observant eye, and learned to respect and reverently investigate the phenomena of nature; and so it happens that Roger Bacon makes his "Opus

---

[1] Vaughan, "St. Thomas of Aquin," pp. 228, 229.

[2] See the Itinerary of Blessed Odoric of Pordenone, in the "Acta Sanctorum," under January 14th. From this book, and from the account of the Franciscan friar, Carpini, concerning the Tartars, Sir John Mandeville filched all that is truthful in his so-called "Travels." See "Encyclopædia Britannica," new edition.

Majus" the forerunner of the "Novum Organum" of his namesake of four hundred years later; in the domain of art, the tender devotion that they inculcated for Mary Immaculate inspired the school of art which flowered into the Madonnas of Raphael.

The Dominicans were established with the formal purpose of occupying themselves with books and studies rather than with the singing of antiphons and responsories,[1] for their sole mission was to preach the doctrines of Christianity and to refute heresy. Their courses of instruction were accordingly thoroughly organized from the beginning. In each convent, four officers were charged with the studies: the prior, who looked after the general conduct and the spiritual and physical wants of the young brothers; the lector and sub-lector, who taught in the schools; and the master of studies, who was always with the brothers, taking part in their exercises, presiding over their repetitions, assisting at their examinations, and even, at times, explaining the lesson.

In the fourteenth century, to these were added a cursory reader and a chief lector. The youthful aspirant to the order was admitted at the age of fifteen, and was supposed to be instructed in all the preliminary branches of education. His novitiate, which lasted three years, was divided between study, spiritual exercises, and manual labor. The novitiate passed, the novice went through a three years' course of logic and rhetoric ; his whole course in logic should

---

[1] Theodosia Drane, "Christian Schools and Scholars," vol. ii., p. 59.

extend to five years. This was known as the *Studium artium.* It corresponded to the course pursued in the university for a bachelor's degree. Its method was comprised in the three traditional words: lectures, study, disputation — *legendo, studendo, ac disputando.* The lector explained the text of the grammar, rhetoric, or logic, which the student had in hand; the student immediately withdrew to learn the lesson. Later, all assembled, and there were repetitions and colloquies or discussions in circles of students of the same capacity. There were semi-annual examinations, and formal disputations were carried on from time to time. By these means the student was prepared for the grand act of disputation.

The young Dominican then passed to the course of ethics and physics, provided he was adjudged "tried, instructed and of good health,"[1] for to none other was the course given. The course was known as the *Studium naturalium.* It extended over two years till 1372 when it was made thereafter a three years' course. It comprised natural philosophy, ethics, mathematics and all the sciences of that day. The treatises of Aristotle were pressed into service rapidly as they were translated. It was the course in which the genius of Albertus Magnus was watered and bloomed into flower and leaf and ripened into fruitful and suggestive thought in scientific matters; and how great Albertus Magnus was in the domain

---

[1] Provincial chapter of Montpelier, held in 1271. See G. Douais, "Organisation des Études chez les Frères Prêcheurs," p. 69.

of natural science only a Poucher and a Humbolt can adequately tell.   Even in that age Albert made permanent contributions to physical science.[1]   St. Thomas availed himself of this course so well that he was afterwards able to speak to the students of the University of Paris upon the construction of aqueducts and machinery for raising and conducting water — *de aquarum conductibus et ingeniis erigendis* — as well as expound the " Timæus " of Plato.[2]

From this course the student passed to theology. The *Studium Theologiæ* lasted three years.   It differed from the previous course in that there was no exemption from its curriculum.   The subject was so vast and so profoundly was it studied, it was never completely mastered.   No member was too old or too learned to say that there was nothing more for him to acquire.   Hence, all were required to follow the course.   "The Friar Preacher," says Douais, "whether student or professor, assisted at the lessons in theology with the two-fold intent of not forgetting what he had already learned and of adding to his stock of knowledge."[3]

Here, also, the method of teaching was in many respects similar to that pursued in the university. A text-book was read and commented upon by the lector.   For a long time the "Sentences" of Peter Lombard was the text.   Later, the commentaries

---

[1] See Echard, "Scriptores Ordinis Prædicatorum," t. i., pp. 162–183.

[2] Bulaeus, "Hist. Univ. Par.," t. iii, p. 408.

[3] "Organisation des Études chez les Frères Prêcheurs," p. 75.

were carefully written before being delivered to the students. Lessons were given every day except feast-days. The customs of the order recognized three kinds of lessons: the public or ordinary lesson at which all assisted; the private lesson given to back-ward students, and the extraordinary or cursory lessons similar to those of the university, generally imparted by bachelors without being seated in the master's chair. There were repetitions, colloquies and disputations as in the philosophy classes. Only a doctor in theology was permitted to preside over the disputations. The times for disputation were Advent and Lent. The rule rigidly insisted that all the brethren be present at these exercises, and it was only after the disputation that they were permitted to go out to preach.

Humbert Romanus, one of the generals of the Order, in calling attention to the defects against which the students should guard, throws further light upon the mode of conducting the exercise. He is unsparing in his censure of those friars, even though they be doctors, who presume to speak at all times in a light, flippant vein, without proper prep-aration, or without sufficient ability to discuss their themes. He is no less severe upon those who pre-serve an obstinate silence during the whole time of the exercise, whether through laziness, or timidity, or dread of defeat. Some debated well, but their vanity was continually cropping out; in season and out of season they aired their knowledge when holy and learned men would have blushed to name the authors that they read. Some there were who

simply sought to get the better of the argument, re-
gardless of truth; others lacked precision and clearness, while not a few were obscure and diffuse.
Even the most penetrating minds, at times, became
lost in minute distinctions that were vain and use-
less.[1] These disputations among the doctors in theology were not conducted merely with a view of
sharpening the wits, or carrying on an intellectual
joust, or as a display of talent. Their aim was higher.
It was for the search after truth, the probing of truth,
the more complete expression of truth.

We have not yet exhausted the educational
resources of the Dominicans. The order had in
reserve other courses of discipline. Each province
was obliged to have two special schools for the
more gifted of its subjects.[2] These schools were
intended solely for those young friars whose aptitude gave promise of their becoming lectors one
day. The friars were sent thither after pursuing
the ordinary three years' course in theology. A
doctor in theology, having under him a sub-lector,
was placed in charge of each school. In 1290, a
lector was appointed to teach special courses in
exegesis and other biblical studies. These schools
were known as the *Studia Solemnia.* The method
of instruction pursued in them was the same as that
pursued in the lower course. The studies were simply broadened and deepened. Those pursuing them

---

[1] " Expositio regulæ B. Augustini," Biblioth. municip. de
Toulouse, MS., 417 (I. 402, fo. 147b.), quoted by Douais, *loc.
cit.,* p. 79.

[2] Douais, *loc. cit.,* p. 127.

were not permitted to remain longer than three years.

Nor was this all. In certain centers, schools of higher study were established. They were called *Studia Generalia.* They were no mere novices in learning who were sent up to these schools. They were men who had been teaching for years, and who now resumed their studies with the intention of winning the doctor's cap and of perfecting themselves in special branches. These schools were established in Paris, Oxford, Bologna, Naples, Montpelier and other university centers. Those who assisted at the course instituted in Paris did so with the view of becoming profound theologians; those who attended the course in Bologna had in view chiefly the study of civil and canon law; those who went to Barcelona intended to become skilled in the sciences of the Moors and versed in the Arabic and Hebrew languages.

The discipline of these houses was severe. There was no vacation as in other schools; the courses were profound, and were carried on without intermission during the whole three years that they lasted. None but brothers of approved health and tried powers of endurance, with a constitution equal to the great strain, were admitted to take up these courses. They were men who had already given evidence of their intellectual prowess as professors of philosophy, theology, Sacred Scriptures, or even as priors. Peter Lombard's book of "Sentences" was read through each year; there was also a complete course of biblical studies, besides the special branches that predominated in each school. Here the friars made a more profound study of the philosophical and theological errors of the day—and the very air was reeking with such errors—as well as of the Sacred Scriptures and the Fathers of the Church.

The professors of the school were picked men. The superior called them together from all parts of Christendom. Once a week they held a solemn dispute. Such a dispute—deep, thoughtful, searching—must have been quite a contrast with the wranglings daily going on in School street at Oxford or the rue de Fouarre at Paris. After fifteen years of study—not counting the years spent besides in teaching or preaching on the mission—these men must indeed have become well equipped to proclaim truth and meet error, no matter the guise under which it should appear. In connection with this solemn and learned body of men discussing the great issues of their day one image fills the mind. It is that of the magnificent tribute which Raphael paid to the Real Presence in his sublime picture, *La Disputa.* There has the artist painted the very men who took part in such solemn discussions. And though Duns Scotus and Dante were more at home in the halls of a Franciscan convent, still we meet there the familiar faces of Albert and Aquinas.

We should never grow weary of repeating the fact that the greatest glory of the Dominican *Studium*, indeed of the mediæval university, is Thomas Aquinas. There was no principle of human reason that he did not lay bare; there was no problem in physical or metaphysical science that he did not grapple with and find a solution for; there was no prevailing error that he did not attack and pursue to its last lurking place. The very construction of the propositions in his most scientific work, the "Summa Theologiæ," the very words in which he formulates objections, are understood only in the light of the history of contemporaneous error. He fought no windmills; he set up no men of straw in order to knock them down. He dealt with living issues. He was in touch with his age upon all its intellectual wants and aspirations. When pondering over his marvelous pages, let us not forget that while much is due to the transcendent genius of their writer, much also is due to the admirable conservative method and rigid intellectual discipline of the Order in which that genius was moulded.

A student once asked Thomas the best method of becoming proficient in science. The rules laid down by the Angelical Doctor are few and simple and to the point, and reflect the serenity of his own life. They bespeak a rare habit of mental cautiousness. They may be summarized as follows:

" Pass from the easy to the difficult; be slow to speak and equally slow to give assent to the speaker; keep your conscience clear; do not neglect prayer; be amiable towards everybody, but keep your own mind; above all things avoid running about from one school to another; let it be your delight to sit at the professor's feet;[1] be more

---

[1] There is here a play upon words that cannot be reproduced: *Sellam frequentare diligas, si vis in cellam vinariam introduci.*

concerned to hoard in memory the good things said than to regard the person speaking; strive to understand what you read, clearing your mind of all doubts as you go along; eagerly seek to place whatever knowledge you can get hold of in the depository of your mind; find out what you can do, study your limitations, and do not aim higher than your capacity permits."[1]

These are golden words to be cherished by every student.

Such suggestions were especially valuable in those days. The spirit of university life was catching, and that spirit was a wild and lawless one.

"The professors in great part," said Archbishop Vaughan, "were reckless adventurers, a sort of wild knight-errants who scoured the country in search of excitement for the mind and money for the pocket. The students were, in the main, disorderly youths living in the very center of corruption, without control, loving a noisy, dissipated life in town. . . . They would rollick and row, and stream in and out of the schools, like swarms of hornets, buzzing and litigating and quarreling with one another, upsetting every semblance of discipline and order."[2]

The picture is not overdrawn. It is merely a garbled transcript from the accounts left us by John of Salisbury, and Cardinal Vitry. "The distinguished traits," says Leclerc, "of this student life, the memories of which have survived with singular tenacity, were poverty, ardent application, and turbulence."[3] The students were as riotous in intellectual

---

[1] "Opusculum," lxi. Opp. t. xvii., p. 338.

[2] "Life of St. Thomas of Aquin," p. 206.

[3] "État des Lettres au XIV. Siècle" (see the whole passage), i. 269-271.

matters as many of them were licentious in morals.
No subject was too sacred for their curiosity;
there was no truth they were not prepared to
challenge. The masters were bold and unscrupulous in their treatment of the holiest doctrines.
Nay, so fond of novelties were they, that they were
known to pay scholars to receive their strange
teachings. The Franciscans and Dominicans, in
the first fervor of their formation, every member
filled with the spirit of charity and zeal, conservative and orthodox in their teachings — more especially the Dominicans — were a standing rebuke to
the masters and scholars who were given to novelties and unwilling to mend their ways. Even the
better class of university men looked askance at the
coming among them of these religious. They were
regarded as intruders. The prejudice extended from
the university to the court. The laureate of St. Louis
attacked the Dominicans. "They preach to us," he
says, "that it is sinful to be angry and sinful to be
envious, whilst they themselves carry on war for a
chair in the university. They must, they will, obtain it. . . . The Jacobins are persons of such
weight that they can do everything in Paris and in
Rome."[1]

But the members of the university were not content with words. They attempted to boycott the
religious. "The masters and scholars of the rival
schools would not permit young men to attend the

---

[1] "Oeuvres Complètes de Rutebœuf," t. ii., p. 251. The
Dominicans were called Jacobins because their convent was on
the St. Jacques.

lectures of the Dominicans, nor allow the young Dominicans to be present at secular disputations and defensions."[1]

The spites and jealousies that were arrayed against them found voice in the pamphlet — "Latter Day Perils" — of William of St. Amour. It was a trumpet blast calling forth all the pent-up feelings that men had been nursing against the friars. We shall not enter into the details of this controversy. Suffice it to say that Thomas Aquinas was deputed to reply to the scurrilous tract, and he did so with all the calmness, scientific precision, and delicate sense of justice that characterize his works above those of his contemporaries. He met the issue in his own direct and simple manner. He asks: "Can regulars be members of a college of secular masters?" and replies that they most undoubtedly can, since the function that seculars and regulars exercise as teachers is based upon that which is common to both, namely, to study and teach.

"The function of teaching and learning," to use his own words, "is common to seculars and to religious men; whence there is nothing to forbid religious men from being associated with seculars in the same function of study and teaching,[2] even as men in diverse conditions compose the same body of the Church, inasmuch as they all agree in unity of faith."

---

[1] Vaughan, "Life of St. Thomas of Aquin," p. 250.

[2] "Opusculum," i., cap. iii. Op. xvii., p. 11, ed. Parma. The same subject is discussed in the "Summa Theologiæ," 2a, 2æ. Quaest. 187, 188. For a detailed account of the controversy see Vaughan, "Life of St. Thomas of Aquin," pp. 208–367.

More regularly organized than the university it-self, these religious schools had a staying influence upon her students, her professors, and her courses of study.

IV.

We shall now descend to the university schools, and from the various side-lights that have been thrown upon them endeavor to catch a glimpse of the manner in which masters and scholars live and act therein. Throughout this intellectual seething mass, there are schools giving instruction in the whole gamut of learning contained in the Trivium and the Quadrivium. Here is a class of youths studying grammar. In the Middle Ages, grammar included literature and composition as well as the technical rules of construction. It covered the whole of the humanities. Hraban Maur defines grammar to be "the science of interpreting poets and historians, and of writing and speaking cor-rectly." [1]

John of Salisbury, who resided in Paris in the latter half of the twelfth century, thus describes the method pursued by his teacher, one of the most competent in his day:

"Bernard of Chartres, not confining himself to grammar, threw in a thousand observations during the reading of his lesson, on the choice of words and of thoughts, as well as on the variety and the pleas-ingness of style. . . . He cultivated carefully the memory of his pupils by obliging them to recite — some more, some less — the most beautiful passages

---

[1] "De Inst. Cler.," lib. iii., cap. 18.

from the historians and poets commented upon in class; and he always questioned them upon the lesson of the previous day. He exhorted them to confine their readings to what was good and edifying, and gave them a daily exercise to compose in prose and verse." [1]

This is an admirable method; it cannot be improved upon even to-day, after the intervening experience of seven hundred years. Bernard of Chartres was an ideal teacher. In the following century the grammarians were not so painstaking. Both masters and scholars were impatient to tread the mazes of logical disputation; in consequence, we find a falling off in the matter of style. "The youths of the universities, but ill-furnished with books, and be it said, but ill-disciplined, passed through the grammar classes rather unprofitably. They remained in them the least possible time, being attracted by the ever increasing vogue of Aristotle." [2]

We enter one of these grammar schools. The scholars are all in one room. Here is one coming from the master after reciting his lesson and having had his exercise corrected. He goes to his place, procures his tablets, a pen and ink and some parchment, and, seating himself at a long table running through the centre of the room, transcribes the corrected exercise upon a small sheet of parchment. The lettering is small and cramped; the words are

---

[1] " Metalogicus," lib. i., cap. xxiv., col. 854, Migne ed.

[2] Ch. Daniel, S. J., " Des Études Classiques," chap. vi., p. 138.

abbreviated. You would like to know the meaning of the line inscribed in this manner:

"Tityre t p r s t f."

The teacher has been alluding to Virgil, and this is evidently a shorthand report of some line in that author's works. Here it is; the word *Tityre* gives the clue:

" Tityre, tu patulæ recubans sub tegmine fagi."

The youth next to him is taking notes in logic. He is evidently quoting an extract from Occham's logic in the following condensed form: " *Sic hic e fal sm qd ad simplr.*" Here is the text: " *Sicut hic est fallacia secundum quid ad simpliciter.*"[1] The less the scholars placed upon parchment, the more they engraved their lessons upon the tablets of memory. Moreover, paper and parchment were expensive commodities in those days and were, therefore, to be sparingly used. Even as late as 1502 the amount of paper assigned to each scholar for the purpose of note-taking was three sheets a week.[2]

Let us pass to another school. This is the Place Maubert—which shall long continue to embalm the name of Albert the Great. That dingy, humid street in the neighborhood is the street that Dante has made immortal in his great poem; it is the rue de Fouarre.[3] It is not an inviting street to enter. From early morning it is the busiest and noisiest thoroughfare in Paris. The students regu-

---

[1] Vaughan, " Life of S. Thomas of Aquin," p. 199.

[2] Pasquier, " Recherches sur la France," t. i., p. 920.

[3] " Paradiso," x., 136–138.

late their rising by the bells of the neighboring churches. The mass-bell of the Carmelites, whose convent you may notice on Place Maubert, gives the first signal at five o'clock. An hour later Notre Dame strikes Prime.[1] Then the student who boards out quits his den, and descending the stairs carefully, takes his shortest course through the by-ways and alleys to the rue de Fouarre. He enters one of these low, ill-ventilated halls, with a damp, heavy smell. The master is seated on a stool; it being a winter morning, three or four candles spread a dim light through the heavily laden air, and the students, seated upon small trusses of straw, take notes of the lecture read by the master.[2] We already had a glimpse of a school of arts; then let us pass to a school of theology.

The room is also low and dingy; the light is inadequate. There are no benches; but here and there are some blocks, and there is an abundance of straw. The master sits in a large chair raised on a platform. The chair has a high, straight back and arms, and can easily seat two. He who is beside the master is an aspirant for the licentiate. But the master predominates over the aspirant and over the school.[3] Now, note the method pursued. It is composed of two parts: the reading and explanation, and the disputation. All teaching is done orally. "The act of instructing by the living voice,"

---

[1] Bulæus, "Hist. Univ. Paris," t. iv., p. 413.

[2] Alfred Franklin, "La Vie privée d'Autrefois; Écoles et Collèges," p. 168.

[3] D'Assailly, "Albert le Grand," p. 186.

says Vincent of Beauvais, "possesses I know not
what hidden energy, and sounds more forcibly in
the ears of a disciple as it passes from the mouth
of a master."[1] The master was at first accustomed
to speak altogether without a manuscript; later in
the history of the university, he read or dictated
from his manuscript a commentary upon the text.
But when, in 1354, Cardinal d'Estouteville reformed
the university, he reverted to the practice of commenting without manuscript. Indeed, the teacher
was placed under oath not to read from a written
commentary upon the text under discussion, lest
he might cease to prepare his lessons properly.

The master is now prepared to give his lesson.
The " Sentences " lies open on his lap ; the students
are seated around in groups ; some are kneeling
upon one knee with tablets in hand, prepared to
take notes ; some few have their own text-book, but
the majority are content with getting a glance at
the copy in the hall for their use. The master first
reads a proposition from the Lombard. In a sub-
dued voice and familiar tone, slightly ascending,[2] he
discourses upon the proposition, the scholars in the
meantime, as rapidly as possible, in that species of
shorthand which we have already been inspecting,
writing down the explanation. Hear how neatly
he gives the reason for each division of the text, for
each paragraph, for each sentence, for the terms
employed, and note how clearly he makes the

----

[1] "Speculum Doctrinale," lib. i., cap. 37.
[2] "De Disciplina Scholarium," cap. v., Migne ed., vol.
lxiv., col. 1234.

E. E.—7

consequences to flow therefrom. The master having ended his explanation, the students compare notes and settle upon the sense and the very words of the discourse that they have heard. Some teachers, more careful than others, in order to avoid misunderstanding, or a garbled version of what they had said, dictate their explanations. In 1492 it was made a general rule that the shorter morning class be devoted to dictation.[1] However, in the thirteenth century, the master whose lessons we are attending was content with explaining the text by a running commentary, leaving the students to carry away from the lesson as much as they could or as they cared to reproduce. The following was the method set down in the Oxford statutes:

" The masters shall read the text in order; then they shall explain it fully and openly as the matter requires. The explanation being duly arranged, they shall afterwards choose notable passages from the text to be remembered. Lastly, they shall raise points for discussion, but only such as naturally arise from the text, so that no prohibited matter be taught."[2]

However, the chief element of university training was not the lecture ; it was rather the disputation. Master disputed with master before the students ; the master disputed with his scholars ; the scholars disputed with one another under the supervision of a determinant who was present to repress quarrels, correct errors, prevent disputes from

---

[1] Du Boulay, "Hist. Univ. Par.," t. v., p. 808.
[2] "Munimenta Academica," vol. i., p. 288.

degenerating into personalities, and mark the in-
dolent ones refusing to take part in the debate. The
exercise was at times abused by teacher and pupils.
Propositions were discussed apart from their connection; distinctions were made and divisions and
subdivisions were entered into with a degree of
ingenuity that only such practice as was then prevalent could achieve. This process of dialectic refining was carried to the farthest extremes.

Thus Stephen Langton, who is known in history
as the champion of English liberties, was previously
known in Paris as a student whose work was no less
solid than brilliant; one of the most enlightened
expounders of the Scriptures, and a powerful
preacher, with a strong musical voice that could
reach any audience. Even Stephen Langton could
not resist the prevailing practice of refining thought
and seeking a new meaning for simple words. And
so we find him taking a well-known love ditty of his
day,—*Belle Aaliz mains s'en leva,*—and with a view
of turning bad into good, writing a commentary
upon it, giving it an allegorical and spiritual sense.[1]
Each professor sought to excel his rival in logical
distinctions, divisions and subdivisions. Each student vied with the other to pick flaws in his arguments; each sought to overwhelm the other and
confuse his mind by subtle distinctions beyond his
grasp. There was no exemption.

---

[1] He makes Alice the Blessed Virgin, and thus speaks of
the name:
Hoc enim *Aalis* dicitur ab *a*, quod est *sine*, et *lis, litis;*
quasi *sine lite*, sine reprehensione.—"Bibliothèque Nationale"
MSS., lat., 16;497.

In Oxford, in 1396, a certain friar from Ireland having omitted a single disputation in his year of opponency was refused permission to read "The Sentences." ("Mun. Acad.," p. 236.) No other road was open to the winning of honors; therefore should each be on the alert to answer every objection with all the vim possible. Should one refuse to take part in the debate, his silence would be imputed to ignorance or arrogance.[1] Disputation was the great field of triumph, and in consequence the greater part of the day was spent in disputation.

What was the daily regulation of university life? We may outline it as follows : The first lesson, as has been seen, was given in the morning early. The students then withdrew and arranged the matter of the last lesson, or prepared for the next, until the hour for dinner, which was generally at ten o'clock. At noon they carried on disputations, which, from the hour, were known as meridionals. At five there were repetitions of lessons and conferences, during which the scholars recited and answered questions put by the master. On Saturdays they had recapitulations and repetitions of the lessons given during the week. These were solemnly carried out under the supervision of the chief master of the school.

There has been preserved for us a daily regulation of college life in Cambridge, which, though mentioned by Lever in the sixteenth century, runs back among college traditions as far as the memory

---

[1] "De Disciplina Scholarium," cap. iv., Migne ed., col. 1234.

of man goeth. We shall put it in the words in which Cardinal Newman expressed it:

The student "got up between four and five; from five to six he assisted at mass and heard an exhortation. He then studied and attended the schools till ten, which was the dinner hour. The meal, which seems also to have been a breakfast, was not sumptuous; it consisted of beef in small messes for four persons,[1] and a pottage made of its gravy and oatmeal. From dinner to five p. m., he either studied or gave instruction to others, when he went to supper, which was the principal meal of the day, though scarcely more plentiful than dinner. Afterwards, problems were discussed and other studies pursued till nine or ten, and then half an hour was devoted to walking or running about, that they might not go to bed with cold feet,—the expedient of heat or stove for the purpose was out of the question."[2]

But we are here trenching upon college discipline and college methods in the universities, a subject that shall claim our attention in another article. In the meantime, let us beware of losing sight of the true proportions of mediæval universities in our eagerness to pry into details concerning them. Looked at in their historical setting, they stand out among the greatest creations of the spirit of Christian truth. They were the institutions of highest culture, the centres whence radiated the latest word in science and the most advanced wave of thought.

---

[1] " A penny piece of beef among four," is Lever's expression. Sermon preached at Paules Crosse, Arber's Reprints, vol. iii., pp. 121, 122.

[2] "On Universities," pp. 330, 331.

UNIVERSITY COLLEGES: THEIR ORIGIN AND THEIR METHODS

UNIVERSITY COLLEGES: THEIR ORIGIN AND THEIR METHODS.[1]

I.

M. COMPAYRÉ concludes the preface to his new volume in the following words:

"I trust also, that the literary dictionaries of the future, if they should grant me a place in their pages, will have the goodness when they mention my name to follow it with this notice: Gabriel Compayré, a French writer, whose least mediocre work, translated into English before being printed, was published in America."

We shall add to this notice : The book of which M. Compayré seems to be so proud is called "Abelard," and yet all that the author has to say about Abelard is confined to twenty-five pages. The book really covers the same ground as Mr. Laurie's work, "The Rise and Constitution of Universities," and is therefore misnamed. The subject was one upon which the author could make a particularly bright book.

---

[1] "Abelard and the Origin and Early History of Universities." By Gabriel Compayré. New York. 1893. "La Sorbonne, ses Origines et sa Bibliothèque." Par Alfred Franklin. Paris. 1875. "The University of Cambridge, from the Earliest Times to the Royal Injunctions of 1535." By J. Bass Mullinger. Cambridge. 1873. "A History of the University of Oxford, from the Earliest Times to the Year 1530." By H. C. Maxwell Lyte. London. 1886. "De Studiis Literariis Mediolanensum." Auctore Joseph Antonio Saxis. Milan. 1729.

Abelard's life, his teachers, his contemporaries, the schools in which he studied, the schools in which he taught, his pupils and his disciples, his doctrines, his methods, his persecutions, his influence—here is matter enough for so many interesting chapters, in which the author need not go over the ground so well tilled by the classic work of M. Rémusat. This is the kind of book we had a right to expect from the title. And we fail to see the intimate connection between Abelard and the University of Paris which the author would establish. Abelard is in no sense its founder. He was to no greater extent its forerunner than was his teacher, William of Champeux. Abelard was a brilliant meteor who crossed the welkin of the twelfth century, throwing around him a lurid glare, awaking minds and creating excitement ; restless, active, superficial, pretentious, bold, with sharpened intellect and a perennial flow of language. But in no sense can the university be traced to him. Had he never lived the university would have grown into corporate existence scarce a day later. There were scholastic disputations before his day ; he may have systematized them more than formerly, but he did not create them. His learning was not at all commensurate with his fame.

M. Compayré may be a good professor ; he certainly is not an apt scholar. When in 1877 he wrote the first book that brought him into notoriety—" Histoire Critique des Doctrines de l'Éducation en France Depuis le Seizième Siècle "—he showed no less a decided proclivity to draw from sources that confirmed his prejudices, than great repugnance towards any authority at all favorable to the school or the system he would condemn. This method of quotation at second-hand led him into very questionable company. He accepted information from sources the most valueless, and in consequence was led into blunders that would shame a schoolboy. Witness the following assertion concerning the Jesuits:

"In metaphysics they suppress some of the questions the most interesting and the most essential, as for instance all that regards the existence of God and the nature of His attributes."[1]

How came he to make this statement? He found a misrepresenting translation of the Constitutions and Declarations of the Jesuits with a hostile appendix, containing garbled extracts from the rules of this distinguished body, and among others, he read these words: *In metaphysica questiones de Deo et Intelligentiis prætereantur.* Now in a footnote M. Compayré avers that he has before him two complete editions of the "Ratio Studiorum." Had he opened either of them, he would have found a prohibition to touch upon those questions concerning God and His angels in metaphysical discussions, which depend wholly or in great measure upon revelation, and which therefore belong to the domain of faith.[2] Père Daniel called his

---

[1] " Hist. Crit.," t. i., p. 196.

[2] *In Metaphysica, questiones de Deo et Intelligentiis, quæ omnino aut magnopere pendent ex veritatibus divina fide revelatis, prætereantur.*

attention to this and other blunders only a little less glaring.[1]

Now, to what degree has M. Compayré profited by this lesson? Let the reader judge from the following extract:

"Thomas Aquinas had composed the 'De regimine principum,' and the 'De eruditione principum.' His disciple, Gilles de Rome, Archbishop of Bruges, who was tutor to Philip the Fair, also followed Aristotle in politics."[2]

True it is that both the volumes here named are to be found among the collected books of the Angelical Doctor, but it is generally considered that only two books of the first-named have been written by Thomas, while the latter work is now universally attributed to the pen of Peraldus, or William of Pérault. Where has M. Compayré picked up the information here so loosely expressed? Surely not from the works themselves. Even the "Histoire Littéraire" loosely written as it is in regard to these books, would have enlightened the author and guided his pen to greater accuracy.

Later on, we shall refer to them for another purpose than to express a platitude about the "Politics" of Aristotle. There is not a clause or phrase in the paragraph from which we quote that does not betray complete ignorance of the subject treated. Now, why will M. Compayré to-day, as sixteen years ago, accept such inferior material and impose it on his readers as something worthy of their intelli-

---

[1] "Les Jésuites Instituteurs de la Jeunesse Française." 1880.
[2] "Abelard," p. 290.

gence? After the wholesome lesson of Père Daniel
one would think that he would be more cautious. It
is just such paragraphs as this that render M. Compayré's book unworthy of a permanent place in
literature, and undeserving of the niche he so mod-
estly looks for. However, the author could not
write an altogether worthless book, nor could he be
dull if he tried.

And when one begins to realize that one is reading a book not on Abelard, but on the mediæval
universities, one finds much to admire and commend
in the sketch. The style is picturesque and brilliant; the outline is clearly traced; the whole subject is cleverly handled. One is enabled to form a
fair conception of the mediæval university life from
a perusal of the book. In this regard and to this
extent may the book be commended. The ordinary
reader may not observe the note of triumph with
which the author records every step towards the
secularization of the university; he may pass over
the antipathy to celibacy that is evinced through
the pages of the little work; he may forget that the
author has overlooked, or treated inadequately, the
influence of the religious orders upon university life;
and when he has finished the perusal of the book,
it may never occur to him that the very elements
which the author ignores or belittles are the soul of
the universities. With the extinction of these elements began the decay of the universities.

II.

Turn we now to university college life. It brings us a step nearer to modern school life. With the advance of the thirteenth century lawlessness grew more and more among university students. They were imposed upon, in spite of ordinance and statute, by the townspeople with whom they boarded; they were frequently in the hands of Jews paying exorbitant interest on moneys loaned; they were daily exposed to become the victims of lewd men and women who were continually on the watch for new victims. Theirs was in many instances a life of hardships that was sustained chiefly by the buoyancy of youth and an insatiable thirst for knowledge. In the meantime, the regular clergy had schools of order and discipline in which youths were well cared for and jealously shielded from the trials and temptations that were constantly assailing the student quartered upon the town. The shining lights of their respective orders lectured in the university and attracted around them youths who from admiring their professors came to love their life of peace and quiet and religious discipline, and ultimately sought admission as members. These youths were generally of bright promise and good family. And so, Carmelite and Augustinian, Franciscan and Dominican—especially the last two— gathered into their novitiates the flower of mediæval youth. Men dreaded sending their sons to Oxford lest they become friars.

In 1358, it was enacted that if any mendicant friar shall induce or cause to be induced any member of the university under eighteen years of age to join the said friars, or shall in any way assist at their abduction, no graduate belonging to the cloister or society of which such friar is a member, shall be permitted to give or attend lectures in Oxford or elsewhere for the ensuing year.[1] Richard Fitzralph, Archbishop of Armagh, who bore the friars no more love than did his disciple, John Wyclif, tells how the friars of Oxford carried off an Englishman's son, then under thirteen years, and how the father was not permitted to speak to his boy except in the presence of the friars. The father was then in Avignon, bringing the case to the notice of the pope.[2] But long before this note of alarm was sounded religious cloisters were the only havens of security amid the turmoil of university life.

Not that the need of safeguarding the student was not felt by the authorities, but all the universities in their early days were poor. Neither Paris nor Oxford up to the middle of the thirteenth century possessed a building that it could call its own. The schools and halls were rented, or were granted by the religious orders, or even by the townspeople. The official dinners of the Masters of Arts were given at the common taverns of the town. So, at Oxford in the thirteenth and fourteenth centuries the Faculty of Arts used to assemble in the Church of St. Mildred, while degrees were granted and other secular business was, by sufferance, transacted in the Church of St. Mary the Virgin.[3]

---

[1] "Munimenta Academica," i., p. 205. This statute was afterwards repealed. Cooper, "Annals," i., p. 109.

[2] "A History of the University of Oxford," p. 174.

[3] Lyte, "A History of the University of Oxford," p. 98.

Still, even at the dawn of university life, we discern traces of efforts made to assist and protect poor youth.   There is a tradition that the Danish College was established as early as 1030, with endowment for one hundred and thirty poor clerks.   In 1187, Robert de Dreux, brother of Louis VII. of France, founded in Paris a house of prayer and a house of studies under the patronage of St. Thomas of Canterbury.   Again, we read that in 1180, Joce of London, on his return from Jerusalem, endowed a room in the Hotel Dieu, in which eighteen students might be lodged.   The college was afterwards transferred to the square of Notre Dame, still retaining its name of Maison des Dix-Huits.[1]   The primary object of these and similar institutions was simply to afford shelter and protection to the scholars.   There was no intention of making them institutions of learning.   Indeed, we may trace their beginning to the hostel in which certain licensed masters were wont to keep students at moderate terms.

"The hostel of the English universities in former times," says Mullinger, "may be defined as a lodging house under the rule of a principal, whose students resided at their own cost. . . . It offered no pecuniary aid, but simply freedom from extortion, and a residence where quiet would be insured and some discipline enforced; advantages, however, of no small rarity in that turbulent age."[2]

Then hostels or inns were comparatively few and wholly inadequate for the numbers that flocked to

---

[1] Lebeuf, "Histoire de la Ville et tout le Diocèse de Paris," t. ii., pp. 129, 130.

[2] "The University of Cambridge," i., p. 217.

the universities. It was but in the beginning of the fifteenth century that Oxford was in condition to forbid clerks from lodging in the houses of laymen.[1]

In the meantime, it became evident that, while the mendicant orders were flourishing and absorbing the best talent in the universities both among masters and students, the secular clergy were decaying. How else could it be, considering the dangers to which youths were exposed upon their entrance into university life? Take those who flocked to Paris. They were badly lodged and poorly fed; their clothes and books were exposed to pillage; usually, at an early stage of their entry into Paris they were relieved of their money. In spite of the vigilance of the officers of the nation under which their names were inscribed, they were cheated, robbed, imposed upon at every turn. The townspeople regarded them as legitimate prey.[2] Designing men and women pursued them, and set snares for them, and made them victims of their wiles till the last penny was extracted.

Many a fond father, in his desire to see an apt son become a learned clerk on the road to preferment and distinction, impoverished his family that the favored son might have sufficient means to live in Paris, and to find that son return one day rich in well-bought experience, but poor in all else. Rutebeuf describes such a typical young man. His father sells some of the patrimony in order to equip

---

[1] Lyte, "A History of the University of Oxford," p. 69.

[2] Ch. Jourdain, "Excursions à travers le moyen âge," p. 249.

E. E —8

him for the university. The youth goes to Paris,
falls into bad company, is soon rid of all that he
had brought with him—even his ambition to study
—and his "money gone and his clothes worn out,
he has to start life anew."

> "Ces argens faux et sa robe usée;
>   Or tout est à recommencer." [1]

Such experiences set men thinking. Why could
not the poor youths struggling under so many difficulties to enter the secular priesthood find some of
that shelter and care that was so lavishly bestowed
upon the candidates for religious life? This question occupied the mind of Robert Sorbon, the pious
and learned confessor to Louis IX. In 1256, with
the assistance of the saintly king and of several
wealthy ecclesiastics about the court, he founded an
institution in which youths aspiring to the secular
priesthood might be housed and fed and their studies
superintended. This institution was from the beginning especially designed for a nursery of theology.
Burses were established for sixteen students, four
from each nation. These youths led a life of economy and regularity. Everything in and about the
house was poor. "Poverty," says Crevier, "was
the peculiar attribute of the house of Sorbonne,
and for a long time it preserved the reality with the
title." [2] Under royal sanction and papal blessing the
institution flourished, and when Robert died, in 1274,

---

[1] "Le Dis de l'Université de Paris," t. i., p. 185. The same
experiences are still bought at the same price. See Alphonse
Daudet's "Sappho."

[2] "Histoire de l'Université de Paris," i., pp. 494, 495.

the Sorbonne had already become the headquarters of the faculty of theology.[1]

The regulations that Robert drew up and applied during the twenty years that he governed the institution prove his wisdom and practical good sense. They remained in vogue until in 1790, the Sorbonne went under in the catastrophe of that year. Robert established a preparatory school, and the students were admitted to the college only after receiving their bachelor's degree, maintaining a thesis called after the founder, a Robertine, and obtaining a majority of votes after three ballotings.

There were two classes of members—the guests and the fellows. ·The guests—*hospites*—were provided with every facility for study, but they took no part in the administration of the house. They were permitted to study in the library, but were not entrusted with the key. They were obliged to leave, in order to give place to others, as soon as they had received the doctor's degree. The fellows —*socii*—had more privileges. They shared in the administration of affairs. Absolute equality reigned among them. Those who were rich paid to the establishment a sum equivalent to the amount received by the bursars. The prior was chosen from among the youngest fellows, and he remained one year in charge. From amongst the most ancient four seniors were chosen. Their duty was to manage difficult affairs and maintain ancient customs. The fellows met once a month to discuss all matters of administration. Robert placed the Sorbonne

[1] A. F. Franklin, "La Sorbonne," p. 16. ·

under the patronage of the Blessed Virgin Mary, but from the fourteenth century we find its patron saint to have been St. Ursula.[1]

The pious founder appreciated the value of a good library in those days when books were scarce and expensive. " He was careful," we are told, " to collect in his college all books necessary for theologians and to install a library."[2] At his death he bequeathed to the college all his books, including the splendid folio Bible inscribed in 1270 and supposed to have been presented to him by Louis IX.[3] In 1289 the library was properly organized. It was divided into two parts. One was called the large library—*magna libraria*—and included the works which were the most frequently made use of; these were chained, and rare and exceptionable were the occasions when it was permitted to remove them. The other part was called the little library—*parva libraria*—and contained all duplicates and works rarely consulted, which might be loaned upon a deposit of a certain sum of money or any article of sufficient value to cover the cost of the book. In 1290 the whole library contained 1017 volumes, among which is the " Romance of the Rose," the only book in French mentioned. A beautiful feature of charity in those days was the bequeathing of libraries for the use of poor students. Thus we read that Gerard d'Abbeville, in 1270, bequeathed not only to the students of the Sorbonne

---

[1] Lebeuf, " Histoire de la Ville et du Diocèse de Paris," t. i., pp. 240, *sqq.*

[2] Ladvocat, " Dictionnaire Historique," Art., Sorbon.

[3] This is now No. 15,467 among the MSS. fonds Latin, in the Bibliothèque Nationale.

but to all lettered seculars his theological works. In the following year, Stephen, Archbishop of Canterbury, left his books to the Church of Notre Dame with the intention that they be placed at the disposition of poor scholars who should find use for them in pursuing their studies.[1]

The counsels that Robert left the students were no less valuable. They were unearthed not many years ago, and as they throw light upon college life in that day it may not be amiss to condense them :

"The scholar," he says, "who would study with profit should observe the following rules : First, to dedicate a certain hour to a specific piece of reading. Secondly, to fix attention upon what he is about to read, and not to pass lightly to something else. 'There is,' says St. Bernard, 'the same difference between reading and studying as exists between a host and a friend, between a greeting exchanged on the street and an unalterable affection.' Thirdly, to extract each day from our reading some thought, some grain of truth, and to engrave it on the memory with special care. Fourthly, to write out an epitome of what one has read, for the words not confined to writing fly like dust before the wind. Fifthly, to confer with one's companions in the disputations or in familiar conversation. This practice is even of greater service than reading, because it results in clearing up all doubts and the obscurities that may have remained after reading. *Nihil perfecte scitur, nisi dente disputationis finiatur.* Sixthly, to pray. In point of fact, prayer is one of the best means of learning. St. Bernard teaches that reading should excite the affections of the soul, and that it should be a means of elevating the heart to God without interrupting study."

---

[1] **Franklin, "La Vie Privée," p. 84.**

This pious doctor cautions young men against wasting their time upon trifles. His words throw light upon one of the greatest weaknesses of mediæval university life.

"Certain scholars," he says, "act like fools. They put forth great subtlety in trifles and prove themselves void of intelligence in important matters. In order to make it appear that they have not lost their time, they form thick volumes of parchment filled with blank pages and have them covered in elegant red skin binding. They afterwards return to the paternal roof with a sackful of science that can be stolen by robbers, devoured by rats and worms, or destroyed by fire or water."

With his eye upon that class of students who do not put their knowledge to good use, he also says:

"Grammar forges the sword of the Word of God; rhetoric polishes it; finally, theology makes use of it. Some there are who unceasingly learn to make that sword, to sharpen its edges, and by dint of whetting to wear it all away. Others keep it entirely confined to its scabbard; when they would draw it forth they find that they have grown old, the iron has rusted, and they can no longer effect anything. As for those who study solely with the intention of reaching high places in the Church, they are greatly deceived, for they scarcely ever attain the objects of their ambition."[1]

These counsels were solid and timely. They left their impress upon the college. A certain number of doctors applied themselves exclusively to the solution of cases of conscience. With practice came skill, and in the course of time people from all

---

[1] "Bibl. Nat. MS. Lat.," 15,971, fol. 197, *sqq.* ; Le foy de la Marche, "Le Treizième Siècle," pp. 50-52.

parts of Europe were wont to send delicate cases for solution, and thus did the Sorbonne come to be regarded as the greatest authority in Christendom in solving moral problems. It was consulted by king and pope.

During the latter half of the thirteenth century, colleges multiplied. In 1262, Walter de Merton, then Lord Chancellor of England under Henry III., obtained a license to assign certain manors for the maintenance of clerks studying in the schools of Oxford.[1] His main object was to secure for the secular priesthood the academical benefits which the religious orders were so largely enjoying. " He borrowed from the monastic institutions the idea of an aggregate body living by common rule, under a common head, provided with all things needful for a corporate and perpetual life, fed by its secured endowments, fenced from all external interference, except that of its lawful patron."[2] Thus was Merton the first to achieve for the secular priesthood in Oxford what Robert of Sorbon succeeded in doing for the same order in Paris. The motives actuating these founders were the same; the regulations enforced are alike in many details.

At Merton, as in the Sorbonne, the students were to be thoroughly grounded in the liberal arts and in philosophy before being permitted to study theology or canon law. Theology is the main object of the foundation of Merton as well as of the

---

[1] Lyte, " A History of Oxford University," p. 73.

[2] Edmund, Bishop of Nelson, " Sketch of the Life of Walter de Merton," p. 22.

Sorbonne; but in Merton a few were permitted to study canon law and as much civil law as was needed to throw light upon the canons. Poor boys of the founder's kin, to the number of thirteen, received a free preliminary education in which they were to be qualified for scholarships. "While he provides for a good liberal education, and a general grounding in all subsidiary knowledge, he jealously guards his main object of theological study both from being attempted too early by the half-educated boy, and from being abandoned too soon for the temptations of something more profitable."[1] It is designed that one of the fellows shall make a special study of grammar, that he shall devote himself expressly to that subject, "that he shall be provided with all the necessary books, and shall regularly instruct the younger students, while the more advanced students are to have the benefit of his assistance when occasion may require."[2]

Other portions of the statutes were evidently inspired by monastic rules. Each scholar was subjected to a year's probation before becoming a permanent member of the society.[3] A spirit of fellowship and equality was cultivated. The students wore a uniform. All dined and supped together while one of them read an edifying book in Latin. They had a share in government and management. The eldest in a dormitory was known as the dean, and presided at the rising and retiring.

---

[1] Bishop of Nelson, " Life of Walter de Merton," p. 22.

[2] Mullinger, " The University of Cambridge," p. 168.

[3] Statutes, Ed. Percival, p. 20.

Three of the fellows acted as bursars, and five as auditors of accounts. Three times a year there was a general scrutiny of conduct, when the behavior of each inmate was minutely examined and all grievances were ventilated. Should any scholar accept a benefice or enter a religious order, he was obliged to vacate his place.[1] All were required to attend the communications of benefactors three times a year.

In 1280 the bequest left by William of Durham, was employed to establish University Hall, and other benefactions enabled the Hall to own a library from which books might be borrowed. The discipline was severe. Disputations were held in the house as well as in the schools. No book was lent out of the house without a deposit of more value than the book, and consent of all the scholars. The scholars were allowed to use a common seal. It was enjoined upon them to live honestly as clerks, in a manner befitting saints, not fighting, not using scurrilous or foul language, nor reciting, singing or willingly hearing songs or tales of an amatory or indecent character, not taunting or provoking one another to anger, and not shouting so as to disturb the studies or repose of the industrious.[2]

The statutes of Balliol, given in 1282, breathe the same spirit, and no doubt were suggested by the Franciscan confessor of Dermguilla. The principal was elected by the scholars from among themselves.

---

[1] Lyte, " Hist. Oxford," p. 78.

[2] " Munimenta Academica," Statutes of William of Durham, i., pp. 56–61.

The scholars were to attend lectures daily and hold
fortnightly disputation in their own house. They
were to attend services in the parish church on Sundays and hear the sermon.   If the weekly allowance
were not sufficient the richer scholars were levied
upon to make up the deficiency, and should any
grumble they were expelled. The food that remained after a meal was to be given to some poor
scholars.[1]

The Sorbonne in Paris and Merton in Oxford
were the types after which all mediæval colleges
were erected. But it took three hundred years
to mature the collegiate system. It was only
about 1550 that it became predominant. The college of Walter de Merton was for some time looked
upon with suspicion, as a dangerous experiment.
In the meantime, there were established boarding-
houses for students having no burses, but able to
pay their way.

Laymen at first rented chambers from the rector
of the university, and prepared some students in
private. Finding the practice lucrative, they enlarged their field of operations. These houses became very numerous and were known as pedagogics.
They were encouraged and were considered far better than the miserable, dingy, close, ill-ventilated
holes and dens into which students were thrust by
the townspeople in various parts of the city. But
with time the pedagogics abused their position.
They neglected the moral and religious training of
the youths confided to them, regarding them as

---

[1] Lyte, 2, 86.

simply so many sources of income. Gerson accused these men of crass ignorance, negligence and immorality. Through fear of losing their pupils they would not correct and punish them. They took no pains to form their boarders to practices of piety and decorum. These youths were as great strangers to the doctrines of Christianity as pagans themselves ; they behaved badly in church, even to the extent of annoying the preacher by interruptions, mockeries, hisses and whisperings.[1]

Cardinal d'Estouteville, when reforming the University of Paris, was severe upon this class of men. He forbade them to run to the inns·and taverns in order to recruit their houses, and he would have them ˉcease speculating upon the food and accommodations of the students, ruling at the same time " that they ask only a just and moderate price for provisions according to their kind and season, and that the food be served up clean and wholesome."[2] In the latter organization of the university we distinguish three classes of students. 1. There were the students boarding outside ; two usually occupying the same room, and frequently the same bed. These were known as *martinets*—the *chamberdekyns* of Oxford—and were looked after by the regent. 2. There were the students under the pedagogues; these were called *camerists*. 3. There were the college students who boarded with the principal and were known simply as boarders. Those elderly

---

[1] "Opera," t. i., p. 110. Letter written about the year 1400.

[2] Du Boulay, "Hist. Univ. Paris," t. v., p. 572.

students who passed from school to school and from
branch to branch, seeming to have no definite aim
in pursuing their studies, and indeed no other aim
in life than to live and die students of the university—shiftless fellows without the ambition of ex-
celling in anything—were called *ga loches*.[1]   In England, as the number of colleges increased the hotels
declined, and were either merged in the colleges or
disused.[2]

III.

The colleges were at first regarded with suspicion,
but as their numbers increased they became the object of special solicitude on the part of the university authorities.   In Paris, the rector was in duty
bound to visit each college at least once a month.
After the seventeenth century, when the university
was losing all hold upon the colleges, these visits
became less frequent.   But when they did occur
they were made the occasion of great rejoicings for
the students.   " If the rector enters a college," says
Pasquier, " there is no telling the joy with which he
is welcomed and the acclamations with which he is
received, evidences of the honor and respect in
which he is held."[3]   On these occasions the rector
made his visitation in state walking through the city
clothed in his scarlet cloak, preceded by two beadles
bearing silver maces, and followed by Masters in Arts
marching two by two in procession.

---

[1] Étienne Pasquier, " Recherches sur la France," liv. ix.,
chap., xvii.

[2] Robert Potts, " Liber Cantabrigiensis," p. 177.

[3] " Recherches sur la France," liv. ix., chap. 22, t. i., p. 937.

Cardinal d'Estouteville, in 1452, empowered the rector to convoke the four nations in order to elect four regents to whom he might delegate this mission of visiting the colleges, inns, and pedagogics, and whose duty it was to ascertain the morals, discipline, teaching, and food of each, and with the aid of the bishop to reform whatever called for reformation.[1]

It were a long and tedious task to trace the story of the relations of the colleges with their university. Suffice it to say that these colleges were established rather as places in which poor scholars were supplied with board and lodging than as schools for purposes of instruction. The principal at first conducted the students to the lecture hall of the professor, and led them back to the college in a body. Here, with the aid of assistants, he superintended their studies. started disputations, occasionally heard the scholars recite, and thus profitably filled that portion of the day which was not spent in attending lectures. But seeing that this passing to and fro was an occasion of disorder and entailed considerable loss of time, the masters, as soon as students became numerous enough, at first privately lectured in the colleges. These lectures afterward became recognized by the university authorities. "We do not exactly know," says Du Boulay, "when this practice began; it is generally thought that the College of Navarre, which was reformed in the year 1464, was the first to open its gates to these public professors of letters." [2]

---

[1] Bulaeus, " Hist. Univ. Par.," t. v., p. 570.
[2] " Hist. Univ. Par.," in loc cit.

And so these institutions grew from their first lowly and unpretentious beginning to be themselves centres of light. Their daily regulation will give clearer insight into college-life than could a lengthy description:

At 4 o'clock, rising. The students were awakened by a member of the philosophy class, who went around the dormitory to arouse those who gave a deaf ear to the bell, and to light the candles at the season when candles were needed.

At 5, the same member saw that the scholars were placed in order around the halls. During the hour from 5 to 6 the regents gave their first lesson.

At 6 o'clock, breakfast, which consisted of a small piece of bread. After breakfast there was rest, but no recreation.

From 8 to 10, the principal lesson of the morning.

From 10 to 11, discussion and argumentation.

At 11, dinner, accompanied by reading of the Bible or lives of the saints. The chaplain said the prayers before and after meals, made mementoes of benefactors, and added thereto pious exhortations. The principal took up the work, gave admonitions, distributed praise or blame among the students, and announced the punishments and corrections determined upon the evening previous.

From 12 to 2, revision and interrogation regarding the morning's lessons.

From 2 to 3, repose, when there was public reading of some poet or orator—*ne diabolus hominem inveniat otiosum.*

From 3 to 5, the principal lesson of the afternoon.

From 5 to 6, discussion and argumentation upon the lesson just attended.

At 6, supper.

At 6.30, questionings upon the lessons of the day.

At 7.30, complin and benediction.

At 8 in winter and 9 in summer, bedtime.

Masters and pupils authorized to do so might keep the candle burning till 11 o'clock. The wild and unrestrained manners of the students became softened by theatrical representations within the colleges, and by outdoor sports and promenades. In the afternoons of Tuesdays and Thursdays the students were given free time, when they were permitted to walk to the Près-aux-clercs. Long promenades into the country were made with great pomp and ceremony. Besides the Landit, there were certain annual ones that were carefully observed. Such were the promenades of Notre Dame des Vignes, Notre Dame des Champs, and a grand promenade in May, when the students, upon their return, assembled before the door of the rector and there planted a tree.

From the regulations here given there were variations. Thus, in the College of St. Barbe, free time was given only after the principal lesson of the afternoon had been gone through.[1] In other schools the whole of Thursday was given to recreation.[2] Feast days were numerous, but they were not idled away. They were passed in devotions and in studies outside the university programme, according to the taste of each student. No leave of absence was granted upon the feast days. An often-mooted question was what constituted servile work for a student on Sunday. Burand de Champagne, in the beginning of the fourteenth century, decided that scholars were not permitted to make complete copies of their notes nor to hire out their labor by transcribing for others, but they might enter notes of lessons to preserve the memory of them, as well as of sermons taken down with the stylus.[3] The students were allowed to go home during the month of

---

[1] J. Quickerat, " Histoire de Sainte Barbe," t. i., ch. x., pp. 83 *sqq.*

[2] Noël du Fail, " Œuvres," t. ii., p. 186.

[3] " Histoire Littéraire de la France," vol. xxx., p. 302.

September.   This period was the vintage-time—*les
vendanges*.   The term "vacation" was confined to
the three summer months, during which the superior courses and examinations of the university were
suspended.

The tuition in the colleges was a variable quan-
tity, and was regulated according to certain statutes
of the university.   It depended greatly upon the
vintage and harvest.   Each year it was definitely
fixed by the rector, the deans of the four faculties,
the principals of the colleges, and two Parisian
merchants.[1]   Another statute authorized the professors to receive from each scholar, without the
exacting or naming of any amount on their part,
five or six gold crowns towards the end of the
school-year.[2]   In the month of June, during the
feast of Landit, each scholar offered his regent a
lemon, upon the rind of which the golden crowns
were arranged, the whole being placed in a crystal
vase filled with sweetmeats.[3]   At one time the
pupils of the whole school, supplied with this offering, marched in great pomp to the playing of fife
and the beating of tambourine, and with formal
ceremony presented them to the regents; but the
custom was abolished in 1600.[4]

Few of the masters and regents were overbur-
dened with wealth.   The colleges, with rare exceptions, retained the primitive spirit with which they

---

[1] Statutes, art. 67.

[2] Statutes, art. 32.

[3] Franklin, "La Vie Privée d'Autrefois," p. 216.

[4] Hazon, "Eloge Hist. de l'Université de Paris," 1771.

were established. They continued to be sheltering schools for poor youths, conducted under the auspices of religion, and the impress of poverty remained stamped upon their rules, the food given and the customs handed down. Mr. Lyte, speaking of Oxford, says: "In its corporate capacity, the University was undoubtedly poor, and it had scarcely any funds applicable for general purposes."[1] The principal and his assistants, in many of the Parisian schools, lived on a pittance of three or four sous a week, and were obliged to resort to other means to eke out a living. When Sir Thomas More, through reverse of fortune, found himself obliged to economize, he wrote to his wife: "But my counsel is that we fall not to the lowest fare first; we will not, therefore, descend to Oxford fare." Oxford fare was the type of poor living. Poor scholars were wont to receive from the Chancellor a license to beg.[2] And Sir Thomas describes them, with bags and wallets, singing *Salve Regina* at rich men's doors. The poor students of Montaigu College went to the neighboring Chartreux Convent for their breakfast, awaiting their turn to be served with the other indigents. It is to be observed that not all college students were obliged to beg. There were two classes in every college, the rich, who paid for their maintenance, and the poor, who worked and begged for it. The meal of the junior students consisted of stale bread with half an ounce of butter, a plate of vegetables, half a

---

[1] "A History of the University of Oxford," p. 97.
[2] "Munimenta Academica," ii., p. 684.

herring, or an egg. The larger students, by reason
of their age and prolonged labor, were allowed one-
third of a pint of wine, a whole herring or two eggs,
and a small piece of cheese or some fruit. They
were never given meat.[1] The rigorous discipline
and extreme abstinence practised in the College of
Montaigu was proverbial, and intellect and appetite
became equally keen with the name:

" Mons acutus, ingenium acutum, dentes acuti."

Erasmus could not find words severe enough
to stigmatize the inhuman treatment and unwhole-
some food that shattered his constitution and en-
feebled him for life, while a student in this college.[2]
Rabelais has no kind words for the same institution and its sparrow-hawks. Ponocrates denounces
the cruelties practised thus: "Criminals and condemned murderers are better treated." And he
ends in this emphatic manner: "If I were King of
Paris I would set fire to the place and burn up both
principal and regents for permitting such inhuman-
ity before their eyes."[3] Francion, in 1630, is no
less severe as regards the fare doled out in the
College of Lisieux. He considered the swineherds
of his native town better nourished. "Withal," he
says, "we were called gourmands, and we should
put our hand in the dish each after the other.
Those who ate sparingly were the favorites." Indeed, Francion's whole description shows that he

---

[1] Félibien, "Histoire de Paris," t. iii., p. 731.
[2] Dialogue, "Flesh and Fish."
[3] "Gargantua," liv. i., chap. xxvii., pp. 119, 120.

had fallen into the hands of a seventeenth century Squeers.[1]

But in order to be understood, mediæval manners and customs are to be looked at with other eyes than those of the nineteenth century. Francis of Assisi, in making poverty his bride, idealized that virtue.[2] His disciples sanctified and exalted begging and caused men to respect poverty. There was no humiliation in being poor; there was no personal degradation in asking an alms. Students no more lost their self-respect in begging for the house, or in doing menial service for their instructors, than did the page in waiting upon his master. This broad and elevated view of poverty established a brotherhood of feeling that inspired the better off to extend a helping hand to those less favorably circumstanced. The bursars of the college distributed their leavings to the poor scholars of their nation. Masters gave their pupils cast-off clothes and shoes.[3] This thoughtfulness extended to their holidays. In 1214, the commonalty of Oxford agreed to pay fifty-two shillings yearly for the use of poor scholars, and to give six hundred and fifty of them a meal of bread, ale, and pottage, with one large dish of flesh or fish on St. Nicholas Day.[4] The poor students themselves resorted to many makeshifts that they might be enabled to pursue their studies. Sometimes they copied books and transcribed

---

[1] See A. F. Franklin, " La Vie Privée d' Autrefois; Écoles et Collèges," pp. 223, 224.

[2] " Paradiso," xi., 64–100.

[3] " De Disciplina Scholarium," cap. iv.

[4] " Anthony à Wood," i., p. 185.

notes; sometimes they swept and garnished the rooms of a rich companion or an instructor to whom they attached themselves; sometimes they kept their lodging-house clean and orderly. Boys with good voices sang from door to door. This was the custom, even in Luther's day.[1]

The cost of instruction was in proportion to the pecuniary resources of each student. He who affirmed under oath that he had only sufficient to pay the expense of board and lodging was charged nothing for instruction. The education of youth ranked among the works of mercy, and indigent scholars were often thought of in men's last will and testament. Chests or funds were established for their temporary relief. Whoever borrowed money from the chest established by the Countess of Warwick, in 1293, was obliged to say the Paternoster thrice in honor of the Holy Trinity, and the Ave Maria five times in honor of the Blessed Virgin.[2] It must be said of the University of Paris, along the line of its whole career that there was a conspicuous lack of economy and forethought in money matters. Just as the bursars threw all surpluses into a common fund for the poor scholars, even so the excess of receipts over expenses was distributed among masters and bedels, and frequently drunk in the taverns.[3] Of course, in these matters, as in all else, there were exceptions; there were students who thought only of

---

[1] Schmidt, "Jean Sturm," p. 39.

[2] "Munimenta Academica," i., p. 63.

[3] Bulæus, "Hist. Univ. Par.," iv., 674; Thurot, "De l'Organisation," 27.

dress and display, and there were masters who extorted money from their students.

The discipline, the exercises and pastimes of college life in its good and its bad aspects have been faithfully sketched by Rabelais in his terrible satire.[1] The colleges continued the traditions of the university schools in the observance of their holidays, games, amusements and customs. The newcomers into the college—*béjaunes*—were severely handled by the old pupils. They were terrorized into the performance of acts the most ridiculous or most dangerous, as suited the whims of their persecutors. Our modern hazing is a relic of these mediæval days. In Germany the custom of formal initiation was somewhat in the following manner: The freshman was seized, arrayed in a garment of coarse stuff, and upon his head was placed a cap with horns or ass's ears. His companions then chased him around, and, having caught him, they pretended to clip his ears with shears, shave him with an axe and stab him with augurs of wood, in order, as an ancient author puts it, that the new student may learn to suppress the horns of vanity, smooth away the rough corners of his nature, and clear the ways to his intellect. The paraphernalia was afterwards deposited in the centre of the hall, to indicate that the student had now cast from him all those evil habits which made him like unto the brute. His hair was then cut. An enormous ear-pick was pointed towards his temple, to indicate that he should listen only to wise and discreet discourses.

[1] "Gargantua," liv. i., chaps. xvi–xxiv.

A wild boar's tooth was extracted by means of long pincers; the operation was intended to show that the student should keep clear of calumny and slander. His hands and nails were cleansed, as an emblem to avoid all quarrels. A black beard was painted on his face, as an image of his entering upon the years of manhood and a warning to him to throw aside the things of childhood. A chorus was sung over him as an emblem of the harmony in which he should live. He went on his knees before those assisting at the ceremony, as a token of respect for authority. The horns having been taken off and laid aside symbolized the fact that the student was changed and rose up a new man. He was then given the wine of gaiety and the salt of wisdom. Here ended the initiation, after which the student was received by his companions to the new life of study.[1] This mode of initiation was one of universal practice in the early days of university life; indeed, the tradition of it may be traced back to pagan times. St. Gregory Nazianzen speaks of a similar ceremony practiced in Athens in his day, in order, as he tells us, to take the pride out of the young men and render them docile.[2]

Before me lies an old engraving representing the process of initiation. The imprint is of 1666, but the scene was at least three hundred years old. Spectators are seated apart. Two subjects are upon the

[1] A. G. Strobel, "Histoire du Gymnase Protestant de Strasbourg." Appendix. No. 8, p. 133.

[2] See Colin de Plancy, "Dictionnaire Feudale," t. i., pp. 57, 58.

floor awaiting the good pleasure of their torturers. The horned caps are thrown to one side. A would-be executioner stands over them with a battle-axe lifted up in the act of striking. Behind this man is a youth subjected to some other' stage of the initiation; in the background others are represented as being led into the hall, each accompanied by his executioner holding a mace.[1] In all these rites and ceremonies masters united with students. They were one in study, one in play, one even in the disorders that arose from time to time.[2] In this manner may we catch a glimpse of mediæval college life far more instructive and suggestive than that revealed by charters and statutes.

IV.

Cardinal Newman sums up the relations of colleges to universities in the following words:

"At first universities were almost democracies; colleges tended to break their anarchial spirit, introduced ranks and gave the example of laws, and trained up a set of students who, as being morally and intellectually superior to the members of the academical body, became the depositories of academical power and influence."[3]

In proportion as the colleges became more perfect, the university began to decay. Some trace the decline as far back as 1380. Disintegration set in very rapidly after the Renaissance. The ecclesiastical character of the university diminished, and it

---

[1] *Ritus Depositionis* Argentinæ, apud Petrum Aubry, 1666.
[2] Thurot, "De l'Organisation de l'Université," p. 39.
[3] "Historical Sketches, Universities," pp. 221, 222.

grew more secular. In 1452, Masters in Medicine were dispensed from celibacy; in 1600, Doctors in Law attached to the university were permitted to marry. The Jesuits succeeded so admirably in perfecting the college system that at their door may safely be laid the chief cause of the decline of the University of Paris. By the end of the seventeenth century they had purchased twelve of its colleges. About 1764, twenty houses of the university were closed because they were not self-sustaining.[1]

Already in the seventeenth century murmurs began to arise concerning the decline and the inefficiencies of the universities. In 1602, there appeared in England an appeal to Parliament to reform the Universities of Oxford and Cambridge. A copy of this petition now lies before me. It is signed J. H., and in all probability is written by the Anglican bishop, Joseph Hall.[2] The author is wholesale in his condemnation of university studies, university methods and university results.

"I could never yet," he tells us, "make so bad an idea of a true university as that it should serve for no nobler end than to nurture a few raw striplings come out of some miserable country school, with a few shreds of Latin, that is as unmusical to a polite ear as the gruntings of a sow or the noise of a saw can be to one who is acquainted with the laws of harmony. And then, possibly, before they have surveyed the Greek alphabet, to be racked and tortured with a sort of harsh, abstracted, logical notions, which their wits are no more able to endure

---

[1] "Thurot," p. 131.
[2] 1574–1656.

than their bodies the strapado, and to be delivered over to a jejune, barren, peripatetic philosophy suited only (as Descartes says) to wits that are seated below mediocrity. . . . And then as soon as they have done licking of this file to be turned to graze in finer ethics, which perhaps, tells them as much, in harder words, as they had heard their mothers talk by the fireside at home."[1]

This is the sum of knowledge that Hall finds in the universities of his day. Evidently the spirit of Bacon and Descartes is abroad.

What does he expect? What would he have? Here is his conception of what a university should be:

"I have even expected from an university, that though all men cannot learn all things, yet they should be able to teach all things to all men, and be able either to attract knowing men from abroad out of their own wealth or at least be able to make an exchange."[2]

He finds the universities lacking in chemistry, in anatomy; there are no masters to make a thorough examination of old tenets, or to review old experiments and traditions; none to make a survey of antiquities or solemn disquisition into history; there is an absence of all ready and generous teaching of the tongues. All these deficiencies he would have supplied, "not by some stripling youngster, who perhaps understands that which he professes as little as anything else, and mounts up into the chair twice or

---

[1] "An Humble Motion to the Parliament of England Concerning the Advancement of Learning and Reformation of the Universities." By J. H. London: Printed for John Walker, at the Starre in Popes-Head Alley, MDCII., pp. 25, 26.

[2] Ibid., p. 27.

thrice a year to mutter over some few impertinences, but by some staid man of tried and known abilities in his profession." [1]

He thinks the university schools "have not yet arrived to the exactness of the Jesuit colleges." Lord Bacon's estimate of the same colleges was no less favorable. In all that regards the instruction of youth, he says, "we must consult the classes of the Jesuits, for there can be nothing better." [2] He beseeches parliament to reduce "those friar-like lists of fellowships" into a fewer number, and those retained "to be bestowed upon men excellent in their particular endowments and peculiar for some use or other so that the number of the professors might increase." [3] He suggests the combining of all the colleges thinly scattered and poorly patronized up and down the land under one or other of the great universities; that there be greater freedom of the press and that two copies of every new book go to the public library; that all medals, statues and other antiquities at the time public property or confiscate to the crown go to the university museums; finally, that learned foreigners be duly honored and encouraged to make their homes in the universities. [4]

An anonymous writer of the same period, evidently intimate with the workings of the University of Paris and anxious for its welfare, sends out a similar cry of warning and bewails the evils he

[1] Ibid., pp. 27, 28.

[2] "De Augmentis Scientiarum," lib. v., cap. iv.

[3] Ibid., p. 29. I have modernized the spelling of these quotations.

[4] Ibid., pp. 30, 31.

would see remedied. He is opposed to any in-
fringement of the old order. He does not like to
see the colleges monopolize university instruction.

" There are," he tells us, " sixty-three colleges or
high schools in the University of Paris. These
were not originally established for boarders, nor
in order that the arts may be taught in them,
as is done to-day, but to feed and maintain
certain scholars whom the ancients called bursars.
These attended public lectures in the rue de
Fouarre." [1]

He would see them return to the old custom. The
regents are no longer adequately compensated. He
tells us that the Jesuits brought about this ruinous
system of gratuitous instruction, "and even the
Jesuits do not teach gratuitously since they secure
such good endowments for their colleges." [2] He
would, therefore, gladly see them expelled from
Paris, and hints at what he considers the proper
mode of treatment for them, by calling attention to
the fact that " Carlo Borromeo took from the Jesuits the seminaries that he had instituted in the
diocese of Milan." [3] He bewails the fact that
neither among themselves have the masters the
proper spirit, nor over their pupils have they the
same influence as of old ; and if they are to do good
as formerly they must reform their present mode of
living and in submission to the statute of September 20, 1577, go back to commons.

---

[1] " Memoires pour le Règlement de l'Université, MDLX."
in the " Bibliothèque Nationale," 1073, 24, 115–2130, p. 2.

[2] Ibid., p. 3.

[3] Ibid., p. 6.

The anonymous author finds fault with the manner in which the students are treated in some of the colleges. He has no good word for the harsh discipline to which the students of Montaigu College are subjected. He advocates the reduction of their number to a third of what it then was, so that they be better fed and better clothed, and that they wear "a dress more civilized and respectable than that they now wear." He bewails the neglect of lessons upon the holidays and fast-days. He says :

"Twenty-five or thirty years ago lessons were taught in the university on feast days and on Sundays, from nine to ten in the morning, and from four to five in the afternoon, and on the feasts of the Apostles there were public declamations—*usance qu'il est necessaire remettre.*"[1]

The regents he finds derelict in duty :

"Each regent should watch in turn over the scholars at play, in order to see that they behave with modesty and reserve, that they speak only the Latin tongue, and that they salute politely all who pass through the ground."

He is dissatisfied with the preparatory schools of the university. They are not doing their duty, they are not grounding the children sufficiently. He tells us that there are thirty such schools in Paris, that the masters of them are frequently ignorant, and that they persist in carrying the children into other fields of study rather than confining themselves to the rudiments. In consequence, he complains bitterly of the difficulty of unlearning children what

---

[1] Ibid., p. 21.

they had been badly taught, and above all of correcting habits of erroneous pronunciation.[1]

Such a foundation can support only a poor superstructure. And what solidity can be found in institutions the principals of which are elected, not through merit, but as the result of canvassing and intrigue.[2] Such was the state of affairs among the colleges of the University of Paris in 1610. Here we part company with the annoymous author, grateful for the glimpse he gave us into the causes that led to the disintegration of that wonderful structure.

The University of Paris had begun to decline in power and influence long before. In the beginning of the sixteenth century while there was slight diminution in the number of her students, a marked change was passing over her spirit. Her prestige was on the wane. She had ceased to be the seminary of Christendom and was simply a national institution.[3] The causes of this decline were both local and general. In the fourteenth century universities were multiplied in nearly every country in Europe. Each nation, sometimes each province or district possessing its own university, naturally students stayed at home and, with few exceptions, availed themselves of the universities established at their doors. The old-time severity exercised in the distribution of academical honors became relaxed and forthwith the degrees from Paris lost their primitive significance and were in consequence less

---

[1] Ibid., p. 22.
[2] Ibid., p. 23.
[3] "Thurot," p. 2.

eagerly sought.   Finally, during the sojourn of the
popes in Avignon, ecclesiastical dignities were
showered upon the professors, who thereupon
threw up their positions and their studies, and in
consequence the work of the university was generally done by inferior men.' Then, as now, it is true
that personal worth and personal influence are the
chief factors in determining the character and prestige of college or university.   Now, as then, a great
educator, or a great body of educators, can establish
themselves in a barn and attract crowds, while the
noblest architectural structures, with the most improved modern school-furniture, may proudly raise
their spires, and yet, if directed by incompetency or
mediocrity, they will be passed by, or will be patronized by that class of parents which judges the merits
of a school by the picture upon its prospectus.

V.

Let us go behind this college life and note the
guide books by which the masters were directed in
their teachings.   We are accustomed to consider pedagogy a modern science.   But let us not be deceived.
In those mediæval days there were wholesome studies
of methods.   Then as now, masters considered the
ways and means by which best results might be
reached.

The manual of the thirteenth century most in
vogue was a small work in seven chapters, known as

---

¹ The first Rotulus Nominandorum was sent in 1316 to
John XXII. See Prof. Shirley's introduction to " Fasciculi
Zizaniorum," p. 11.

" De Disciplina Scholarium,"[1] and attributed to Boëthius, but not written till the University of Paris had
been fully established. The book is quoted by Roger
Bacon in 1627.[2] The name of Boëthius rendered it
popular and gave it a prescriptive standing that it
might have never otherwise attained. Still there is a
goodly share of sound advice running through its
pages.

The unknown author would have instruction con-
tinuous, uninterrupted, riveted in the brain by frequent repetition until the verses of the poets and the
sentences of the philosophers find a fixed place in the
memory. The master should not be content with
the teaching of mere words, which makes sophists,
nor with purely mental activity which develops the
judgment and originates science, but he should also
with both of these combine common usage that comes
with habit. Science without practice is of small
avail, whereas practice without science availeth
greatly. He should be erudite, affable, strict, grave,
and careful without arrogance.[3] The scholar should
always be subject to the master, for only he who
knows how to obey knows how to govern himself.
This submission has a threefold character; attention
in practice, docility of mind, and good will of the
soul; the student should ever be attentive to listen,
docile to understand, and ready to retain. It behooves the master to understand his scholars and direct each according to his talents; the obtuse mind

---

[1] "Patrologia Latina," vol. lxiv.
[2] In the "Opus Majus."
[3] "De Disciplina Scholarium," cap. vi., col. 1235.

to mechanics, the mediocre to politics, the acute to philosophy.[1]   Masters and scholars should constitute one family, and if the master is obliged to administer corporal punishment it must be with permission of the parent.   In all that has been here transcribed very little can be improved upon after an experience of six centuries.

The Carmelite, William Whetely, made a careful study of this little volume, and according to its principles during five and twenty years directed the schools of Stamford, and under his efficient management Stamford grew to such prominence that it was considered a rival of Oxford and Cambridge. The historian of Stamford says of the Carmelite convent :

" Certain it is this convent was as happy in the famous men it produced, as their schools and house itself were remarkable for the strictness of their discipline." [2]

Whetely wrote an elaborate commentary upon the manual attributed to Boëthius, whence Leland calls him " Boëtianus." The commentary is still extant in manuscript in Pembroke College Library, Cambridge. [3]

A voice out of the same age, speaking to us from Brescia, the voice of a judge learned in the law, Albertans Albertani (circa 1250) among some moral prosings discusses the subject of education with the

[1] Ibid., cap. v., col. 1233.

[2] Peck, " Academia Tertia Anglicana," lit. viii., p. 44.

[3] See J. Bass Mullinger, " University of Cambridge," pp. 637, 638.

practical sense of a man of affairs. In a tract titled "Of Speaking and of Silence"—*De Loquendi et Tacendi Modo*—the author lays down the requisites for study (cap. xi.). According to him there are three essentials that enter into the acquisition of knowledge, namely, doctrine, use, and exercise, and practical application. The mind is afterward aided by forcible thoughts on doctrine, which should be committed to memory; by constant reading, by writing, and by chewing and masticating the science that one learns. While studying one should over-look or despise no science, no written document; one should never feel ashamed to learn from any person that can give information, and finally one should not despise others because one has become familiar with some science.[1]

Another manual of pedagogy is the treatise "De Eruditione Principum," from the pen of William Pé-rault, who was contemporary with Thomas Aquinas. He died about 1275. For a long time his book was attributed to St. Thomas, and is still to be found in all the printed editions of his works.[2] Echard proved conciusively that the treatise belongs to Peraldus.[3] The work is divided into seven books. The first is made up of moral reflections considered suitable to a young prince. It dwells upon the vanity of

---

[1] See an analysis of this little work by Vicenzo di Giovanni in " Nota," published at Palermo, 1874. A copy of the work itself is to be found in the Mazarin Library. See also Ever-ardo Micheli, " Storia della Pedagogia Italiana," pp. 79, 80.

[2] " Opusculum," XXXVII., vol. xvi., Parma edition, 1865.

[3] " Scriptores Ordinis Prædicatorum," i., pp. 131-136. Paris. 1719.

worldly riches, praise and glory, and the risks, mis-
eries and responsibilities that accompany earthly
power, and inculcates clemency, piety, wisdom and
the other qualities becoming his earthly power and
true nobility.[1]   The second treats of the relations of
the prince towards God and the Church.   It dwells
upon the faith, hope, charity and the fear of the
Lord that should possess him.   It lays stress on the
rules and motives urging one to the love of God and
of one's neighbor[2]   The third unfolds the care the
prince should take of himself.   While engaged and
occupied with others it behooves him not to neglect
his own interior life.   He may possess all knowledge
of men and things, but not knowing himself he
would only be building upon a ruinous foundation.
He is not wise whose wisdom does not extend to
the attaining of his own salvation.   In his every act
he should ask himself, "Is it lawful?   Is it expedient?   Is it proper?"   He should frequently enter
into himself and ask himself who he is, what he is,
and what manner of life he leads.   He proves himself stronger in overcoming himself than in conquer-
ing an army.[3]   The fourth book treats of a prince's
relations with others.   It shows the misfortunes and
temptations to which princes are exposed when surrounded by designing and currupt men; it lays
stress upon the necessity of wise counselors, and
having honest men at the head of affairs, of being
above the acceptance of rewards, of doing justice

---

[1] "S. Thomas Opera," vol. xvi., p. 391–403.

[2] Ibid., pp. 400–414.

[3] Ibid., pp. 414–422.

by the poor and never coveting whatever may be theirs.[1]

The fifth book is the most important. It is composed of sixty-six chapters, and may be regarded as a complete treatise upon education. Peraldus lays down the elementary principle that parents owe it to their offspring as a primary duty, the lacking in which were inexcusable, to see that they are educated. This discipline is not merely one of words; it must also be a training by means of the whip — *nec sufficit ut eruditis verborum, immo necessaria est etiam disciplina verberum.* The child is taken from his tender years and his dispositions are studied and his habits are formed accordingly. The advantages of bearing the yoke of the Lord from the days of youth are clearly laid down. Five things are required on the part of the master; namely, that he be endowed with fair talent, that his life be upright and honorable, that he be possessed of knowledge accurately acquired and well digested before instructing others, that he be possessed of an eloquent manner of imparting information, and that he have experience as a teacher. The instruction imparted by an experienced teacher has five qualities ; it is plain and simple so as to reach the feeblest intelligence ; it is imparted in the fewest possible words; it is useful; it is presented in such a variety of lights as to render it agreeable ; and the subject-matter is neither too long drawn out nor too rapidly passed over. This is a valuable pedagogical chapter[2] upon the

---

[1] Ibid., pp. 422–427.

[2] Ibid., cap. ix., pp. 431, 432.

form and method of teaching. No less instructive is the succeeding chapter upon the qualifications of a good student.

The good student should be of good life. Pride, anger, envy, sloth, gluttony, love and hatred are all impediments in the way of learning. The good student endeavors to overcome every deadly vice. He prays much ; for wisdom being a gift of God, he constantly beseeches the Divine Source for an abundance thereof. He brings humility to his studies, especially to all studies concerning Holy Writ. This humility leads him to that honest love of truth, possessing which he is not ashamed to confess ignorance when he does not know, and is ever ready and willing to learn. As he who receives from everybody becomes all the richer, so he who learns from everybody becomes all the wiser. The good student ever cherishes the fear of God in his heart. This fear, which is the beginning of wisdom, leads him to walk carefully in the right way, and guards him against error, presumption and negligence in study. He is meek, ever receiving instructions, especially the lessons of the sacred Scriptures, with docility. He is diligent in his studies ; for he who hastily passes over the words of a text does not perceive all its meaning or appreciate all its beauty. Here the student is cautioned against that curiosity which would sacrifice the important for the trivial; against fickleness and instability in reading ; against quarrelsome disputations and verbal hairsplittings.

The good student is methodical. Where there is an absence of method, there may indeed be hard work, but there is very little progress. He is persevering in his studies; this is the essential condition of all advancement. Perseverance has been called the mother of the arts, negligence the stepmother of all learning. Another requisite, very essential for youths, is continued practice. The unused iron rusts. Hence the value of disputations amicably conducted; they polish and sharpen intellects. Furthermore, the good student impresses upon his memory whatever he reads; otherwise his labor would be in vain. What avails it that the dog catches the game, if forthwith he lets it go? Water easily receives impressions, but to no purpose, since it does not retain them. The mind discovers wisdom, the memory preserves it. Intellectual slowness may be aided by assiduity, and defective memory improved by frequent repetitions and taking notes. The scholar should ever regard his teacher with esteem and respect and be towards him submissive and affectionate. Finally, he should be careful to thank and glorify God for the talents and the knowledge with which he has been favored.[1]

The remainder of the book is devoted to the discipline of youth as regards behavior, clothing, food and drink, marriage and virginity. The author dwells upon the temptations to which young men are exposed; the puerilities that they should avoid; the virtues that they should practice, especially patience, humility and obedience. He commends matrimony and speaks in glowing terms of the love and esteem that should mutually exist between

[1] Ibid., cap. x., pp. 433, 434.

husband and wife. But he pleads most earnestly for freedom of action among those young men who would lead a life of celibacy and serve God in a religious order. Several chapters are devoted to the education of daughters. They should not be allowed to gad about, should never be idle, and should devote themselves to study. They should be brought up chaste, humble, pious, meek and reserved, and their virtue carefully guarded. They should prize goodness and moral worth above physical beauty and consider the spiritual adornments of the soul superior to those that set forth the beauty of the body. The honor of widowhood is commented upon; the state of virginity is lauded and shown to be far above that of matrimony; its beauty is compared to the lily and its efficacy and special glory are extolled.[1]

Of the remaining books little need be said. The sixth is devoted to the relations of the prince to his subjects. The author begins by picturing the magnitude of the evil an impious prince can inflict upon his subjects, and the punishment he is liable to incur. Afterwards the blessings that accompany the reign of a good prince are eloquently depicted. The seventh and last book is devoted to the relations of the prince to his enemies, and to the various duties belonging to a military life. The only recognized avenues to honor and position in those days were the military and the clerical life. So it is here stated that "as in the body of the Church the clergy constitute the brain, so the military organization is the

---

[1] Ibid., pp. 427-466.

hand . . . from the clergy it has direction and accordingly owes the clergy protection."[1] Here ends this remarkable treatise on education from the pen of William Pérault. Petit-Radel, after giving a very inadequate account of the book, says with truth: "We can praise the lucid style, the wise maxims, the noble and beautiful sentiments, the good order in details, that pervade the work."[2] The recognition of Pérault as a great educator and an eminent writer is a tardy act of justice.

Another Dominican who preserved the educational traditions of the Dominicans in his writings, and still more with his pupils in the school-room, was Fra Bartolomio da San Concordia (1262–1347), of whom the Pisan chronicle speaks in terms of admiration as a teacher. The highest tribute the chronicle pays him is this: that while he stimulated genius he did not neglect youths of mediocre talent; that he was accessible to all; that he communicated what he had learned without distinction and without pretension; and so well did he succeed that the most unpolished minds went forth from his school so carefully instructed that their skill seemed to be natural and their efficiency to come from art. Besides conducting the studium of his convent, he established a school of oratory and poetry for the laity. In his " Ammæstramenti degli Antichi," he gathered together about two thousand passages

---

[1] Ibid., cap. iii., p. 472.

[2] " Histoire Littéraire de la France," t. xix., p. 315. See " Bibliothek der Katholischen Pädagogik," vol. iii., p. 212. Also Von Ketteler, " Die Pflichten des Adels," Mainz, 1868.

from one hundred and twenty different authors, and through the quotations he has interspersed his own beautiful and practical suggestions.   There is little that is new in his method, but when treating of the natural dispositions of soul and body, of the actions that lead the way to virtue, of studying and teach-ing, and of the mode of speaking, he says things that every student of pedagogy might read with profit.[1]

Another volume breathing the spirit of St. Thomas, and written in the same key-note with that of Pérault, is the " De Regimine Principum " of Egidius Romano of the Colonna family (1241–1316).   Egidius, though an Agustinian, had sat at the feet of the Angelical Doctor for several years, following him from chair to chair.   He afterwards became general of the Augustinians and Bishop of Bourges.   Having been charged with the education of the Dauphin of France, who was afterwards known as Philip the Fair, he wrote this treatise on the education of a prince.   The book was written before 1285.   It is divided into three parts : the first treating of self-government, or morals; the second of government of the family, or economics ; and the third of civil government, or politics.   The second part includes the subject of education.   Felix La-jard pronounces it "a complete treatise on educa-tion, physical, intellectual, and moral, adapted to the different ages of the child from the cradle up."[2] Going over the same ground that Pérault cultivated, and going over it in the same spirit and according

---

[1] See Milanese, " Storia della Pedagogia," vol. ii., p. 1491.

[2] " Histoire Littéraire de la France," t. xxx., p. 521.

to the same principles, it naturally follows that the same ideas are enforced in the work of Gilles. The author begins by laying stress upon the care and prudence with which the parent should guide the steps of the child in the path of truth and virtue. He dwells upon the love between father and son, which love should be the principle of obedience on the part of the son. He afterwards speaks of the instruction that should be imparted. The first and most essential is everything pertaining to religion, then good habits and good manners, then correctness of speech, and finally science. He goes through the gamut of the Trivium and Quadrivium, and adds thereto, as essential for the education of a prince, metaphysics, theology, politics and ethics. Nor must we conclude from this elaborate programme, that the truly learned author—*Doctor Fundatissimus* he was called in his own day—was an impracticable theorist. He discriminates. He says:

"The sons of princes should know enough of theology to confirm them in their faith; they should know well the moral sciences in order to learn therefrom how to govern themselves and others. From certain sciences they should know all that is necessary for their moral development; from grammar, enough to understand the idioms in which the truths of religion and morality are taught; from rhetoric and dialectics, all that can render their intellects prompt to apprehend, and give them facility of expression; from music, whatever can aid good manners. For the other sciences a slight acquaintance is sufficient."[1]

------

[1] "De Regimine Principum," p. 310.

The teacher should possess three essential qualities : he should be learned in the science of philosophy ; he should know all matters that man can and
ought to do, and he should be good and upright in
his life. He should teach children how to speak,
how to listen and how to see. Rules are laid down
regarding eating and drinking and all the wants of
the human body, and great caution is given concerning the avoidance of bad company. The author
divides the educational period of life into three
parts : first, from birth to the seventh year ; second,
from the seventh to the fourteenth year ; third, from
the age of fourteen upward. He then lays down,
even to minute details, all that is requisite for the
development of the body, the instruction of the
mind and the education of the heart in each stage of
growth. Above all, is it recommended that the
teacher study the bent of the child's mind, and see
that it follows that bent in a special manner. Herein Egidius agrees with the unknown author of the
teacher's manual that had been attributed to Boëthius. From this principle it follows that those who
have a taste for reading and study and science should
be afforded every facility to pursue their studies,
while those who have no inclination for books should
be exercised in arms, that they also be able to benefit their country. Finally, in the last chapter the
author treats of the education of girls, and therein
lays greater stress upon their being adorned with
every virtue than upon their being learned in every
science ; he sets his face against dancing, public
promenades and loitering on the porches ; instead,

he would have them simple and modest, always occupied, and gracious and becoming in their manners.
This book was translated by Henri de Gauchi, at the
request of Philip, for the benefit of his people, and
it thus became popular at an early day.[1] Thomas
Ouleve embodied the chief portion of the work in
his poem "The Governail of Princes."

But it was not only Dominicans who gave us insight into the methods of teaching practised in those
days. There were Franciscans who were not less
alive to the wants of the day. Take Roger Bacon
(1214–1292). He saw deeply and clearly into the
reality of things and the value of systems. He distinguished between what was solid and substantial
in the studies and teachings of his day and the mere
varnish and veneering that was frequently substituted for real knowledge. He does not conceal his
impatience when in presence of what he considers
mere pretension. Throughout his writings he keeps
up a constant fusilade against his contemporaries.
He finds fault with the groundwork given to boys in
his day. He assures us that thousands of boys entered the Mendicant Orders unable to read their
psalter or their Latin grammar, and that forthwith,
without other preparation, they were set down to
the study of theology. And then, even in the study
of theology, he found Peter Lombard held in greater
esteem than the Sacred Scriptures. Indeed, he was
disgusted at seeing how men abandoned the study
of theology for the more lucrative study of civil
law. " Every first-rate man," he says, " having an

---

[1] "Histoire Littéraire de la France," t. xxx., p. 531.

aptitude for theology and philosophy, betakes himself to civil law, because he sees that civilians are honored by all prelates and princes." He may be ignorant of theology and canon law, but he is held in higher esteem than the master of theology and sooner elected to ecclesiastical dignities.

Bacon had no sympathy with the roundabout methods by which, at great expense of money and time, a small modicum of knowledge was acquired. He avers that in one year he could teach a promising boy all that it takes the schools twenty years to impart. He discourages the study of light literature and considers the moral writings of Seneca and the Vulgate a better training for young men than the amatory poems of Ovid. He regards the method of teaching geometry as needlessly long and tedious. He bewails the paucity of good mathematicians. He would apply experiment and mathematical calculations to physics. Natural science does not depend upon authority, but upon experiment as the only sure road to certainty. He advocated as the key to all knowledge the careful study of languages and of mathematics. Did men know the languages better there would be more precision in thought. Mathematics purges the intellectual vision and fits the learner for the acquirement of all knowledge, for mathematics is the connecting link between all the sciences.[1] Logic he did not consider so important ; for we know it naturally, and even the uneducated syllogize.[2] He goes back to the workings of the

[1] "Opus Tertium," p. 37.
[2] Ibid., p. 102.

human mind, and considers the obstacles that stand in the way of acquiring human knowledge.

"In the way of acquiring truth," he says, "there are four stumbling blocks which impede all wisdom whatever and scarcely permit anybody to arrive at true wisdom. They are: the force of weak and unworthy authority, prolonged custom, ignorant popular opinion, and the hiding of one's ignorance by the semblance of knowledge."[1]

Thus, out of the stray remarks running through the works of this great but too outspoken Franciscan might one construct a whole methodology far in advance of his day and generation.

Another eminent man who, for the instruction and edification of master and pupil, wrote in Latin verse a little treatise on school-life, was Bonvicino da Ripa. His is one of the most honored names in Milan. He had been set down as a Dominican,[2] and it had been surmised that he was a ·Franciscan; but he was neither; his monument tells us that he was a distinguished member of the Third Order of Humiliati.[3] In May, 1291, we find him assisting at a general chapter of his Order. The old chroniclers speak highly of him as an eminent teacher in the Palatine school, in Legnano, where he erected a hospital, and in Milan. In addition, he was the first to establish in Milan and the surrounding district the pious custom of recalling the memory of the Incarnation at the ringing of the bells, as his eulogist expresses

---

[1] "Opus Majus," lib. i., p. 2.
[2] Echard et Quetif, "Script. Ord. Praed.," t. i., p. 419.
[3] Argelati, "Bibliotheca Scriptorum," t. ii., p. 187.

it,' in the words of his epitaph: "qui primo fecit pulsari companas ad Ave Maria Mediolani et in comitatu." That same epitaph adds: "Dicatur Ave Maria pro anima ejus."[2] Let us not forget the pious bequest. Bonvicino was courteous, generous, devoted to the noble work of educating youth. Though he wrote Latin in a style that Sassi compliments, he was none the less an enthusiastic cultivator of the Italian, which he sought to polish, and in which he wrote, among other things in verse, a little book laying down the rules of courtesy and good behavior for children. These rules have been edited by Mr. Michael Rossetti, and published by the Early English Text Society.

Let us now glance at the poem "De Vita Scholastica."[3] The pious author begins by stating that he would place in the hands of every student the keys by which in the pursuit of his studies he may best unlock the gate of wisdom. The edition of the poem from which the abstract is made, is subdivided under various headings. Now, the first key the author would place in the student's hands is the fear of the Lord. He lays stress upon an active faith which is based on this fear. "The devil believes, but he is wanting in this living faith." The poet next counsels the student so to control his thoughts and intentions that whatever he learns shall be for the honor of God. It is the part of wisdom to be dis-

---

[1] Sassi, "De Studiis Literariis Mediolanensium," Milan, 1729, p. 94.

[2] Argelati, loc. cit.

[3] "Fratris Bonvicini Mediolanensis Vita Scholastica," Brixiæ, 1585.

creet in the use of the tongue. One should never slander; never deceive; never be vain; never boastful; never flattering; never false; never indulge in proud prating.'

The author next dwells upon the observance of humility and the avoidance of pride. He would have the student fly from jealousy; would have him grateful for favors, and forgiving of injuries; he would have him make all studies subservient to the glory of God and the salvation of his soul. The poet here tells the legend of that Master Serlon of Paris, whose disciple took undue pleasure in sophisms and undue pride in his power of logical disputation, and who, terrified at the apparition of this disciple damned for his vanity, and wearing a cloak of sophisms which crushes him to earth and consumes him, forthwith becomes converted and retires to a monastery, saying: I leave frogs to their croaking, rooks to their cawing, and things of vanity to the vain, and henceforth I pursue that logic which fears not the Ergo of death—

> " Linquo coax ranis: croc corvis: vanaque vanis,
> Ad logicam pergo: quæ mortis non timet Ergo.'

Another section of the poem exhorts the student to avoid luxury, and that vice of sodomy which was then prevalent among masters and students, and for which Dante placed his own teacher in hell. The student is counseled to be abstemious in eating and drinking, and is cautioned against gluttony,

---

[1] " Lingua tibi non sit detractrix: subdola: vana: grandis: adulatrix: falsa: superba loquax," p. 3.

the wearing of delicate clothing and sleeping in a bed that is too downy and comfortable; against games of chance; against frequent balls and dances; against avarice and cupidity; against extravagance in giving, the student knowing always to whom he gives. He should regulate his senses, and fix his thoughts upon heaven that they may become worthy of heaven and filled with goodness. Stress is laid upon avoiding bad company, upon being charitable towards all, especially one's companions; the duties to be performed morning and evening, the the prayers to be said; upon making the sign of the cross when one eats or drinks; upon the love and reverence due to father and mother; upon prayer to the saints and the frequent hearing of mass—*ut videas Christum virgine matre natum.*

Nor does Bonvicino overlook the teacher's duties.[1] To be worthy of his position, the first thing the master should do, "If he would control his pupils, is discreetly to correct his own defects." He is to avoid all vanity, and perfect himself in his studies. The master who is lacking in sound learning, is preparing to live dishonestly. He should be discreet in correcting, nor be easily overcome by anger. Where peace and discipline are united, there are studies properly conducted. Such is the substance of this rare book.[2]

We shall find summed up in the writings of Dante what was best in the educational methods of that

---

[1] Incipit liber secundus de Regimine Magistrorum.

[2] The volume from which I took this sketch is in the Mazarin Library, Paris.

day. Dante (1265–1321) was born and raised in a republic in which education was general. According to Villani, fully 12,000 children out of a population of 90,000, which Florence then contained, attended school. Of these, the large majority received only an elementary training; the girls, at an early age, learning from their mothers all the various household duties, and the boys apprenticed to the trades of their fathers, who transmitted to them that skill which made Florence so famous. Seven hundred young men received the higher education. The very spirit of the arts was scholastic in Dante's day. You read the story in the oratory of Orsanmichele, in which each art with its masterpiece receives a crown; you read it in the chapters of Santa Maria Novella, in Gaddi's painting of the Trivium and Quadrivium; you read it in Giotto's sculpture of the same subject upon his marvelous campanile. Here was the atmosphere in which Dante's boyhood and early manhood were passed.

It is the mission of the poet to reflect in his work the predominant, all-pervading spirit and views of his age. Now, in his day, the universities were the controlling element in thought, in art, in politics, moulding the thinkers and rulers of the age both in church and state. But Dante was a life-long student. He traveled from land to land and from school to school, and sat patiently and humbly at the feet of masters, imbibing whatever knowledge they could convey. He disputed in public. His bright eye and strong, sombre, reserved features attracted the attention of fellow-students as he wended his way, absorbed in his own thoughts, through the rue de Fouarre, and entered the hall in which Sigier was holding forth.[1]   Tradition has it that he was no less assiduous a frequenter of School street in Oxford.   He has left us no distinct treatise on education, but he who embodied all the science of his day, who was supreme in teaching so many other lessons, could not be silent in regard to pedagogy.   From his writings a whole volume of rules and principles bearing upon education might be gleaned.   In "Il Convito" he expresses himself fully on the different ages of human growth and development ; speaks of obedience as an essential requisite for the child ; after his father he should obey his masters and his elders.[2]   He should also be gentle and modest, reverent, and eager to acquire knowledge ; reserved, never forward ; repentant of his faults to the extent of overcoming them.   As our soul in all its operations makes use of a bodily organ, it behooves us to exercise the body that it grow in grace and aptness, and be well ordained and disposed in order that the soul may control it to the best advantage.   Thus it is that a noble nature seeks to have a sound mind in a sound body.[3]

Dante is as faithful a disciple of St. Thomas Aquinas as is Gilles of Rome.   He holds with the Angelical Doctor that the soul was made to know truth, to love and possess the good, and to enjoy the beautiful.   The heart was created for the good.   All

---

[1] "Paradiso," x., 136–138.
[2] "Il Convito," Tratt. iv., cap. 24.
[3] Ibid., cap. 25.

indistinctly apprehend the good towards which the
soul aspires and in which it would rest :

> " Each one confusedly a good conceives
> Wherein the mind may rest, and longeth for it;
> Therefore to overtake it each one strives." [1]

Elsewhere he beautifully likens the soul seeking
the good to the traveler in a strange land going from
door to door expecting that each house he enters
will be the inn in which he is to take lodgings ; even
so does the soul turn its eyes now upon one thing,
now upon another, and because its knowledge is
limited and fragmentary, and it sees not things in
their true light, it not infrequently accepts as a
great good that which in reality is very small and
insignificant. [2]

As the heart seeks the good, so does the intellect seek the true. The intellect was made for truth
and rejoices in possession of the truth:

> "And thou shouldst know that they all have delight
> As much as their own vision penetrates
> The Truth, in which all intellect finds rest." [3]

So also does the soul rejoice in the contemplation
of the beautiful. But, as there are different degrees
of goodness, so are there different degrees of beauty.
The spiritual beauty of religious dogma and doctrine,
for instance, as explained in the science of theology
—she who " betwixt truth and mind infuses light " [4]
—and symbolized in Beatrice, is far above beauty

---

[1] " Purgatorio," xvii., 127–129.
[2] " Il Convito," Tratt. iv., cap. 12.
[3] " Paradiso," xxviii., 106–108.
[4] " Purgatorio," vi., 46.

that appeals to the senses, and so absorbs the soul that it turns aside from all earthly forms of the fair. Here is how the poet expresses this truth :

> "Then by the spirit that doth never leave
> Its amorous dalliance with my lady's looks,
> Back with redoubled ardor were mine eyes
> Led unto her : and from her radiant smiles,
> When as I turned me, pleasure so divine
> Did lighten on me, that whatever vail
> Of art or nature in the human flesh,
> Or in its limned resemblance, can combine
> Through greedy eyes to take the soul withal,
> Were to her beauty nothing." [1]

But man's senses and the faculties of his soul are developed for other purposes than that of self-gratification. Since he is made for society, and society requires various duties, various functions, various aptitudes in the arts and sciences and the diverse walks of life, then is it in the nature of things that there should be among men diversity of talents. This is the teaching of Aristotle :

> "Whence he again : 'Now say, would it be worse
> For men on earth were they not citizens?'
> 'Yes,' I replied ; 'and here I ask no reason.'
>
> 'And can they be so, if below they live not
> Diversely unto offices diverse?'
> 'No, if your master writeth well for you.'" [2]

Upon this principle, based upon the nature of man as a social being, Dante builds up the great pedagogical truth that natures should not be forced into grooves for which they are unfitted ; that in the

---

[1] "Paradiso," xxvii., 88–97, Cary's tr.

[2] "Paradiso," viii., 115-120.

choosing of a state of life one's tastes and inclina-
tions should be consulted ; that it were unwise to
compel one with a love for study and retirement to
assume the career of arms, or one whose tastes are
for outdoor life and industrial activity to confine
himself to books. He would have him with a mechanical turn of mind devote himself to a trade ; him
with a bent for science devote himself to scientific
pursuits ; him fond of books and reading devote
himself to a life of letters, and so on with other talents and other callings. In this manner will the designs of Providence be best carried out and most
good accomplished. To this effect spake Charles to
the poet :

> " Evermore nature, if it fortune find
> Discordant to it, like each other seed
> Out of its region, maketh evil thrift,
> And if the world below would fix its mind
> On the foundation which is laid by nature,
> Pursuing that, 'twould have the people good.
> But you unto religion wrench aside
> Him who was born to gird him with a sword,
> And make a king of him who is for sermons :
> Therefore your footsteps wander from the road.'"[1]

But the whole poem recognizes the necessity of
education. Dante in his own person represents humanity. He is unable to extricate himself from the
dark wood or to overcome the many obstacles that
beset his way without the guidance of Virgil, whom
he calls his master[2] and his pedagogue.[3] Even so,

---

[1] Ibid., 139–149.
[2] "Inferno," i., 85.
[3] "Purgatorio," xii., 3.

humanity cannot of itself get out of the wood of
error and vice and ignorance and prejudice without
the aid of a master who will guide it safely and
reveal to it the knowledge of things in heaven and
on earth.   With the schoolboy and with humanity
the road to progress and liberty is through a severe
tutelage.

The Franciscans made the language of the people the vehicle of spiritual thought.   Dante in a
happy hour made that language the medium of the
highest philosophical thought and fixed its structure
as a classic form of expression for all time.   From
that memorable twelfth day of August, in the year
1373, when the citizens of Florence petitioned the governors of the Republic "to make provision for the
choosing of a man learned, capable and well-versed
in the doctrine of the 'Divina Commedia,' to read
and explain the said poem every day not a holiday
during the year," and the governors selected Boc-
caccio; and Bologna, Pisa, Ravenna, Piacenza, and
other cities, following the example of Florence, established chairs for the study of Dante—from that
day Dante became the schoolmaster of Italy, keeping alive the fire of patriotism, accustoming the people to the sublimest truths sung in noblest verse, and
through good and bad fortune ever keeping before
the Italian mind such a high standard of thought
that whoever was familiar with Dante was possessed
of an education far more complete than that imparted
by Homer to the Greeks of old.   There were inter-
vals when the study of Dante was neglected, still the
nation owning such a classic might become extinct,

but it could not continue to live and neglect the precious lessons contained in that priceless treasure. Dante is no longer the educator exclusively of Italy ; he is fast becoming the schoolmaster of the most cultured among the other nations of Christendom. In taking leave of Dante we shall also take leave of college life and college methods as they existed when the college was still in touch with the university.

THE PRIMARY SCHOOL IN THE MIDDLE AGES

THE PRIMARY SCHOOL IN THE MIDDLE AGES. [1]

I

THE Abbé Alain has made a specialty of the history of education prior to the Revolution of 1789 in France. The volume before me is one among several from his pen. It is not only a compendious summing up of the labors of others in the same field; it is also based upon original research, and has brought to light facts and figures that may not be ignored. The learned Abbé is indefatigable. The amount of reading that has gone into any of the least chapters of this modest book is sufficient voucher for the conscientiousness of the work done. The book will prove a revelation to many readers.

Time was, and that not very long ago, when men were convinced that in France primary education began after the Revolution. They could see nothing previous to that epoch but an ignorant people, deprived of all educational facilities for their children. That there was primary education, and gratuitous primary education prior to 1789, is still to

[1] *Educational Review.*

"L'Instruction primaire en France avant la Révolution, d'après les Travaux récents et des Documents inédits," par l'Abbé Alain. Paris: Librairie de la Société Bibliographique, 1881, pp. xvi., 304.

many an unknown fact. Nonetheless is it true, nor will it be denied by any person presuming to know aught of the history of education in Europe. The spontaneous enthusiasm with which men, in different parts of France, found themselves working upon this subject is in itself quite phenomenal. I cannot undertake to make a complete record of the books that have been produced, teeming with scholarship and all unanimous in their results, but I will glance at a few of the more important works.

The first, to my knowledge, to let in light on the subject of the education of the people, was the erudite Director of the National Library of Paris, M. Leopold Delisle. In his learned essay, called "Études sur la Condition de la Classe Agricole, et l'État de l'Agriculture en Normandie au moyen âge" (Evreux, 1857), he dwelt upon the intellectual status of the peasantry of Normandy, and from original sources proved that people to have been well cared for as regards education. This was a side light, revealing an unexpected state of affairs. The book is a model of its kind, and has been largely so utilized in France.

The next author to deal with the subject was M. Fayet. In 1858, he read before the Scientific Congress of France his first memoir on the state of primary education in Auxerre during the past centuries. On the same occasion we find a similar memoir from the pen of M. Quantin.[1] Since that time M. Fayet has been indefatigable in collecting docu-

---

[1] "Congrès Scientifique de France," 15e Session, tenu à Auxerre en 1858, t. ii., pp. 115, 130.

ments throwing additional light on the subject, and he has written some other valuable works concerning it.[1]

In 1868 M. Maggiolo read at the Sorbonne his important essay, "De la Condition du Maître d'École en Lorraine avant 1789." Since then he has issued papers and volumes, all bearing on the question of primary education ; but the main results of his investigations are to be found in valuable articles of his scattered through the pages of Buisson's "Dictionnaire de Pédagogie."

Other works on the subject began to multiply with astonishing rapidity, and they furnish a striking example of what may be achieved when method and scholarship and untiring research are brought to bear upon a disputed or ill-understood issue. Thirty years ago, men might inform you concerning the Colleges of the Jesuits, or the Oratorians in France during the sixteenth and seventeenth centuries, but on the state of primary education, or whether it had existence at all prior to the Revolution, they were in total darkness. To-day, he would be a very daring or very ignorant man who would assert, in presence of an intelligent audience in any part of the civilized world, that there was no primary education before the end of the eighteenth century. It was with the sole view of refuting this assertion that the whole library of educational literature just referred to was produced.

---

[1] Among others, we may mention " Les Écoles de la Bourgogne, sous l'Ancien Régime," Langres, 1875 ; "Recherches historiques et statistiques sur les Communes et les Écoles de la Haute-Marne," Paris, 1879.

There is scarcely a province in France in which archives have not been overhauled ; and facts and figures of all kinds have been pressed into service, and made to reveal results as astonishing as they were unlooked for. I shall not attempt an exhaustive enumeration of them. Beaurepaire has unfolded in three volumes the history of public instruction in the diocese of Rouen before 1789.[1] Quantin did the same for the department of the Yonne.[2] De Charmasse gave us invaluable documents bearing on the state of education in the ancient diocese of Autun.[3] Babeau brought to light the state of education in in the department of Aube.[4] Armand Ravelet, the brilliant editor of *Le Monde* of Paris, in the introductory portions of his history of Blessed John Baptist de la Salle, summarized such of these as had been published at the time of writing, and added new matter, the result of his own research.[5] These are but a few of the many works that I might quote. They have all been utilized to the best advantage by the Abbé Alain.

---

[1] " Recherches sur l'Instruction publique, dans le Diocèse de Rouen, avant 1789." Évreux, 1872, 3 vols., 8vo.

[2] " Histoire de l'Instruction primaire avant 1789, dans les Pays formant le Departement de l'Yonne," Auxerre, 1874.

[3] " État de l'Instruction primaire dans l'ancien Diocèse d'Autun pendant les XVIIe et XVIIIe Siècles," Autun, 1871 ; second edition, Paris, 1878.

[4] " L'Instruction primaire dans les Campagnes avant 1789," Troyes, 1875.

[5] " Histoire du Vénérable J. B. de la Salle, Fondateur de l'Institut des Frères des Écoles Chrétiennes," Paris, 1874. Leon Gautier has made further additions to this portion of Ravelet's work in a new edition, which he edited in French and which was afterward translated into English by the late Kathleen O'Meara.

I shall now endeavor to give some idea of the primary school in the Middle Ages as we find it outlined in such works and documents as have been mentioned.

II.

There is no time in the history of the Christian Church when schools did not exist, now of one kind, now of another. Even down in the catacombs we find next to the little chapel the schoolroom for the catechumens, where they had their own teachers, distinct from those who gave instruction to the faithful.[1] In the East we need only mention the schools of Edessa and Alexandria. We have seen that wherever monastic institutions were established, schools flourished. Then there were the episcopal school, the cathedral school, the parish school, the burgh school, the rural school, schools attached to the hospitals for the poor,—all of which flourished at one or other time during the Middle Ages, throughout Christendom.

In the graphic pages of Gregory of Tours (539–593), we read accounts of poisonings, murders, wars, intrigues at the royal court, while Chilperic is discussing Arianism and writing bad verses. But even in those lawless days there are indications that schools abounded. Chilperic turns grammarian and adds to the alphabet. Gregory says of him :

" He sent orders to all the towns in his kingdom that the new alphabet be taught the children and

---

[1] Padre Marchi, " Monumenti delle Arti Christiane Primitive nella Metropoli del Christianesimo," Rome, 1844, p. 172.

that all books formerly written be effaced by the pumice stone, and written anew." [1]

Again, Guibert of Nogent, born about 1065, writing of education in his day, says :

"Somewhat before this time, and even since, there was so great scarcity of schoolmasters that hardly a single one could be seen in the country, and not many in the large towns; and even these were so backward in learning that they could not be compared with the class now (1110) to be found in the country schools."

He witnesses a general revival of learning,—"seeing how on all sides men give themselves zealously to the study of grammar, and the ever-increasing number of schools renders knowledge easy of access to the rudest men." [2] From this time on evidences of the existence of the rural school become more frequent.

M. Simeon Luce, in the course of his historical researches, feels bound to notice its existence in the fourteenth century. He says :

"It is a grave mistake to imagine that there were no primary schools. Mention is made of rural schools in all the documents, even in those in which we would least expect to find it, and we can scarcely doubt that during the most stormy years of the fourteenth century most villages had their masters, teaching children reading, writing, and some arithmetic."

Elsewhere the same author places before us a little scene, which she represents as occurring in 1377,

---

[1] " Histoire," V., 45.
[2] " History of the Crusades," Preface.

that brings home to us the schoolmaster of that dis-·
tant day finding difficulty in collecting his dues.
Tassin de Loitre, such is the master's name, after
drinking wine in the tavern of one Thomas D'Aunoy,
refuses to pay. "And why not?" asks the hostess.
"Because," replies Tassin, "you keep a cleric at
my school for whom you owe me more than forty
pence."[1]

In the thirteenth century out of a population of 90,000 in Florence, we find 12,000 children
attending the schools, a ratio of school attendance
as large as existed in New York City in the year of
grace 1893. A statute of the diocese of Rouen, issued in the year 1230, reads: "Let the clergy frequently exhort their parishioners to be careful and
exacting in sending their children to school."

James Grant bears witness to a like multiplicity
of schools in Scotland:

"Our burgh schools," he says, "were not created
by an act of Parliament; they had their origin in
connection with the church, or were called into
existence by the people themselves; but in whatever way they were founded, undoubtedly, toward
the end of the fifteenth century, schools were planted
in every considerable town in Scotland; and the
memorable Act of 1496, which has been so frequently quoted, assumes the existence of schools
enough for supplying the people with knowledge of
art, 'jure,' and 'perfect Latin.'"[2]

---

[1] "Histoire de Bertrand du Guesclin et son Époque: La
Jeunesse de Bertrand (1320–1364)," p. 15.

[2] "History of the Burgh and Parish Schools of Scotland,"
p. 25.

E. E.—12

Babeau, as the result of his researches, finds this state of affairs everywhere throughout France. "According to a great number of traditions," he says, "school was as much frequented, if not more so, formerly, than it is to-day."[1]   As early as 1500, in the Middle Rhine province, there were schools every two miles.   In the annals of Wesel, under the year 1494, there were charges for five teachers "to instruct the youth in reading, writing, figures, and church music."[2]

Nor were the parents of mediæval days as indifferent to the education of their children as some would lead us to suppose.   In the burghs and villages it was customary with fathers, when binding out a young son to learn some trade, or hiring him out to do manual labor, to impose on the master conditions obliging him to send the child to school at certain times and seasons, and to procure him elementary instruction.   Thus we read that in 1398 one Jean Milles, in apprenticing his son as servant to a certain William Louvet, stipulates that the master shall find the child in all the necessaries of life ; among others so named are : "eating, drinking, shoes, clothing, and the being kept at school."

Again, we read that in the year 1399, among the stipulations under which a minor is bound to his uncle for nine years, is one that the latter shall keep him at school during the whole time and shall see

[1] "L'Instruction primaire dans les Campagnes avant 1789," p. 41.

[2] Janssen, "Geschichte des Deutschen Volkes," i., pp. 23, 24.

that he be tonsured — *faire avoir couronne.*[1] This solicitude extended to the time when they could no longer look after their education. A customary expression, found in the wills of merchants and artisans of the thirteenth century in regard to a child was : " Volo quod sibi provideatur in scholis."[2]

The clergy were equally interested in the education of the children. In the rural districts they were wont to teach school themselves. And in the eighth century we find a bishop of Modena, when investing one of his priests with an important parish in the city, exhorting him " to be diligent in keeping school and educating the children."[3] A statute of the diocese of Rouen, of the year 1230, reads :

" Let the clergy frequently exhort their parishioners to be careful and exacting in sending their children to school, since no one without instruction can be admitted to ecclesiastical benefices."[4]

Dederich Goelde, a Friar Minor, in a catechism which he wrote in 1470, thus speaks of the duties of parents toward their children :

" Children should at an early age be sent to school, to honorable and worthy teachers, in order that they learn to be respectful and to save them from learning sin and bad habits in the streets."[5]

---

[1] Tonsure admitted to the benefit of clergy, and was greatly sought after by parents for their children. We read that in the diocese of Rouen, from the Michaelmas of 1465 to the Michaelmas of 1466, there were tonsured 3954 children. Cf. Beaurepaire, " Recherches sur l'Instruction publique dans le Diocèse de Rouen, avant 1789," pp. 53–62.

[2] Louis Guibert : " Dictionnaire de Pédagogie," Art., Limousin, p. 1594.

[3] Cerruti, " Storia della Pedagogia in Italia," p. 95.

[4] Beaurepaire, op. cit., p. 53.

[5] Cf. Janssen, op. cit., I., p. 22.

The Church was ever solicitous to maintain a supply of teachers especially for the primary schools. The Council of Vaison, held in 529, decreed that, as was the general custom throughout Italy, each pastor should have in his house a class of young men studying for the priesthood. These young men were also engaged in teaching the small children. And so, in the ninth century, one of the questions to be asked when the bishop makes a visitation of his parish, is : " Whether the parish priest has with him a cleric who can teach school—*qui possit tenere scholam*—and assist him during the divine services." [1]

Riculf, the bishop of Soissons, admonishes his priests that among other things they pay particular attention to the scholars confided to them, and so teach them grammar that they will not destroy its fruit by inaccuracy in their conversation. [2] The good bishop, in asking his priests to find a method of teaching grammar by which pupils could speak correctly, was giving them a problem that very few of the schoolmasters of the present day have been able to solve. Later on we find the statutes of Troyes decreeing that every parish priest shall have dwelling with him a cleric who shall teach school, and that said priest shall notify his parishioners to send their sons to the church to be properly instructed by this cleric. [3]

---

[1] Hincman, " Statutes of 852, XI., Acts of the Province of Rheims," I., p. 211.

[2] " Constitutions of the Diocese of Soissons," 889, Art. xvi.

[3] Statutes of the Synod of Troyes, beginning of thirteenth century, cf. Babeau, op. cit., p. 8.

Monasteries also supported a certain number of young clerics with a view of their becoming teachers.[1] And in each large monastery there were generally two schools, one for those intending to enter the service of the Church, and the other for youths who were to continue to live in the world. In 817 the Council of Aix-la-Chapelle issued a decree which shows that masters were looked after in those early days. The decree reads:

" If it should happen that the Brother who shall be charged with the care of the children should take little or no pains to instruct them, or should teach them other things than the subjects they ought to learn, or should have injured them in beating, let such be severely punished and removed from his office, and let this office be committed to some other Brother who shall keep the children innocent by the example of his life, and shall excite them to the performance of good deeds." [2]

In the cities, as early as the eleventh century, chapters took charge of the schools.[3]

The schoolmaster in the Middle Ages, we may infer, was, up to the fifteenth century, generally a young ecclesiastic or a cleric who dwelt with the pastor, helped him to sing the divine offices, aided him in many ways, and generally acted as sacristan. Flodoard tells us of such a cleric who, in order to study, or for some other purpose, was wont to steal the oil from the lamps burning before the relics of

---

[1] " Beaurepaire," op. cit., II., p. 28.

[2] " Statuts et Réglemens des petites Écoles de Grammaire de la Ville. Cité, Université, Faux-bourgs, et Banlieuē de Paris," Paris, 1672, p. 214.

[3] Choron, 2d fascic., p. 54.

certain saints. His pupils, to whom he was teaching the psalter, informed on him.

Even when not a cleric, the schoolmaster still performed certain functions in the church. Thus, we read the following articles of agreement, bearing date of July 25, 1699:

"The said Gaillardet promises to teach reading, writing, cyphering, plain chant . . . and obligates himself to ring the bells when storm, wind, or hail threatens, and to sing at benediction during Advent and Lent."[1]

This formula embodies the traditional occupations of the schoolmaster for centuries. A similar document has been handed down to us from the Catholic days of Scotland. It reads:

"Master Harry Henryson is taken bound to be the good, true, and thankful servitor of the abbot and convent, and their successors, during his lifetime, and to attend to high mass and even-song at the high solemn festival times, with his surplice on."[2]

In Paris, the master was expected "to preach on Palm Sunday in the Church of Notre Dame," or to pay out of his own purse for one to replace him.[3] At Pavilly, the master and his pupils were wont to attend mass on Sundays and solemn feasts in the chapel of the priory, where they chanted, and after mass both master and pupils dined with the prior.[4]

---

[1] L. Maglio, Art., Bourgogne in Buisson's "Dictionnaire de Pédagogie."

[2] Grant, "History of the Burgh and Parish Schools of Scotland," p. 23.

[3] "Mémoires de la Société de l'Histoire de Paris," t. xiii., p. 47.

[4] Beaurepaire, op. cit., p. 28. This dinner was called *Truée.*

The connection of the schoolmaster with singing in the church dates far back. Thus we read that when Charlemagne would change the system of music from the Gallic to the more efficient Roman system, he ordered all the schoolmasters to bring their antiphonaries to the chanters Theodore and Benedict to be corrected. Hence we generally find that the precentor of the cathedral is also the superintendent of the schools. But we must not for a moment imagine that because of the offices he filled around the church the schoolmaster of mediæval days was not held in honor. Such offices were not considered to be in any sense degrading. In those ages of faith it was thought an honor to be employed in the humblest manner with anything connected with the worship of God.

"Men have been amused," says the Abbé Alain, "they have even feigned indignation upon seeing our old schoolmasters both teachers, chanters, and sacristans. These good Christians took quite another view of the matter. The humble duties they performed in the church were great in their own eyes, and far from making them fall in the estimation of pupils and people they added to their respect."[1]

The General Assembly of the clergy of France, held in 1685, decreed that "the schoolmasters, clothed in their surplices, should be incensed in the church and should hold the place of honor above all the laity, even the aristocracy of the parish."[2] The

---

[1] "L'Instruction Primaire en France avant la Revolution," p. 132.

[2] "Collection des Procès-verbaux du Clergé," t. v., pp. 602, 603.

teacher was, according to Merlet, "after the pastor, the man of the parish. He saw the child born; he added his congratulations to the young couple pledging their love at the foot of the altar; he joined the last prayers uttered over the tomb that was closing down on some departed one." [1]

He was the counselor of families, the confidant of secrets; when a letter was to be written, to him men and women had recourse. Not infrequently did he exercise some civic function in connection with that of teaching; now that of notary public, now that of registrar, now that of lawyer, now that of mayor of the town.[2] He was held in respect during life, and his memory was cherished after death. Nor was the schoolmistress less esteemed. There is pathos in this inscription bearing date of 1687:

"Catherine Ravigné, schoolmistress, was buried in presence of the chapter assembled, bearing with her the esteem of the whole congregation for her many offices of charity done to each and all." [3]

Moreover, the schoolmaster enjoyed many privileges from the state. He was generally exempt from taxation and from military services.[4]

The manner in which he was paid varied with the locality. Sometimes he received a certain stipend from the burghers or the parish. Sometimes he taxed each pupil according to the subject studied.

---

[1] Merlet, iii.

[2] For these and other instances see Alain, op. cit., pp. 144, 145.

[3] C. Post, "Dictionnaire de Maine-et-Loire," t. iii., p. 379.

[4] Babeau, "Le Village," p. 231, *sqq.*

A document of the thirteenth century thus regulates the stipends of a grammarian: The town was to be responsible for the payment of all the younger children within its limits not studying grammar, and the master should exact from them no salary. From those outside, the sum of five sols was required. Those studying grammar should pay seven sols and six pence; and the grade extended to twenty sols.' The poor were always enabled to receive instruction gratuitously.

A decree of the town of Worms in 1260 reads as follows: " No one shall be excluded from the schools on account of indigence." Frequently the master received payment in kind, according to the local products. The Abbé Alain, after summing up the results of those authorities who entered into details on the subject, says:

"All things considered, the position of our ancient educators, as regards ease and competence, was scarcely inferior to that of their important successors in our own days."'

III.

Such was the schoolmaster. What of the school itself? The primary or rural school was at first frequently held in the church, and it was only after a long struggle and reiterated synodal decrees that it became located elsewhere. Thus Reginald of Durham, writing in the twelfth century, assures us that

---

¹ Compayré, "Études Historiques et Documents inédits sur l'Albigeois," Albi, 1841, p. 209.

² " L'Instruction Primaire," p. 133.

it was the custom to hold school in the church, and mentions the incident of a boy who thought he would get rid of all his school troubles by throwing the key of the church into a deep pool of the river flowing near by.[1] The Bishop of Bayeux in 1662 forbids the holding of schools in churches and chapels.[2] If the pastoral residence was large enough, school was held there. The children of all grades were assembled in the same room, and it was only after stringent legislation that the boys were separated from the girls. In the cities this arrangement was more readily brought about.

The school books were few. The child had one book containing the alphabet and his prayers in Latin. It was sometimes called the A B C; but because it bore the image of the cross, it was more generally known as the *Croix de par Dieu.*[3] The next book placed in his hands was the psalms and offices for Sunday.[4]

"It is undoubtedly to the study of the psalms," says De Charmasse, "made on the school benches, that we must attribute the universal taste which all classes of society in the Middle Ages preserved for the almost daily recitation of the psalter."[5]

---

[1] James Grant, "History of the Burgh and Parish Schools of Scotland," p. 5.

[2] "Lettre Pastorale," p. 56. The little book on **Method** attached to this letter is rare and valuable.

[3] "Croix de par Dieu" is equivalent to "Croix *de parte Dei.*"

[4] It was called the "petit Latin," and from its peculiar form the "Longuette." Cf. Babeau, op. cit., p. 39.

[5] "État de l'Instruction primaire dans l'ancien Diocèse d'Autun," 1878, p. 22.

The child was invariably taught to read Latin before he had learned to read in the vernacular. In England the custom was changed during the sixteenth century.[1] In France this was considered the natural method, inasmuch as the Latin tongue was the foundation of the French. In consequence of this method, children were frequently withdrawn from school before they had learned to read in their mother tongue. The custom had begun at a time when Latin was the vulgar tongue.[2] It was only in the seventeenth century that La Salle succeeded, amid great opposition, in changing this order, and teaching the French first.

The old arrangement may seem to us a great hardship, but we must remember that we are dealing with a period in which newspapers were not in existence and books were scarce and expensive. Those in the mother tongue were comparatively few and costly. Strolling bards made the people familiar with the substance of popular song and legend— the romantic literature—that ran side by side with the spiritual and theological writings of the period. Even for those who were taught to read in the vernacular, the amount of available reading matter was scanty, and did not extend beyond their catechism, with some Bible history, and an occasional pious book.

In the thirteenth century a code of politeness was added. Advanced pupils were further taught to read charts and manuscripts. We find mention made

---

[1] Mulcaster, "Positions," p. 31.

[2] "Essai d'une École Chrétienne," Paris, 1724, p. 293.

of prizes given for excellence in the reading of documents.[1] When the student could decipher old registers and dusty parchments, often set down in writing difficult to read, his education was considered complete. The master had nothing more to teach him.[2] Teachers have been rejected because they could not decipher the deeds, charts and documents of a township.[3] Those of my readers who have had any experience in deciphering all such documents cannot fail to respect the intelligence and patience of the teacher or pupil who had become expert at the work. In the seventeenth century pupils were taught to read books printed in the black-letter or Gothic characters. Thus, one of the earliest hand-books of pedagogy says :

"While they are learning politeness and to read manuscripts, the master shall teach them how to read in some book printed in Gothic letters, showing them once a day the characters, ligatures, abbreviations, and capitals in this kind of printing."[4]

Arithmetic in the primary school did not extend beyond a knowledge of numeration. Far into the Middle Ages the Roman system of learning figures and letters by means of pebbles was employed.[5] Alcuin, as well as Isidore, sought rather the mystical meaning of numbers than their practical utility.

---

[1] Maggiolo, "Les Archives scolaires de la Beauce," p. 19.

[2] Babeau, "L'Instruction primaire dans les Campagnes," p. 40.

[3] Sérurier, p. 54; "Archives de la Gironde," C. 328z; Alain, op. cit., pp. 168, 169.

[4] "L'Éscole Paroissiale," p. 253.

[5] Cf. "Etymologia" of Isidore of Seville.

Only in computations bearing on the ecclesiastical year was any serious use made of them. Even Gerbert gives only the teaching of Boëthius, and though he simplifies the abacus, he does not introduce Arabic numbers, as had been frequently asserted.[1]

It was in 1202 that Leonard Febonacci, a merchant of Pisa, published his books on arithmetic and algebra, in which he introduced the Arabic figures, decimals, and another modification of the abacus.

Vincent of Beauvais, one of the most encyclopædic men of his day, popularized the system. Up to 1581 we find no mention of arithmetic in the primary school.

Mulcaster speaks only of "writing and reading" as the two things which children might easily learn "for religion's sake and their necessary affairs."[2] An arithmetic published in 1719, in France, contains numeration and the first three fundamental rules. The examples are all in the concrete, dealing with yards of cloth, casks of wine, and the like. The book was then considered a novelty.[3]

Writing was taught in the primary school. But as the schoolmaster was frequently the scribe of the village, and in the employment of his pen found an additional source of income, he was very slow in

---

[1] Chasles, " Mémoires de l'Académie de Science," 1843.

[2] " Positions," p. 139.

[3] It was called " Instruction nouvelle pour enseigner aux Enfants à connoitre le chiffre et à sommer," Lille, 1719. Resbecq has an analysis of it in his very instructive and valuable work, " Histoire de l'Instruction primaire dans le Departement du Nord," Paris, 1878, pp. 84, 85.

teaching writing to his scholars, fearing lest they would afterwards supplant him as public scribe.'

In the fourteenth century writing is but little practiced among the people ; it still belongs to an exclusive profession.   In the fifteenth century it ceases to be so exclusive, and we find that the *bourgeoisie* write.   In the first quarter of the sixteenth century the signatures of all kinds of artisans begin to appear. At this period also do we find the writing masters organized into guilds, apparently for mutual protection against the encroachments of other teachers.

By a decree bearing date of July 2, 1661, primary teachers are circumscribed as to the amount of writing they may teach their pupils and prohibited to teach special pupils unless they are licensed to keep a writing school, all being in accordance with a decree made in the year 1600.   And in like manner, the writing masters were forbidden to teach any subject beyond writing, arithmetic, and orthography — " for which purpose only they were permitted to use books in print or in manuscript, without abusing them or using them to teach reading except in the manuscripts assigned and for the purpose only, without fraud or subterfuge." [2]

It was Jean Baptist de la Salle who broke up this monopoly, about twenty years afterward.   In addition, the girls were taught sewing and knitting, and all the children were taught singing.   Religious

---

[1] E. Rendu, " De l'Éducation populaire dans l'Allemagne du Nord," p. 8.

[2] Cf. Charles Jourdain, " Histoire de l'Université de Paris," p. 215.

instruction pervaded the school from morning till night. The last quarter of an hour was daily given to Christian doctrine, and on Wednesday and Saturday afternoons the children were taught the catechism of the diocese. Later on, in Paris, as complaints were made that the children were devoting too much time to catechism lessons, those of Saturday were transferred to Sunday.[1] And that teachers be imbued with the spirit of faith and piety, they were expected to read daily in some spiritual book. The precentor of Notre Dame prescribes the following books : " The Imitation of Christ," "Lives of the Saints," "Introduction to a Devout Life" by St. Francis de Sales ; Catechism of Cardinal Bellarmine, Catechism of the Archbishop, the Old Testament — especially Proverbs, Wisdom, Ecclesiastes ; the New Testament. This is the spiritual food with which their piety was nourished. In addition, they were recommended to read two valuable works on methods of teaching, " Le Pédagogue Chréstien " and " L'Escole Paroissiale." [2]

Such were the subjects taught in the primary schools of the Middle Ages. Let us not censure them for their limited scope. We find it no better elsewhere. We turn, for instance, to the Moorish primary schools in Spain, and we find the children of the poorer classes learning, in their way, what our Christian children had been learning in theirs. They

---

[1] " L'Escole Paroissiale," p. 113.

[2] Statuts et Règlements des Petites Ecoles de Grammaire de la Ville, Cité, Université, Faux-bourgs et Banlieuë de Paris, 1672, Preface.

are taught reading, writing, and religious doctrine.
The child first learns the Arabian alphabet.   He is
then taught the difference of letters according to
punctuation, accentuation, sound, the composition of
letters, and the other elements that enter into the
study of Arabic words.   He is afterward carefully
drilled upon pronunciation.   Finally he learns to read
the Korân, which is for the Arabian the Alpha and
Omega of all study.   Here his education finishes.[1]

It is evident that the Christian mediæval primary
schools were not always and in all places kept up
with uniformity.   Nor were these the only schools
in which children might learn the elements of
knowledge.   There were numerous private schools
kept by a class of teachers who were known as
grammarians.   These grammarians seem to have
been a restless class, passing from town to town.
They were subject to pay a tax.[2]   Erasmus has
pictured them with a pen dipped in gall.   He calls
them :

"A race, of all men the most miserable, who
grow old at their work surrounded by herds of boys,
deafened by continual uproar, and poisoned by a
close, foul atmosphere ; satisfied, however, so long as
they can overawe the terrified throng by the terrors
of their look and speech, and, while they cut them
to pieces with ferule, birch and thong, gratify their
own merciless natures at pleasure."[3]

---

[1] Henricus Middeldorpf, " Commentatio de Institutis litter-
ariis in Hispania quæ Arabes Auctores habuerunt," Goet-
tingæ, 1810, p. 53.

[2] Choron, " Recherches Historiques, Bulletin de la Société
Archeologique," fascico 2, p. 69.

[3] " Encomium Moriæ."

This might have been a scene of frequent occur-rence, and yet there might have been, and no doubt there were, many worthy men belonging to the profession.

Throughout the Middle Ages the level of edu-cation varied with times and places. The ravages of war, the terrible scourges of plague and famine that devastated whole peoples, were as disastrous to the progress of education as they were to that of life and civilization. The school, being sustained by local enterprise, varied with the fluctuations of local energy.

What we might call the public school in France was created only in the fifteenth century, reached its highest state of efficiency in the sixteenth century, declined in the seventeenth century, and, under the new impulse given to all primary education by La Salle, revived in the eighteenth century. We are told that during the eighteen years of the reign of Louis XVI. more schools, both large and small, were founded and legislated for than during the whole French monarchy in twelve hundred years.[1] Paris was always a specially favored city as regards edu-cation.

Independently of the schools attached to churches, eleven masters and one mistress figure in the roll of the land tax levied on the inhabitants of Paris by Philip the Fair, in 1292. In the fourteenth century we find record of forty-one masters and twenty-two mistresses; in the fifteenth century,

---

[1] Boutiot, "Histoire de l'Instruction publique et popu-laire à Troyes, pendant les quatre derniers siècles," pp. 7-15.

there are a hundred; and at the close of the sixteenth century, the precentor, Claude Joly, enumer-
ates no less than five hundred schoolmasters and
schoolmistresses. The statutes regulating these
schools date back to the year 1357.[1] It should be
remembered that this was the period — from the
thirteenth to the sixteenth century — in which the
great University of Paris flourished and counted
its students by the tens of thousands.

IV.

And now, let us take a rapid glance at school life
as revealed to us. Then, as now, there was little
uniformity in the age at which children were sent to
school. The old French romances generally speak
of the hero being sent to school and taught to read
and write. This is true of Hervé de Metz.[2] It is
true of Garin, who knew how to read in Romance
and in Latin.[3] Of another hero we are told that
"when he had attained his twelfth year he was a
full-blown bachelor . . . and had passed four years
at school."[4]

---

[1] Ravalet, "Life of Blessed de la Salle," illustrated edition, p. 27.

[2] Bibliothèque Nationale, MSS. française, 19,160.

[3] Le Loherains fut a escoles mis   .   .
Bien savoir lire et roman et latin.
          —"Garin le Loherains," I., 179, 180.

[4] Quant ot xii. ans moult fu biax bachelier
D'esches de tauble fut bien en doctrinez
Et a l'ecolle fut bien iiij. ans passez.
          —Bibl. Nat., MSS., fr. 19,160, f. 3, § 7.

Sometimes the hero was fifteen years before his schooling was finished, as was the case with the son of Parisi la Duchesse.[1]

James Melville, of Scotland, born in 1556, tells us that in the fifth year of his age the "grace-buik" was put in his hands at home, but he made little progress in it. At the age of seven he was sent to school at Logie Montrose.[2] During the first five or six days the pupil was placed apart from the other scholars and no lessons were assigned him. Afterward he was supplied with his A B C book, which he carried hung to his belt.[3] He also brought the rod with which he was to be punished.[4] The use of the rod was universal. We read of its employment in England in the eleventh century.[5] St. Louis, King of France, when a boy, was beaten with rods once a week.[6] Guibert of Nogent, tells us of the harsh treatment he received, and when his mother, seeing the welts and bruises on his back, wept and said she no longer wished him to learn grammar, he replied that even though he should die he would continue to learn and become a clerk.[7] All were not equally harsh.

---

[1] Quant l'anfes ot quinze ans et compliz et passez—
Premiers apprist a letres tant qu'il en soi assez.
—" Parisi la Duchesse," ll. 964-65.

[2] James Grant, "History of the Burgh Schools of Scotland," p. 59.

[3] Bibliothèque Nationale, MSS., fonds latin, 15,955: Anonymous sermon.

[4] Grant, op. cit., p. 61.

[5] Alfric's "Colloquies."

[6] Henry Martin, "Histoire de France," 4me ed., t. iv., p. 133.

[7] "Vita Sua," lib. i, cap. 6.

Bishop Bertram speaks of St. Germanus of Auxerre as a kind teacher, who not only gave him knowledge, but by his prayers led him to the honor of
embracing the priesthood. Fortunatus draws a
beautiful picture of this same saint in his cathedral,
surrounded by the ancients as well as by the youths
whom he is training for the priesthood.[1] Anselm of
Bec stands forth pleading for mildness and stoutly
protesting against the rod as the sole means of training the child. " Can you by beatings," he says, " form
the heart of the child and lead it to good principles?"[2] But the men of that day and generation
believed in the efficacy of the rod as an essential
factor in education.

School opened at half-past seven in the summer
months, and at half-past eight in the winter months.[3]
The child was there generally half an hour earlier.
On entering, his first act was to say a prayer on his
knees.[4] One of those prayers has been handed down
to us from the Catholic days in Scotland. It will
bear repetition :

"I thank Thee, heavenly Father, that Thou hast
willed that the past night hath been prosperous for
me ; and I pray that Thou wilt also be favorable to
me this day, for Thy glory and the health of my
soul ; and Thou who art the true light, knowing no
setting, Sun eternal, enlightening, supporting, glad-

---

[1] "Carmina," lib. ii., 8.

[2] Cf. "Christian Schools and Scholars," vol. i., pp. 418,
419; Choron, fascic. 2, p. 74.

[3] Recueil des Ordonnances Synodales du diócèse d'Autun.
1685.

[4] "L'Escole Paroissiale," p. 67.

dening all things, deign to enlighten my mind, that I may never fall into any sin, but, by Thy guiding, arrive at life eternal. Amen."[1]

The children began the day's study by assisting at the mass. On their return from the church they took their breakfast. In those days, it was customary for every child to bring not only his own meal but also something for the very poor who had none to bring.

Now that school has begun it would interest us to know the methods pursued in teaching. There lies before me an old woodcut of the sixteenth century representing the interior of a school. As customs were slow to change, we may take it for a type of the school in the Middle Ages. The teacher is seated in a large arm-chair, with a low-crowned, broad-brimmed hat on his head and a mantle on his shoulders. He holds in his hand a bundle of rods, and in his lap a large folio lies open. The boy whose lesson he had been hearing stands aside while the master is talking very earnestly to another boy with hat in hand, and we infer that the latter has come late and is to be duly punished. A long table runs down the center of the room, at which the other boys stand in various attitudes with open books before them. There is a low stool destined for the new comers. A small boy has his book laid upon the stool, while he himself is engaged with balls or marbles on the floor. In another engraving, bearing date of 1493, the same low stool is found, and on it sits the same small boy, holding his book out to a

---

[1] Directory of Aberdeen Schools, cf. Grant, op cit., p. 60.

little terrier as though he would have the dog to read. In this engraving it is evident that the teacher employs exclusively the individual method. He knew no other. Each boy in turn stood before the the teacher, recited or read his lesson, and resumed his seat to give place to another. In the meantime, the remainder of the school was doing as it liked. The assiduous ones were occupying their time in reading or spelling, or arithmetic or writing; the giddy ones were disturbing the others as far as they might do so with impunity. Much time was lost and only slight results were achieved.

An anonymous pamphlet, issued about 1680, bewails the loss of time that is the consequence of this individual method. "In our colleges," he says, "we find pupils of the same capacity placed in the same class; why is not the same done in our primary schools?"[1] Another anonymous work, a teacher's manual, advises that children be taught writing at as early an age as possible so that they may have occupation, and to avoid disorder while the master is engaged with the lessons of each one.[2] Still another manual recommends that the more advanced pupils call up their less advanced companions every half hour to recite a lesson—a method "making as many masters as there are pupils."[3] On the whole, the

---

[1] "Avis touchant les Petites Escoles." It is to be found in the Bibliothèque Nationale.

[2] "Essai d'une École Chrétienne," p. vi., chap. 14. This essay is not to be confounded with the "Conduite de l'École Xtienne," a work on the same subject by Jean Baptiste de la Salle.

[3] "L'Escole Paroissiale," Paris, 1654, p. 75.

individual method was the only one known and applied up to the seventeenth century in the primary
school. This led to great waste of time. Jean
Baptist de la Salle was the one to revolutionize the
whole system of primary teaching by introducing the
simultaneous method.[1]

With the individual method there was necessarily an absence of emulation. During the Middle
Ages we meet with few modes of recompense for
work done in the primary school. In 1585, we come
upon a class of Abecediaries, who, in presence of
several wrote the same sentence, and he whose pen-
manship was declared best received from the hands
of the mayor "two pens and a penknife."[2] In more
advanced classes books were given as prizes. But
the best boy in the school was otherwise honored.
And this leads us to consider the sports and recre-
ations of the schoolboy of that day.

I have now before me a most interesting old
print, taken from a book of Hours, bearing the date
of 1523. The subject is boys coming out from
school. Some are flying a hawk; others have hurl-
ing-sticks and a ball, and one of this party has fallen
down; others again are testing their strength by
standing on one leg and placing the soles of their
shoes flat against each other and then pushing till
one gives way. Another schoolboy game was this:
At one end of an alley-way a suspended stick

---

[1] Cf. André, " Nos Maîtres d'hier : Étude sur les progrès de
l'Éducation et sur les Developpements de l'Instruction populaire en France," Paris, 1873, p. 295.

[2] Maggiolo, in Buisson's " Dictionnaire de Pédagogie," i.,

supports a crown decked with ribbons. At the other end stood the scholars, and each in turn sought to knock down the crown. He whom luck or skill favored received compliments from his companions, and was crowned king of the *Neude*. As such he enjoyed many privileges during the year.

But the game that crowned all other games with mediæval students of all grades, from the primary school to the universities, was cock-fighting. It was emphatically a schoolboy sport, and had its origin in the school.[1] The annual recurrence of the day of *les joutes de coqs* was keenly looked forward to. We find the custom established in London about 1174. We learn that about that time, every Shrove Tuesday the boys were wont to bring their fighting-cocks to the master and during the whole morning they had cock-fighting in the school-room.[2] After dinner they indulged in the game of football. In France, on the day appointed, all the students assembled in a large hall. Their birds were fasting, and were nourished with some drops of generous wine. The two first champions were placed facing each other over a plate of oats. They eyed each other for some time and then began to attack. The defeated one was withdrawn and replaced by another. The cock that floored the greatest number is victor ; his master is proclaimed king and is carried through the town in procession amid universal rejoicings. During the remainder of

---

[1] Leopold Delisle, "Études sur la Classe Agricole en Normandie au Moyen Age," p. 185.

[2] Fitz Stephen-Pogge.

the school year he takes the lead in all religious ceremonies and public reunions.[1]

In the rural districts and in the poor schools of the towns, where each boy could not afford to keep his own bird, the students indulge in the sport known as " Killing the Cock." In this case the bird was pursued and beaten to death. In many places it was the schoolmaster who, by stipulation, furnished the cocks for the occasion. Thus, in 1282, we find a schoolmaster at Dieppe held indebted for no less than four.[2] In 1353, the schoolmaster of Rameru was bound to furnish his pupils annually with a cock to be thrown at with sticks.[3] The practice was continued down to recent days in some of the districts of France — and this in spite of protest and interdict on the part of Church authorities. Thus, as early as 1260 we find the barbarous amusement condemned by the synod of Coprigni, presided over by the Bishop of Bordeaux.[4]

A day which the younger children celebrated with great pomp and ceremony was the feast of St. Nicholas. On that day they chose a bishop from among their number. In many places the honor was reserved for the best and most studious boy. The chosen one was dressed up in gorgeous pontificals and borne in procession to the church with the accompaniment of fife and drum and violin. He ruled as king of all celebrations during the day, and in honor

[1] "Histoire de Chateau Theirry," p. 168.
[2] Delisle, op. cit., p. 185.
[3] Ibid. cf. Boutiot, op. cit., p. 18.
[4] Labbe, " Concilia," xi., c. 800. D.

of him the children of the school received presents and were feasted. Afterward a play was enacted in which St. Nicholas figured as savior and protector of person and property. He was frequently represented, as in our modern pictures of him, in the act of restoring life to three children. But the playing of this rôle led to so many abuses that it was suppressed by act of parliament, and the schoolmaster permitting naked children to appear on the stage was heavily fined. The saint was also represented as finding stolen goods that had been placed under his protection. Champollion-Figeac brought to light one of those plays dating back to the twelfth century, written by one Hilary, an Englishman, and a disciple of Abelard. It is one at which Abelard himself might have been present. The play is very simple and rude, and is written in a mixture of Latin and French. It had been for centuries the tradition to write comedies, farces, and plays in the Latin tongue. We have now arrived at a point where there is a breaking up of the tradition. Latin is becoming more exclusively confined to the schools. But in the cities and large towns it was still understood by the people.

Few were the boys there present who could not have taken in the whole sense of this play. And what with the robbers carrying off the stolen goods and what with the spectacle of a rude, angry man, loud in words and fierce in gesture, the play must have greatly amused the little ones. Barbarus, who impersonates a rude and ignorant man, confiding his treasures to the protection of St. Nicholas, places them at the foot of his statue. The treasures are stolen. Thereupon, Barbarus grows furious, and frets and fumes and bemoans his sad lot in having placed his goods in such bad keeping. He goes up to the statue, and with violent gestures tells Nicholas that he must return the goods or he shall pay for them :

> Mea congregavi,
> Tibi commendavi ;
> Sed in hoc erravi.
> *Ha! Nicholas!*
> *Sé ne me rent ma chose, tu ol comparras.*

But words having no effect, he takes a whip and threatens to beat Nicholas if the goods are not forthwith coming. Nicholas goes after the thieves, and induces them to repent of their evil ways ; which they do, and they forthwith make restitution. In fear and trembling these men bring back the goods to the place from which they had been taken. Barbarus thereupon becomes jubilant :

> Nisi visus fallitur
> *Io en ai*
> Tesaurus hic cernitur,
> *De si grant merveile en ai.*

In a transport of gratitude, Barbarus offers Nicholas all the goods, but Nicholas appears to him and exhorts him to thank God alone: " Not to me the merit; that belongs to God alone ; bless Him and bless the name of Christ." Whereupon Barbarus becomes converted.[1]

---

[1] " Hilarii Versus et Ludi." Paris, 1838, pp. 34–39.

And now that the play is over, let us also return from our short excursion to the primary schools of the Middle Ages. From the close, narrow, badly-lighted, and poorly-ventilated schoolroom of those days, with its dingy walls and low ceiling, we pass into the light, spacious, well-ventilated schoolrooms of our own times. But let us remember that in other days there were other manners, other customs, other standards of comfort, and another order of ideas. Our own progress is only of recent growth and has been very slow. Moreover, the seeds of that growth have been sown elsewhere, as the Abbé Alain has shown by placing within the scope of all the result of researches scattered through many volumes bearing especially upon education in the sixteenth and seventeenth centuries.

THE SIMULTANEOUS METHOD IN TEACHING

THE SIMULTANEOUS METHOD IN TEACHING.[1]

R. W. T. Harris conceived the happy idea of editing an international educational series of books on the same plan as the well-known international scientific series published by the Appletons. This volume of Prof. Painter's is a contribution to the series. We regret that we cannot recommend the volume to our Catholic readers. It is evidently modeled after the "Histoire Universelle de la Pédagogie" of Paroz. But our recollections of Paroz's volume are that it was far more fair-spoken than the one before us. Had the professor contented himself with translating Paroz, he would have given us a better book.

In treating Catholic education, he has imported into his work all the bile and bitterness of Raumer. But scant justice is consequently done to the grand rôle played by the Church and by great Catholic educators in the work of education. If Fénelon is praised, it is because the professor has mistaken him for a Jansenist. We do not accuse the author of deliberately misrepresenting us. In all probability

---

[1] *American Ecclesiastical Review.*

"Management of Christian Schools." By the Brothers of the Christian Schools. New York, 1887.

"A History of Education." By F. V. N. Painter. New York, D. Appleton & Co., 1887.

he never set foot within a Catholic institution; still less likely is it that he ever made a careful study of our Catholic schools and their methods. The sources from which he drew were poisoned.

"It was in the library of the University of Bonn," he tells us, "nearly four years ago, as I sat before an alcove of educational works and leisurely examined the admirable histories by Raumer and Karl Schmidt, that the thought and purpose of preparing this work were first conceived."[1]

Later on he acknowledges his indebtedness to these works. Most valuable aids they are to the student of pedagogy, when he has antidotes to counteract the bigotry and prejudice pervading them. Pity it was he did not give more attention to Stöckl, and the great work of Father Denifle, then just published.

The author's omissions in treating his subject are conspicuous. He ignores the educational development of Spain, and yet La Fuente, among others, would have enlightened him upon the great part Spain took in the education of Europe. He has no word upon the educational progress of Italy. A glance at Tiraboschi would have shown him the magnitude of Italy's claims as an educator. The smaller works of Everardo Michele, Ceruti, and Milanese would have brought the subject home to him still more directly.

True, all three are Catholic writers, but we can assure him that they are none the less trustworthy. Even when treating of education in France, the professor finds no place for the work of Blessed de la Salle.

---

[1] Preface.

And yet, in another volume of this same series, we find that educator characterized as follows:

"A man of progressive, modern thought, he introduced, besides normal schools, gradation and object-lessons, and established industrial schools, polytechnic institutes, and reformatories."[1]

Blessed de la Salle is especially identified with the Simultaneous Method. It shall be the purpose of the present paper to trace this method from its first dawnings to its full application by Blessed de la Salle. It is a study that has not been made in any pedagogical work that has come under our notice; it therefore cannot fail to interest the educator.

First, let us explain what is meant by the Simultaneous Method. There are three recognized methods of teaching.

The first is that of hearing and explaining the lesson of each child apart, while the others may be studying. It is called the Individual Method.

The second is that of having the more advanced pupils in a class to teach the less advanced ones under the general supervision of the master. This method was brought from India by Bell and was popularized by Lancaster. It is known as the Mutual Method.

The third is that of grading the children according to their capacity, putting those of the same capacity in the same class, and having them to use the same book and follow the same lesson under one and the same master. It is the Simultaneous Method. Now, all teaching is done by one or other

---

[1] Boone: "Education in the United States," p. 126.

E. E.—14

of these methods, separately or combined.[1]　But at the present day, the method most in vogue, and which has best stood the test of time and experience, is that with which the Brothers of the Christian Schools are identified, and which is known as the Simultaneous Method.

Like all fruitful ideas, the Simultaneous Method is not the exclusive property of any one man.　Others discerned its value, and even partially applied its principles, long before Blessed de la Salle made it live in his work.　We do not find it in the university methods of the Middle Ages.　The mere listening to a lecture, taking notes upon it, and holding disputations over it, is far different from the Simultaneous Method.　Nor does it seem to have been followed in the Grammar Schools.

The Jesuits organized each class in subdivisions; each division being headed by an advanced pupil called a *decurion*, to whom the boys recited their lessons at stated times, while the master corrected exercises or heard the lessons of special boys.　The whole class afterwards received explanations from the master.　Order and discipline reigned.　Emulation prevailed.　The unpleasant picture drawn by Erasmus became an impossibility in their schools. But still this is not the Simultaneous Method.　And above all, it only slowly dawned upon the masters of the primary schools to introduce these improvements into their methods of teaching.　Theirs was exclusively the Individual Method.　Each pupil passed in turn before the master, said his lesson, returned

---

[1] See "Management of Christian Schools," p. 34.

to his place, and moped, or studied, or amused himself as best it pleased him or as dread of the birch permitted.

Such a system necessarily brought with it disorder and confusion in the school, and led to loss of time on the part of the scholar. The consequent evil was irreparable for the poor child, whose schooldays were limited. He quitted school, fortunate if he learned his catechism and how to spell through his Psalter; rarely fortunate if he had advanced sufficiently to read in his mother-tongue and to write a letter. The child preparing for college spent seven or eight years endeavoring to learn that which might have been mastered in half the time.

Mulcaster, in 1589, laid stress upon grouping the children of the same capacity upon the same bench. ("Positions," p. 234.)

In 1610, the evils of the old system are spoken of in a memorial dealing with the government of the university. It is beginning to dawn upon men's mind that the old way might not, after all, be the best way. This memorial is the first emphatic protest in France that we have come across against the old way. The memorialist feels the necessity of some method for regulating the studies and the teaching of children, and for preparing youths better for their university course.

" Since our members," says he, " depend principally upon the primary institutions, just as good health and natural complexion depend upon the milk we take in infancy, it is due to the prudence of the magistrate, with the aid and counsel of experts, to provide some method to be used in the education of the children ; for doctrine without method is like a torch under a barrel, consuming itself without giving out a profitable light.'"

He sees no reason why children might not learn in four years all that, in his day, it took them eight or nine to learn. He appeals to experienced teachers to devise some means out of this roundabout method, which consumes so much valuable time.' To realize an evil is one thing; to remedy it is quite another.

The university was too taken up with the struggle for its own existence against the encroachments of the separate collegiate system, to occupy itself with elementary schools. The evil grew apace. Elementary education in France reached its lowest degree of confusion during the first half of the seventeenth century.' The numerous wars of this period left little time and less inclination for the cultivation of peaceful pursuits. The eyes of the natural custodians of society were so dimmed by the dazzling brilliancy of the court of the Grand Monarch, they could no longer perceive the evils festering at their own doors.

---

[1] "Mémoires pour le Règlement de l'Université." 1610. Bibl.Nat. Printed Matter. Paris Université (Generalités), 1073. 24.115–2130, p.17.

[2] Ibid., p. 19.

[3] Boutiot, " Histoire de l'Instruction publique et populaire à Troyes pendant les quatre derniers siècles." Troyes 1865. P. 9.

II.

Blessed Peter Fourier (1565–1640) saw in Christian education the remedy for many of the disorders existing among the poor and the laboring class.[1] He was a far-seeing man, and anticipated more than one of our modern social improvements. In 1597, he attempted to organize a religious teaching order for boys. But the four young men whom he had brought together for the purpose abandoned him. The work was reserved for another no less worthy.

However, Peter Fourier was more successful in organizing religious teachers for girls. Providence blessed and fructified his labors in this direction beyond his greatest hopes. He lived to see all Lorraine peopled by the Congregation of Notre Dame, which still remains a monument and a witness to his zeal and his enlightened views. He gave this sisterhood a rule and constitution. It was first printed in 1640. The second edition, bearing date of 1694, now lies before us.[2] Therein the saintly author lays down rules for the management of scholars and methods of teaching such branches as are usually taught in elementary schools. To attempt to trace the history of pedagogy without allusion to this

[1] Rev. P. Jean Bedel, "La Vie du Rev. Pierre Fourier." Paris, 1666.

[2] "Les vraies Constitutions des Religieuses de la Congregation de Nostre Dame." Séconde Edition. A Toul. 1694. At the end of the volume we read : La présente copie des *Constitutions* . . . a été fidèlement extraite sur son vray original sain et entier, et écript de sa propre main, et se conforme de mots à autres, par le subscript Notaire Apostolique. Ainsi signé, F. Tabourin.

remarkable book were an unpardonable oversight. There is wisdom in every line. It ranks by incontestable right and title the parish-priest of Mattaincourt among great educators. We shall note its salient points.

Therein the principle of Simultaneous Method is, for the first time, clearly stated :

" The inspectress, or the mistress of class, shall endeavor, as far as it possibly can be carried out, that all the pupils of the same mistress have each the same book, in order to learn and read therein all together the same lesson; so that, whilst one is reading hers in an audible and intelligible voice before the mistress, all the others, hearing her and following this lesson in their books at the same time, may learn it sooner, more readily, and more perfectly." [1]

Read it how we may, it is the principle of the Simultaneous Method whole and entire. And yet, when this great man — who was in advance of his age upon every subject that he touched — entered into details of practice, he lost sight of the principle which he had laid down. In the very next paragraph, it is regulated that the mistress call up two pupils at the time and place them one at each side of her seat. Then, the author continues :

" The more advanced shall read her lesson ; the other shall listen to her, shall correct all the faults she may make, whether in using the wrong words, or in pronouncing badly, or in not making the proper pauses. When she has finished her lesson, the other one shall read hers, and her companion shall likewise correct all her mistakes." [2]

---

[1] Ibid., p. iii., ch. xi., sec. 6, p. 54.

[2] Ibid., sec. 7, p. 54.

These two having read, two others shall come forward, and so on till the class is all heard. And here enters a rule that throws light on the source whence the European peasantry imbibed that gentleness and urbanity for which they are noted :

"According to the number of mistakes she has made, she shall say an *Ave Maria* for the companion who has corrected her." [1]

Elsewhere in the same chapter we read :

" If any mistakes are made in reading, and they are not corrected by the companions of the readers— *leurs compagnes apariées* — the mistress shall gently correct them at the time." [2]

The nearest the saintly author comes in practice to the Simultaneous Method is when, speaking of the younger children, he says :

" In order the more easily to make the very young children profit of the lesson, the mistress shall take four or six at the time, of about equal capacity, and while one is reading, the other five shall follow in their books, saying after her the same words in a low tone." [3]

With beginners, he would have the Simultaneous Method practised on particular occasions :

" Sometimes they shall be exercised all together, by pointing out to them on a large card, and making them say, all the letters in a syllable and all the syllables in a word." [4]

---

[1] Ibid.
[2] Ibid., sec. 2, p. 52.
[3] Ibid., sec. 4, p. 53.
[4] Ibid., p. 53.

Again Blessed Fourier devotes a special chapter to his method. The chapter is an admirable one. It grades the school into three chief divisions;[1] it assigns special teachers to each bench when there is need for them;[2] it places pupils of the same capacity on the same bench;[3] it attempts to inspire at the same time devotion to the Blessed Virgin and an *esprit de corps* among the pupils of the same bench, by putting each under the patronage of Our Blessed Lady according to her feasts;[4] it seeks to create emulation by having a bench of honor and a bench of disgrace.[5] Here, also, the method that runs through the whole book — the method that is peculiar to Blessed Fourier — is distinctly stated:

"*Each mistress shall pair all her pupils, placing them two by two, one with the other;* placing together those most alike, not in age, or quality, or affection, but in knowledge; in order that they may hear and correct each other, and piously compete for the first place, in recitation of prayers and catechism, and in reading."[6]

Such is the method of Blessed Peter Fourier. Sometimes he would exercise a class of beginners all together from large reading cards hung up in a conspicuous place; sometimes he would have all those learning to spell to work together under the dicta-

---

[1] Ibid., chap. vi., sec. 2, p. 19.

[2] Ibid., sec. 7, p. 20.

[3] Ibid., sec. 7, p. 20.

[4] Ibid., sec. 8, p. 21.

[5] Ibid., sec. 11, pp. 22, 23, 24.

[6] Ibid., chap. vi., sec. 10, pp. 21, 22.

tion of the same mistress; sometimes he would have the more advanced, when learning to read Latin, brought before the teachers in groups of four or six at the time; always he would have the most advanced pupils heard two by two, each reciprocating the corrections of the others. This is indeed a great improvement upon the Individual Method.

We are greatly indebted to Abbé Pierfitte [1] and to M. G. Du Bois [2] for having called the attention of the pedagogical world to the rich treasures contained in the "Constitutions." But when they tell us that this is the Simultaneous Method pure and simple, they are calling it that which it is not. Equally great a misnomer is it to call the act of two children correcting each other under the eye of a teacher the Mutual Method. The essence of the Mutual Method is the dispensing with the teacher altogether. It is the pupil instructing the pupil. In the method of Peter Fourier it is still the teacher who instructs. The pupil's corrections are only for the purpose of keeping up attention.

We may well call that method the Reciprocal Method. It is this method we find recommended in the teacher's manual for the city of Paris, the "Escole Paroissiale," edition of 1654:

"Those who go to the master to read shall present themselves *but two at a time.* . . . The master shall call the writers to his desk, *two by two*, to correct their exercises." [3]

---

[1] Paper read before the Congress of Blois, 1884.

[2] *L'Univers*, Dec. 17, 1887.

[3] 3me partie, chap. iv.

III.

Another thinker and educator, in another part of Europe, about the same time, in the midst of wanderings and persecutions, sought to solve the problem of educating the greatest number, in the least time, and with the smallest pains. Komensky (1592–1671)[1] was an ardent admirer of Bacon, and applied his inductive method to its solution. From the physical world he drew analogies for the intellectual world. This led him to fanciful and extravagant inferences. But he was observant; he learned much from the systems of others, and feared not to borrow from them whatever he considered good and useful. Upon the " Janua Linguarum " of Father Bathe, of the Irish College at Salamanca — a book which had been translated into eight languages by 1629 — he modeled, even to the very name, his more popular " Janua Linguarum Reserata."[2] From Ratich he learned to unite the study of words with the study of things. From the " Ratio Studiorum " he inserted many a detail of practice and principle in his " Didactica Magna."

Komensky asks: "How can one teacher suffice for any number of pupils whatever?" He replies

---

[1] Komensky — Comenius — takes his name from his native village of Komna, in Moravia. He suppressed his family name on account of the persecutions to which he was subjected as a Moravian bishop. He held wild philosophic vagaries, which he pretended to draw from the Old Testament. (See Franck, "Dictionnaire des Sciences Philosophiques," Art., Comenius.)

[2] "Inasmuch as they (the Jesuits) were the prime inventors, we thankfully acknowledge it." Preface to Anchoran's translation, 1639. See Quick's " Educational Reformers," pp. 63–65.

by saying that not only can he suffice, but that it is
for the benefit of the class that there be a large
number, inasmuch as it excites sympathy and emulation.[1] As the sun sheds its rays upon the whole
earth, so should the master instruct his whole class;
each and all, intent of eyes and ears and minds, receiving from him whatever instruction he imparts.
Therefore he should not instruct single pupils privately, outside of school-hours, nor publicly in
school, but — *omnes simul et semel* — all together at
one and the same time.[2] All of the same capacity
should have the same book. All should listen in
silence to the master. In order to lessen the fatigue
of the master, he should be assisted by *decurions*
in correcting the exercises. That he may control
the attention of his pupils, he should frequently
question them promiscuously on what has been said.[3]
One teacher, one book, one lesson for all in the same
grade : this is an approximation to the Simultaneous
Method. Charles Hoole (1610–1666) introduced this
method of Komensky into England with most success.[4] His school was efficient and a model of good
order. He attempted to propagate the method
in a little work called "The New Discovery of the
Old Art of Teaching."[5]

But the method did not take root in England.
Indeed, the influence of Komensky was not lasting.

---

[1] See S. S. Laurie, "John Amos Comenius," p. 105. Eng.
Ed.

[2] "Didactica Magna," Amsterdam, 1657. Col. 103.

[3] Ibid., col. 104. His whole method is embodied in chap. xix.

[4] "Quarterly Journal of Education," 1867, p. 262.

[5] There is a copy of this rare book in the Bodleian Library.

Rousseau and Pestalozzi followed in his track, and, unawares re-discovered many of his principles. "Comenius," says Buisson, "established nothing durable and definite ; he was simply an admirable precursor." [1]   The only part of his system that has survived, may be summed up in the formula :   "Let all things be taught to all."   Now this is an educational fallacy.   The mind simply stuffed with facts is not an educated mind.   The mind so trained and disciplined that it knows how to use its knowledge to purpose and advantage, is alone the truly cultured mind. [2]

Mgr. de Nesmond (1629–1715), Bishop of Bayeux, independently of Komensky, was working at the same problem of method.   In 1672, he distributed among his clergy a "Plan of Instruction and Education for Primary Schools." [3]   We have before us, for our use, a beautiful copy, bound in vellum, of the Pastoral and the Method.   The Pastoral bewails the absence of schools and the lack of competent masters.   It recites the strenuous efforts made by the early Fathers and the Councils of the Church in behalf of Christian education.   It prohibits the holding of schools in churches and chapels. [4]   This was at one time a general custom in country places and villages.

Next comes the bishop's method.   He also would answer to the question : How may large classes be taught in a short time by a single master?   He enters

---

[1] "Dictionnaire de l'Pédagogie," Art., Comenius.
[2] See S. S. Laurie on Comenius, p. 220.
[3] "Dict. de Péd.," Art., Nesmond.
[4] Ordonnance 1662, p. 56.

into so many practical details, and puts such good
sense into all he says, one feels that if he were not a
bishop he might have become an eminent educator.
In the first place, he would classify all the children of
the school. "The master shall divide his school into
four or five benches, according to the number and
capacity of his scholars."[1] He then assigns to the
same bench children of the same capacity occupied
with the same subject. The division is instructive as
revealing an order of things different from that prevailing to-day. The most advanced scholars are placed
on the first bench, and they are supposed to learn
how to read French and manuscripts, and how to
write and work arithmetic. In the second bench are
placed "those who read passably well in their Hours."
The book of Hours contained certain offices of the
Church in Latin, and the child was to read therein
before he had learned to read in his mother-tongue.
A few years later, Blessed de la Salle—amid much
opposition and many protests from bishops and
clergy — introduced the method of teaching the child
to read his mother-tongue before reading the Latin.

In the next place, to each bench he would assign
the same book.

"We give the same book to each bench," he
says, "simply in order that all the children on that
bench may receive the same lesson, and when one
begins to read, the others may read in a low voice
at the same time."[2]

---

[1] "Méthode pour instruire en peu de Temps les Enfants,"
p. 59.

[2] Ibid., p. 60.

This is a decided improvement on Peter Fourier's system of reading by twos. Like Komensky, Mgr. de Nesmond goes to the root of the difficulty connected with this method, by showing how the children's attention is to be sustained; for, he adds in another place, without this attention, "the method would not only be a delusion, but irksome, and even unbearable."[1] The means he would adopt is the only rational one: "And in order to oblige those children — who should all have the same lesson and the same book — to read in a low tone of voice what one of their companions reads aloud, it were well sometimes to take them by surprise, and to make those least expecting it continue the lesson."[2]

The wisdom of his remarks has not grown old. They are as true to-day as they were in his own day. They apply as well to our class-rooms in America as to the little country schools for which he was legislating. In order to awaken the child's intelligence, he suggests that the master be not too prompt in naming a word over which the child hesitates, but rather to let the child spell it and make it out for himself.[3] He would have the lessons short.[4] It is of great advantage, he tells us, for children to do a little and to do that little well.[5] Commence by the more advanced pupils, so that the others may learn from them, and that the

---

[1] Ibid., p. 65.
[2] Ibid., p. 64.
[3] Ibid., p. 65.
[4] Ibid., p. 66.
[5] Ibid., p. 68.

former may be occupied during the remainder of
the school-hours in writing and arithmetic.[1]

The daily regulation is no less instructive. It
reveals customs that are gone out of use. School
opens at seven in summer and at eight in winter.
The scholars bring their breakfast with them. They
are taken to mass two by two. Upon returning to
the school, they shall say grace before breakfast,
standing; during the meal, one of the more advanced
scholars shall make public reading either from the
" Lives of the Saints" or some other pious book,
unless the master himself should choose to entertain
them with their defects or their duties.[2] Here the
page is lit up with a beautiful trait of Christian
charity. It is recommended that a pupil go around
with a basket and collect food for the poor scholars
having none, taking care that insinuating or flattering
children do not deprive themselves in order to gain
the good graces of the master or of him making the
collection. To this little touch of nature is added
this other touch of grace : " And the poor shall say
a *Pater* and *Ave* for those among their companions
who have acted so charitably."[3] La Salle regulated
the matter after a more gentle manner — and one
less calculated to take away the merit of the act of
charity by vanity or other human motive. The
master should see that the pupils bring some breakfast, without, however, forcing them to do so. A
basket is placed in the corner for whatever the

---

[1] Ibid.
[2] Ibid., p. 72.
[3] Ibid., p. 75.

children cannot use. This is distributed to the poor children who have come without any breakfast, and the master shall exhort them to pray to God for their benefactors. They must understand, further-more, that if they are allowed to eat in school, "it is that they may learn to eat with wisdom, modesty, and in a becoming manner, and to pray to God before and after their meal."[1] All this brings us back to other days, when poverty was generally allied to scholarship. In the fourteenth century we find the children of the College called Bons Enfans going out daily to beg for their sustenance.[2]

In the fifteenth century the poor students of Montaigu College went to the neighboring Carthu-sian monastery to beg their daily pittance with the other indigent poor. We know how mercilessly Rabelais lashes these Montaigu sparrow-hawks — *esparviers de Montaigu* — as he calls them.[3] The spirit of charity and prayerfulness reigned everywhere during these ages of faith, and healed the misery and supplied the indigence of poor master and poor scholar. These things are of the past; but they are the welding and cementing elements that have made of the past a strong foundation on which to build up the present and the future. This inculcating of charity and gentleness and unselfishness was the refining and educating factor in mediæval life.

---

[1] "Conduite des Écoles Chrétiennes," 1720. Chap. ii., art. i., p. 8.

[2] "Dit des Crieries de Paris:"
Les Bons-Enfans orrez crier: ´
Du pain ! n'es veuil pas oublier."

[3] "Gargantua," liv. I., ch. 37.

But we cannot linger over the interesting little book of Mgr. de Nesmond. We have found it a precious landmark in the history of pedagogy. The author groups and classifies the scholars; with Peter Fourier, he gives those on the same form the same book; with Komensky, he appoints officers to hear repetition of catechism, serving at mass, and other memory-lessons, while a class is reading before the master; but he has not conceived the Simultaneous Method.

IV.

About 1675, Charles Demia, a zealous and enlightened priest, founder of the Brethren of St. Charles, drew up rules for the schools of the city and diocese of Lyons.[1] They run along the same lines as those of Mgr. de Nesmond. The scholars are divided up into bands according to their capacity. The more advanced pupils taught those less advanced.

"M. Demia," says Ravelet, "had the intuition of the mutual system of teaching; at least he appealed to the good will of the older pupils, and established among them dignitaries who aided the master."[2]

In his general remarks upon reading he lays stress:

"1. That children of the same band be of the same capacity; 2. that they have the same book, in the same print, and the same lesson; 3. that each one follow, holding his finger or marker on the word that is being read."[3]

---

[1] "Règlements pour les Écoles de la Ville et Diocèse de Lyon."

[2] "Histoire du Vénérable J. B. de la Salle," Ed. 1874, p. 64.

[3] Buisson, "Dict. de Pédagogie," Art., Lecture.

E. E.—15

He further introduced a system which Venerable Cæsar du Bus had borrowed from the Jesuits, and had applied to the free schools that he began to establish in 1592 ; namely, that of public disputation among the pupils on all the branches taught—catechism, arithmetic, spelling, politeness, and we are told, even "the method of making mental prayer" —those distinguishing themselves receiving clothes or other necessary articles according to their wants.

In this manner were earnest educators groping towards the light, and out of chaos seeking to make order.   But these were the exceptional souls of this period.   The large majority ran in the old grooves. Small pay-schools multiplied.   Even many of the clergy, especially in country places, kept pay-schools for small boys, as a means of subsistence.[1]   It had been decreed by law that no child should be retained in a private school beyond his ninth year completed.[2]   But the statutes were ignored or defied.   Boys were retained years beyond their limitations.   Professors were engaged for various branches, and the private elementary school soon grew into an academy rivaling the university colleges.   The university complained.   Its halls were becoming deserted.   We find it bringing action at law against that most active, most domineering, and most combative of Precentors, Claude Joly, for licensing so many boarding-schools. In the course of its argument, the university says:

"Method-mongers, like searchers after the philosopher's stone, have always been in vogue, but it

[1] See Babeau, "La Ville sous l'Ancien Régime," p. 484.
[2] Statutes Henri IV., 1598, Art. 10.

does not seem that they ever succeed. . . . It is safer and more advantageous to have children pass regularly through the ordinary college classes. It may be longer, but it is surer." [1]

The university here alludes to the charlatanism practiced in many of these private schools. Every professor had his nostrum. Some pretended to be able to teach Latin in three months, and in six to have the student competent to interpret all classical authors.[2] Circulars as flaring as any of our own day were issued, announcing wonderful results and advertising for situations for students who should finish with the master.[3]

In spite of these strenuous efforts to introduce method into primary education, we still find the old disorderly ways prevailing. In the latter half of the seventeenth century, a voice in Paris cries out against the inhuman discipline to which young

---

[1] "Factum pour l'Université de Paris contre M. le Chantre de l'Église Cathédrale et ses Permissionaires tenans École à Pensions." Seconde Partie, pp. 22 *sqq.* (Bibl. de l'Université. H. F. a. u. 9, 1675–1677).

[2] Jourdain. "Histoire de l'Université de Paris," p. 240. This, I dare say, was the foible of Ratich, which must have penetrated the schools of Paris about that time.

[3] Here is one snatched from oblivion: "L'orthographe françoise imprimée de puis peu, a rendu nos petits escoliers si sçavans dans l'orthographe, qu'ils sont tout prêts de combattre contre les plus grands maistres de cet art, mesme avec party du double contre le simple. Le champ de bataille est ouvert à tous venans, et à toute heure.

"Si quelcun a besoin, pour son service, de petits garçons tout faits et bien instruits dans le Christianisme, bons lecteurs, écrivains, et parfaits orthographes, nostre escole luy en fournira à son choix.

"C'est dans la rue Bourg-l'Abbé à l'escole de charité." Bibliothèque Mazarine. 274 A [13] in-fol.

children are subjected in the primary schools. It is still another protest against the old, confusing, roundabout manner of teaching a school full of children one by one. It is the voice of an educator —evidently a layman—of forty years' experience, whose labors, he tells us, were found worthy of the approval of gentlemen of the university, of the Jesuit Fathers, and of the professors of St. Nicholas de Chardonnet. It is a memorial pleading for a school in which to apply the same principles that Komensky, Peter Fourier, Mgr. de Nesmond, and Charles Demia had applied—"proposing to myself," says the author, "no other end than the glory of my God, and asking no other reward than His mercy."[1] The voice comes to us out of a miscellaneous collection of pamphlets of the seventeenth century. The collection is a recent acquisition of the Bibliothèque Nationale of Paris.

In the midst of schoolboy exercises, by way of translations from French into Latin, a eulogy upon Henry of Matignon in 1658, an account of the canonization of Peter of Alcantara in 1671, and other tracts, is found this memorial, well written and clearly reasoned, but without name or date. M. Leopold Delisle, Director of the Library, kindly examined the pamphlet for us, and after carefully considering type, style, and matter, came to the conclusion that it could not be of later date than 1680. It certainly must have been prior to 1690, for by that time the method of Blessed de la Salle

---

[1] "Avis touchant les Petites Écoles." Bibl. Nat., (p. Z. 320) p. 6.

was becoming the admiration of the people and the envy of the schoolmasters of Paris.

The voice that speaks from the pamphlet has the ring of sincerity. After exposing the difficulties that beset children in their first attempts at learning, the anonymous author justly and considerately asks:

"Were one designedly to oppose the good of children, and cause them to consume time uselessly and with great trouble, could one have acted otherwise?"[1]

He sees students classified according to capacity in colleges, and he wonders why no one thinks of applying the same method to the elementary school.

"Why," he asks, "are these little ones deprived of the light, the beauty, the comfort, and all the advantages that order and grading produce?"[2]

He pictures the ease with which a great number might be taught by the method in which "one master, one book, and one voice teach."[3] Farther on, in stating his method, the first principle which he lays down is the principle of the Simultaneous Method.

"The primary school," he tells us, "should be so disposed that one and the same book, one and the same master, one and the same lesson, one and the same correction, should serve for all, so that each scholar would thereby possess his master wholly and entirely, and occupy all his care, all his time, and all his trouble."[4]

Still, although the principle is clearly stated, when we remember what these little schools were, and how

---

[1] "Avis," p. 4.

[2] Ibid., p. 13.

[3] Ibid., p. 13.

[4] Ibid., p. 19.

they contained all grades of scholars, from those learning their A B C out of their primer decorated with
the sign of the Cross,[1] to those reading in manuscripts,
we perceive at a glance the impossibility of carrying
out this principle under a single master. The anonymous author does not get beyond the regulations
laid down by Charles Demia and Mgr. de Nesmond.
They also speak of one book and one master.

The voice is the voice of a precursor, feeling
acutely the wants and shortcomings of his age in
educational matters, but unable to remedy them.
He advocates strongly public examinations as a
means of exciting emulation.[2] He considers such
examinations a powerful corrective upon both
teacher and pupil. He feels the necessity of training teachers before allowing them to assume charge
of a school:

. "A shoemaker or blacksmith must learn his
trade, but young men without experience, and who
are themselves studying, are allowed to try their
prentice-hand at the expense of those poor little
ones."[3]

At the very time that this cry is going up in
Paris, a saintly priest is quietly evolving the solution
to all these problems. In 1681, Blessed John Baptist de la Salle had organized the Brothers of the
Christian Schools, and had given them the Simultaneous Method of teaching. What Blessed Peter
Fourier touched, what Komensky and Mgr. de

---

[1] Hence the name to the child's Primer of that day, Croix
de par Dieu;" i. e., de parte Dei.

[2] "Avis," p. 10.

[3] Ibid., p. 13.

Nesmond, and Charles Demia had glimmerings of; what the anonymous memorialist could nowhere find and thought to realize, had become a fact.

There is no uncertainty about the language of Blessed de la Salle in regard to the method he would have his disciples follow. It is no longer a single master governing a whole school; it is two, three, or more, according to the number of pupils; each taking those of the same capacity and teaching them altogether. In order to give effect to this method he regulates the duty of the masters in their respective classes:

"The Brothers shall pay particular attention to three things in the school-room: 1. During the lessons, to correct every word that the scholar who is reading pronounces badly; 2. to cause all who read in the same lesson to follow therein; 3. to have silence strictly observed in the school."[1]

The pupils follow in the same lesson; they observe strict silence; the master, in correcting one, is correcting all: here is the essence of the Simultaneous Method. Glancing over the pages of the admirable manual of school management which Blessed de la Salle prepared, we find scattered through them this principle inspiring all the rules of wisdom and prudence in which the book abounds. In one place we read: "All the scholars in the same lesson shall follow together, without distinction or discernment, according as they shall be notified by the master."[2]

---

[1] "Règles Communes des Frères des Écoles Chrétiennes." Translation from the MS. of 1718, signed and authenticated by Brother Bartholomew, Second Superior-General.

[2] "Conduite des Écoles Chrétiennes." Avignon, 1724. P. i., ch. iii., art. i., sec. i., p. 19.

On the page following it is said ; " All the scholars
in each lesson shall have the same book and shall be
given the same lesson."[1] A few pages further on
we find the same thing repeated: "All shall have
but one lesson, and whilst one spells or reads, all the
others shall follow, those who spell and read as well
as those only reading."[2] Again he generalizes the
principle for all the lessons :

"In all the lessons from alphabet-cards, sylla-
baries, and other books, whether French or Latin,
and even during arithmetic, while one reads, all the
others of the same lesson shall follow; that is, they
shall read to themselves from their books without
making noise with their lips what the one reading
pronounces aloud from his book."[3]

Note the expressions: *in all the lessons . . . all
the others . . . shall follow.* The four or six pupils of Peter Fourier, or the whole bench of children
of Charles Demia and Mgr. Nesmond, following that
which one is reading, whilst all the others are occupied as best they may, is a far different thing from
that of the whole class following in silence the one
who reads, whilst the master corrects, or has the
pupils to correct, the mistakes that are made. In
order to sustain the attention of the pupils, the saintly
founder would have him who is called upon to continue not to repeat a word or syllable that has been
read.[4] With truth has Matthew Arnold said, in speak-

---

[1] Ibid., p. 18.
[2] Ibid., p. 33.
[3] Ibid., p. 120.
[4] Ibid., p. 10; see also p. 120.

ing of this handbook of methods: "Later works on the same subject have little improved the precepts, while they entirely lack the unction."[1]

We might quote pages from this precious handbook, applying the Simultaneous Method to all the details of school life with a precision and directness that bespeak the master-mind. But it is needless. The method has not only been embedded in a book, it has also been embodied in a living organism, that has preserved its traditions with the greatest fidelity, and that still applies them the world over. Because we all of us have been trained according to this method, and see it practised in nearly all our public and many of our private schools throughout the land, and have ceased to find it a subject of wonder, we may be inclined to undervalue its importance. Not so was it regarded in the days of La Salle. Then a Brothers' School was looked upon with admiration. Strangers were shown it as a curiosity worth visiting. It is thus that two merchants of Marseilles are introduced into the Brothers' Schools of Avignon. On their return, so highly did they speak of the "discipline of the schools, the piety of the masters, and the novelty of the method,"[2] that they induced their townsmen to establish similar schools, which in their turn also became the admiration of all who witnessed their working.[3]

---

[1] "The Popular Education of France," London, 1861, p. 15.

[2] "Ravelet," p. 369. What especially struck the Marseilles merchants was the manner in which a large number of children was taught altogether and at the same time, with very few words on the part of the masters.

[3] Ibid., p. 383.

This method, as practised by the Brothers to-day, is still the same in principle with that taught by their Blessed Founder. The requirements of the present may have enlarged the course of studies; the accumulated experiences of two centuries may have modified some details and added others; but the broad outlines and working principle have remained unchanged. Speaking of the teaching manual of La Salle, Ravelet says with truth:

"If we take a recent copy of this little book, and go back from edition to edition up to the first type, noting in each what has been suppressed or added, we shall be astonished to find how almost alike the latest one is to that emanating from the founder's hands. The rules are the same; the hints and counsels are the same; the expressions, many of them, are the same. In these latter days more stress is laid upon developing the child's intelligence and making less use of mechanical processes. The minds of our children, having in their present environments an earlier development than those of children formerly, admit of this amelioration; but withal the principle of the method has not changed. La Salle had at first glance discovered all that should be done, and there remained but to follow in the path traced out by his genius."[1]

Not that La Salle did not make a careful study of the schools and methods within his reach, and take from them whatever he found good and useful. His was too practical a mind to do otherwise. We are told in the earliest edition of the school-manual that has come down to us — that of 1724 — how from

---

[1] "Histoire du Vénérable J. B. de la Salle," Ed. 1874, pp. 260, 261.

time to time hints and suggestions were adopted, according as the work progressed and the Brothers were gaining experience, and his own observations multiplied. In 1708, he writes to Brother Gabriel Drolin in Rome, asking for information concerning the rules, management, and government of the Piarist schools there established by St. Joseph Calasanzio.[1] In 1714, we find him stopping over at Lyons for several days, in order to examine the working of Charles Demia's schools.[2]

We take in hand the latest English version of Blessed de La Salle's admirable school-manual. We open it at the fifth chapter, dealing with teaching and method. We there find, within the compass of eight pages, as clear, concise, practical, and efficient a body of rules for teaching with method and drawing out the intelligence of the child, as can be found in the whole range of the literature of pedagogy. First, we are told what method is, how it is based upon principles, and therefore not arbitrary ; how these principles "are grounded in the subjects to be imparted, and in the intellect to be taught." Then method in teaching is defined "to consist in the selection, arrangement, and employment of means and processes the most fitting to bring the minds of pupils in certain branches of study to a certain degree of development."[3] Already the student of Methodology has opened up to him a field of speculation on

---

[1] Ibid., p. 345.

[2] Ibid., p. 447.

[3] "Management of Christian Schools," New York, 1887, p. 31.

which volumes have been written and fruitful volumes still remain to be written. The practical rules for teaching with method are simply and concisely stated.

"The master who teaches with method observes the following rules: 1. He determines the relative intelligence of every child in his class. 2. He adapts his language and explanations to the general capacity of his class, and is careful never to neglect the duller pupils. 3. He makes sure that the pupils know the meaning of the words they employ. 4. He advances from the simple to the complex, from easy to difficult. 5. He makes it a special point to insist greatly on the elementary part of each subject; not to advance till the pupils are well grounded on what goes before. . . . 9. To state but few principles at a time, but to explain them well. . . . 10. To speak much to the eyes of the pupils, making use of the blackboard. . . . 11. To prepare every lesson carefully. 12. To place no faulty models or standards before the pupils; always to speak to them in a sensible manner, expressing one's self in correct language, good English, and with clearness and precision. 13. To employ none but exact definitions and well-founded divisions. . . . 18. To assert nothing without being positively certain of its truth, especially as regards facts, definitions, or principles. 19. To make frequent use of the system of question and answer." [1]

Then come twenty rules laid down concerning the mode of putting questions and receiving answers:

"Every question should be clear, brief, special, and adapted to the capacity of the pupils. . . . Questions should generally begin according to a

---

[1] "Management of Christian Schools," chap. v., art. ii., pp. 31-33.

certain order, so as to retain the connection of all the parts, and lead up to the proper development of the lesson; in recapitulations, however, this rule might be profitably departed from. . . . The pupils should be taught not to answer too hastily, but to reflect first on the question put to them. . . . When the master gives an answer it should possess the following qualities: it should be brief; it should be clear and exact; it should be adapted to the capacity of the average, and even of the most deficient pupil; it should express a complete meaning, independently of the question." [1]

The rules that we have omitted from these extracts are no less to the point. They all bespeak the same practical good sense. They reveal an intimate knowledge of boy-nature. Written to cover the requirements of men engaged in elementary teaching, the rules of this school-manual stand for all time, and are equally applicable to the teaching of higher studies. They are the same rules by which Blessed de la Salle prepared the sons of the noblemen who followed James II. to France for positions of trust in the land of their exile. They are the principles by which, under his supervision, his disciples made the boarding-school of St. Yon the most successful and advanced polytechnic school of its day. They are the principles with which he indoctrinated the young teachers he sent forth from the normal schools which he had established.

They prevail to-day in the workshops of St. Nicholas at Paris, and in those of the Catholic Protectory of New York; in the chemical laboratory

---

[1] "Management of Christian Schools," chap. v., Art. iv., pp. 35-38.

of the Brothers' house at Passy, and in the science room of their college at Tooting ; in their language courses at Cairo, and in their literary and philosophic courses at Manhattan. They prevail, above all, in the innumerable parish schools that the Brothers conduct the world over. They prevail in all the class-rooms of all the lay religious teaching orders of men and women, who have now more or less modeled their methods upon that of Blessed de la Salle.

They have become the principles which, I doubt not, are daily inculcated in this hall, and on which all sound teaching is conducted at the present day.

The Church, in crowning him Blessed, has most fittingly given to popular education a patron. He is the benefactor of the modern schoolmaster. He it was who raised primary teaching out of the ruts of never-ending routine, carried on in the midst of time-honored noise and confusion, and, in giving it principles and a method, made of it a science. He hedged in the dignity of the schoolmaster. He was the first to assert the exclusive right of the master to devote his whole time to his school-work. Prior to him, teachers, if clerics, were ecclesiastics with a varying round of parish-duties to perform likewise, or were students making their own studies for the priesthood ; if laymen, they sang at the public offices of the church, rang the bells and performed the functions of sacristan. Not that such functions were at all considered as degrading. On the contrary, in those ages of faith it was thought an honor to serve in the house of God in any the most menial

capacity.¹ Here was the usual formula of agreement to which the teacher subscribed:

"The aforesaid Gaillardet promises to teach reading, writing, ciphering, and plain-chant. . . . He
also obligates himself to ring the priory bells when
storms, tempests, or hail-showers threaten, and to
sing in the said priory during Advent and Lent."²

These terms sound strange to modern ears; but
they bring us nearer to, and throw light upon, other
times and other customs. The outside services were
distracting. They left little or no time for preparation of lessons. Blessed de la Salle, through much opposition and no small persecution on account thereof,
withdrew the Brothers from all such distractions. He
brought home to them that their calling was one
worthy of their whole energy and their undivided
attention. "The new institute set out with this
thought, that teaching is less a career or instrument
of fortune, than that it is the most elevated expression of the spirit of sacrifice and devotedness."³ Nor
is this all.

La Salle broke down the barriers of exclusiveness
that confined the schoolmaster to certain subjects,
beyond which he dare not go, to the detriment of
poor children. Thus, a decree of 1661 forbade the
teachers of elementary schools to instruct their pupils
in writing beyond the merest elements, without a

----

¹ Alain, "L'Instruction Primaire avant la Révolution," p.
132.

² L. Maggiolo, Art., Bourgogne, in Buisson's "Dictionnaire de Pédagogie."

³ De Charmasse, "L'Instruction Primaire dans l'Ancien
Diocèse d'Autun," p. 41.

writingmaster's license; while on the other hand writingmasters were also restricted in their subjects.[1] By ignoring these distinctions, introducing the modern, simple, and more efficient method of writing, and enlarging the whole course of popular instruction, Blessed de la Salle drew upon himself and his disciples the enmity of the writingmasters, and emancipated the youth of France from their thraldom. Still more: in making, for the first time in the history of education, the mother-tongue the basis of all instruction, he appealed to the intelligence of the child, prepared the way for the study of national literature, and opened up to the grown man avenues of knowledge and amusement that had hitherto been encumbered with rubbish. His was the merit of the pioneer. And if to-day the artisan and the workingman, the world over, can read and write and discuss intelligently all the political and social issues of the hour, they owe it in great measure to the method of teaching completed and perfected by Blessed de la Salle and his disciples, the Brothers of the Christian Schools.

---

[1] Ch. Jourdain, " Histoire de l'Université de Paris," p. 215.

BEGINNINGS OF THE NORMAL SCHOOL

I.

FOR more than half a century Dr. Henry Barnard has been active in sowing broadcast the seeds of educational wisdom. "Declining numerous calls," says a friend and admirer, "to high and lucrative posts of local importance and influence, he has accepted the whole country as the theatre of his operations, without regard to State lines, and by the extent, variety and comprehensiveness of his efforts, he has earned the title of the American Educator."[2] He went abroad and studied the educational systems and the educational methods of the various countries of Europe, and returned laden with the experiences of the older civilization. He explained to his countrymen what was being done for all grades of education in France and Germany, in Italy and Austria and Switzerland, and England and Ireland; he brought home valuable documents giving facts and figures and suggesting improvements in methods. Nor did he confine his observations to state institutions. He also sat on the benches of the schools conducted by the Jesuits and the Christian Broth-

---

[1] "Normal Schools, and other Institutions, Agencies, and Means designed for the Professional Education of Teachers." By Henry Barnard, Hartford.

[2] John W. Stedman in the *Massachusetts Teacher*, January, 1858.

ers, and found much to admire in their educational methods, and without prejudice revealed the secrets of their great success. He went back to the educational traditions of the early Christian schools, and feared not to speak the truth, so far as he knew it, concerning the efforts of the Catholic Church to preserve learning and maintain schools during the ages of violence through which she was striving to civilize the barbarians who overran Europe. Pamphlet after pamphlet and volume after volume has he issued, embodying the past and the present of educational reformers and educational schemes, for the study and reflection of American teachers. This was a noble work, and nobly and well, according to his lights, did Dr. Henry Barnard perform it. All educators, knowing the man and his work, knowing the devotedness and the singleness of purpose with which he labored during the past fifty years, will agree that he is worthy of any recognition, no matter how emphatic.

The present volume on Normal Schools occupies 659 closely printed pages. It makes a survey of the workings of teachers' seminaries in Europe and the United States, and gives a rapid historical sketch of their establishment in various countries. We in America borrowed our conception of the normal school from Germany, but the idea was conceived long before Germany had begun to make it a reality. As Dr. Barnard has not traced the origin and growth of the professional school for teachers, it may be of interest to do so and afterwards dwell upon the scope and function of such an institution.

II.

To every thoughtful teacher, in every age and clime, there must have frequently occurred the all-important question, " How can I best convey instruction to my pupils?" And every successful teacher, after much experimenting and overcoming many difficulties, has managed to hit upon the method best suited to his talent and temperament on the one hand, and on the other to the capacities of the children under his charge. With religious orders, from the days of St. Benedict to the present time, teaching has held an important place, and educational traditions embodying the combined experiences of several successful members were handed down from generation to generation, and acted upon and developed to a certain extent.

A century after the time of St. Benedict we find the Benedictine Common Rule insisting that the master who instructs the young religious shall be skilful.[1] Alcuin did much in his day to simplify instruction ; on one occasion we come upon him giving the Archbishop of York a leaf out of his experience as regards the best method of dividing and grading the classes of a school. Later on, educational traditions are carefully cherished by the Brothers of the Common Life. Both John Sturm and the Jesuits learned from them many points in their systems of instruction. It is amusing to hear Sturm, forgetting

---

[1] Cap. i. See Mabillon," Études Monastiques," Paris, 1691, p. 47.

the common source, speak of the method of the Jesuits as "a method so nearly like ours that it appears as if they had copied from us."[1] Now, while we would not detract one iota from the merits of Sturm as an organizer and educator, we must confess that we look upon the Jesuits as the legitimate depositaries of the traditions in which Thomas à Kempis was educated, for they were preservers of the faith that inspired "The Imitation," while Sturm was organizing an adverse force to destroy that faith.

Before the close of the sixteenth century the Blessed Peter Fourier of Mattaincourt, who possessed advanced ideas upon every subject to which he gave thought, prepared an admirable school-manual for the Congregation of Notre Dame, which sisterhood he had organized. Alain, speaking of primary education in France during the two centuries preceding the Revolution, says: "In reality, the first normal schools were the novitiates of the teaching orders established during the last two centuries."[2] But these methods and traditions did not become public property; they were confined exclusively to the members of the religious orders possessing them. Lay teachers had no share in them beyond the glimpses they got when receiving instruction as children. Lord Bacon saw the necessity of proper methods of teaching in his day, and wrote: "The art of well delivering the knowledge we possess is among the secrets left to be discovered by future generations."

---

[1] Barnard, "Education in Germany," p. 233.

[2] "L'Instruction Primaire en France avant la Révolution," p. 129.

When we undertake to seek in our educational literature the origin of the normal school we are met with vagueness and absence of documents. We turn to Buisson's " Dictionnaire de l'Éducation." This is on the whole a valuable work. Many of the articles are solid and trustworthy. Many also are mere rubbish. M. Buisson and some of his co-laborers have their intellectual vision limited by the Revolution; and so we are told in all seriousness that, in France, " this generous thought is due to the National Convention. . . . The history of normal schools dates from the year iii."(1795).[1] The school established by the Convention was most abnormal. The ablest men in France were installed as professors—that is, such as had escaped the guillotine. But these men had not the least conception of their duties. Laplace and Lagrange gave a few lessons in elementary mathematics, and then started off explaining to a bewildered class their most recent mathematical discoveries. The Abbé Sicard was named professor of grammar; but he was content to interest his class in the methods by which he taught his deaf mutes. Laharpe made literature the cloak with which to cover his political disquisitions against the Jacobins. And so on with the others. The young men learned anything and everything except methods of teaching. The courses have been published, and they are a standing monument to the inefficiency of the work done. Within a few months the school was closed. The Convention, judging from the failure, could not

---

[1] T. ii.,p. 2,058.

appreciate the value of such an institution, and voted against the establishment of normal schools in each district as chimerical. Fifty years before this vote was taken Hecker had demonstrated the success of normal schools in Stettin and in Berlin. But the first conception of the normal school of which we have any record dates one hundred and fifty years back of the foundation of Hecker's institution.

III.

This conception originated with Richard Mulcaster. Mulcaster was for twenty years head-master of the Merchant Taylor's School, an experienced teacher, and a severe disciplinarian, to whom Fuller bears this testimony: "It may be truly said (and safely from one out of his school) that others have taught as much learning with fewer lashes."[1] He was favorably looked upon by Queen Elizabeth—his boys played twice before her—and was good-naturedly bantered by Shakespeare.[2]

Edmund Spenser was under him, and imbibed some of his enthusiasm for English literature. Now, in 1581, Mulcaster published a valuable work on education, known as "Positions,"[3] in which, through much clumsiness of diction and no small share of

---

[1] "Worthies," vol. ii., p. 431.

[2] "I protest the schoolmaster is exceeding fantastical; too too vain; too too vain."—Love's Labor Lost, act v., sc. I.

[3] The full title is: "Positions wherein those primitive circumstances be examined, which are necessary for the training up of children, either for skill in their booke, or health in their bodie." 1581. A facsimile edition of this volume was reproduced by Mr. R. H. Quick in 1887. It is from this edition we quote.

pedantry, abound many wise suggestions. Among others does he suggest in his own awkward manner, and with apology as though he were too bold in his views, that a way might be found for the establish- ment of a seminary for excellent masters, either with- out or within the universities. He throws the hint out with the hope that the more it is thought of the better it will be liked.[1] The suggestion was beyond the reach of the educators of his day and generation. All the more credit be his for having conceived and expressed it.

The next allusion made to such an institution oc- curs in the annals of the University of Paris. At the beginning of the reign of Louis XIV. there was found to be a great lack of competent professors for the large number of colleges then existing in Paris. And so we are told that in October of the year 1645 the rector, Doumoustier, " occupied with the best means of encouraging vocations for professorships,

---

[1] We here give this remarkable passage in all its quaintness of expression: "There were a way in the nature of a seminary for excellent masters in my conceit, if reward were abroad, and such an order might be had within the university: which I must touch with licence and for touching crave pardon, if it be not well thought of, as I know it will seem strange at the first, be- cause of some difficulty in performing the devise. And yet there had never been any alteration to the better, if the name of alteration had been the object to repulse. This my note but by the way, though it presently perhaps do make some men muse, yet hereafter, upon better consideration, it may prove very familiar to some good fantasies, and be exceeding well liked of, both by my masters of the universities themselves and by their masters abroad. Whereby not only schoolmasters, but all other professors also shall be made excellently able to perform that in the commonweal which she looketh for at their hands when they come from the university. '—" Positions," pp. 236, 237.

proposed to raise at the expense of the university a certain number of poor and promising children, who might afterwards become regents or professors."[1] But the suggestion remained fruitless. Doumoustier's was a voice crying in the wilderness. Forty-odd years later another voice is raised, this time in the shape of a petition to Louis XIV., coming from M. de Chennevières, who styles himself "a priest serving the poor—*prestre servant les pauvres.*" In a rather prolix style this zealous priest advocates the establishment of what he calls seminaries for schoolmasters and schoolmistresses in every diocese of France, for the good of religion and the benefit of the state.[2] The memorial bears no date, but there is internal evidence that it was written after the revocation of the Edict of Nantes. It remained unheeded.

But when this good priest was indicting his memorial the experiment had already been made. Shortly after Blessed de la Salle had organized the Brotherhood of the Christian Schools, the fame of the schools taught by them in Rheims spread far and wide. Their wonderful method of teaching was the subject of loud encomiums. Several of the clergy in the towns and hamlets applied for a single Brother to take charge of their schools. This could not be, as the founder had established the rule that not less than two Brothers teach in any school. Accordingly, he offered to open, under the title of a

---

[1] Jourdain, "Histoire de l'Université de Paris," p. 157. Quintane records the original Archiv. M. Reg. xvii., fol. 361. This MS. is now to be found in the Library of the Arsenal, Paris.

[2] Alain. loc. cit., p. 128.

seminary for schoolmasters, an institution in which young men would be trained in the principles and practices of the new method of teaching. The school was opened in 1684. The clergy sent thither intelligent and virtuous young men, and Blessed de la Salle soon reckoned twenty-five under his direction.[1] This was the first normal school ever established.

About the same time the Duc de Mazarin, nephew of the great cardinal, having consulted Blessed de la Salle in regard to carrying out the pious intentions of his uncle, was advised by the servant of God to found a normal school similar to the one then established in Rheims, for the training of teachers for every town and hamlet upon his vast estates. The duke had visited the Brothers' schools, had admired their methods, and hastened to meet the wishes of Blessed de la Salle. Accordingly, in a deed of contract testified to before the notary at Rethel, we find the duke agree to endow seventeen burses in perpetuity for young men "destined to be instructed in the true maxims of Christian pedagogy, as also to read, write and sing well, in order that they may afterwards teach the youth throughout the burghs, villages and hamlets in the Duchy of Mazarin."[2] The school was to be directed by two competent Brothers deputed for the purpose by "the aforesaid Sieur de la Salle."[3]

---

[1] "Conduite admirable de Providence envers le Vénérable J. B. de la Salle." MS. in Archives of the Régime, Paris.

[2] Minutes de Me. Mistris, notaire à Rethel.

[3] Minutes de Maître Aubert, notaire à Renwiz, chef-lieu de canton (Ardennes). See "Vie du Vénérable de la Salle," par F. Lucard, t. i., p. 75.

This was a certainly noble work, and nobly and generously was it begun. But it was considered so new-fangled a notion, so great a departure from the old ways, so impracticable and unfruitful in its results, that it aroused opposition where opposition should have been least expected. Monseigneur Letellier, the bishop of Rheims, refused to sanction the work. When La Salle and the duke submitted to him their articles of agreement and asked his approval, the good bishop looked at them amazed, and gave vent to his feelings on the subject in memorable words, which history has preserved: "And so you are two fools—*Vous êtes donc deux fous!*" Other influences were brought to bear upon Mazarin; they prejudiced him against the scheme, and for a time his ardor cooled. The articles of agreement were annulled. But his better judgment again prevailed; again he sought La Salle. His vast territory extended beyond the jurisdiction of Monseigneur Letellier. The marquisate of Montcornet, also Mazarin's, was in the bishopric of Laon, and the bishop was a friend of both the noble lord and the eminent educator. He entered warmly into their project of establishing a normal school, and gave them sympathy and encouragement in the undertaking. Thereupon new articles of agreement were drawn up. The territory not being so extensive, the number of burses was reduced. The document goes over the same ground as the one previously annulled, and bears the date of September 22, 1685. We learn from it, furthermore, that La Salle solicited letters-patent for the establishment in Rheims "as well as for the normal school." [1]

Nor were these La Salle's only efforts to establish normal schools. In 1699 he opened one in Paris, in the faubourg St. Marcel. This had attached to it a poor school, in which the young masters were exercised in the practice of teaching under the guidance of an experienced Brother. In 1708, he opened another at St. Denis, which was the admiration of Cardinal de Noailles, deeply interested Madame de Maintenon, and caused Louis XIV. to grant the house, as a personal favor, exemption from having soldiers billeted upon it. [2]

The course of studies in these institutions included simply the branches taught in the elementary schools for which the teachers were preparing. When, in 1851, the government of France established primary normal schools throughout the kingdom, it laid down practically the same course. Here are both programmes:

1684.	1851.
Catechism.	Moral and religious instruction.
Reading of printed matter.	
Reading of manuscripts.	Reading.
Penmanship.	Penmanship.
Grammar and orthography of the French language.	Elements of the French language.
Arithmetic, including the system of weights and measures then in use.	Arithmetic, including legal system of weights and measures.
Plain chant.	Religious music.
	N. B.—In 1865, geography and the history of France were made obligatory in this course.

---

[1] M. Lepine. "Monographie du Marquisat de Montcornet." See "Vie du Vénérable J. B. de la Salle," par F. Lucard, 1874, pp. 41–46. See also "Annales de l'Institut des Frères des Écoles Chrétiennes, t. i., pp. 32–40.

[2] "Annales," t. i., p. 243.

Under the guidance of the saintly La Salle the young men possessed an advantage which the state schools could not supply. Their spiritual life was cultivated by prayer, meditation, spiritual reading, and daily conferences. The result was in keeping with the training. The rector of the Seminary of St. Nicholas du Chardonnet bears witness to the merits of four young men who had been trained for his schools:

"They went forth," he says, "so zealous and so well formed, that if the clergy with whom they were placed had cultivated the good dispositions with which they were animated, they might have established one of the most useful communities in the province. Both myself and my country are under never-ending obligations to M. de la Salle."[1]

Such, in brief, is the story of the establishment of the first normal schools. That which Mulcaster timidly alluded to one hundred years before, Blessed John Baptist de la Salle made a living reality. Withal the work of the great educator did not survive. It was the seed sown upon parched earth. It sprang up, soon to be nipped. In the meantime, the necessity of preparing teachers for their profession is dawning upon men's minds. As early as 1687 Des Roches established a normal school in Brussels.

Hermann August Francke, an educator whose name should ever be held in benediction, in 1697 organized at Halle a teachers' class, composed of poor students who assisted him in return for their board and lodging. From this class, in 1704, he selected twelve pupils who gave evidence of "the right basis

---

[1] " Vie de M. J. B. de la Salle," 1733, t. ii., p. 179.

of piety, knowledge, and aptness to teach." These he constituted his *Seminarium Præceptorum.* Their course of training ran through two years, and so great was his success in forming them hundreds flocked from all parts to witness and to study his methods.

In 1698, Frederick II., Duke of Saxe-Gotha, decreed that ten of the most experienced teachers in his duchy should assemble promising youths in their houses in order to initiate them into proper methods of teaching. The father of the normal school in Prussia was the eminent educator, Johannes Hecker. A disciple of Francke's, thoroughly imbued with his spirit, he was no less devoted as an educator. He established his first normal school at Stettin in 1735.

In 1748, Frederick the Great called him to Berlin, where he established another, and organized the schools of the city upon such a footing that they became the admiration of all Europe. The necessity of the normal school is again being felt in France ; and so we find Madame Guillard, a wealthy lady of Dunkirk, give in 1753 " eight thousand livres to the commune of Saint Waast, Pas-de-Calais, for the purpose of founding a novitiate in which might be formed good schoolmasters, whom the boys so sadly need."[1]

The idea spreads. It takes root in Hanover in 1757; it becomes transplanted in Brandenburg in 1767. Bishop Felbiger is deeply interested in the problem of education. While still a young priest, he hears of the wonders wrought by Hecker in Berlin.

[1] " Société des Antiquaires de la Morinie," t. ix., 2e partie, p. 28.

He visits the Prussian capital in order to see for himself ; he sees and is rejoiced ; he finds description to fall short of the reality ; and forthwith the Catholic priest sits at the feet of the Protestant educator and learns his methods. In this manner was cemented a life-long friendship between kindred souls. He returns to Sagan, and with renewed energy continues the work of regenerating his schools till they become models.

In 1764 the Royal Board at Breslau, under his advisement, decreed the establishment of normal schools in each province, to defray the expenses of which every newly-appointed pastor should pay the first quarter of his revenue ; and furthermore, that every newly-ordained priest qualify himself in a normal school so as to be able to direct and counsel the teachers of his parish ; and till such time as the normal schools are established that he repair to Sagan to familiarize himself with the reformed method as introduced by Felbiger.

So great was the bishop's reputation as an educator, he was called to Austria by Maria Theresa with the view of reforming the school system of the empire. In 1770, he organized a normal school in Vienna, with a special course of lectures and practice for teachers, extending over four months. When recalled to his native land, he had left the schools of Austria in a flourishing condition and with a uniform method—the Simultaneous Method of Blessed John Baptist de la Salle.

Thus it was that, two centuries from the first suggestion of the normal school—one hundred years after the first of its kind had become a reality—this institution came to be regarded, especially among the German-speaking nations, an essential factor in the work of education. Teaching was placed on a footing with other professions requiring a course of preparation. To-day, throughout the whole civilized world, the normal school is of primary importance. There are one hundred and fifty of them in the United States.

IV.

The Rt. Rev. Bishop Spalding has recently advocated the establishment of Catholic normal schools among us.[1] It is a want that must be supplied in the near future. He who so successfully sounded the necessity of a Catholic university and labored so arduously to see it become a reality, cannot bring his graceful pen or his eloquent voice to bear upon this greater want without evoking enthusiasm and coöperation in the work. It is only normal schools can give our Catholic teachers the standing and the aptitude for their profession that will insure them complete success. Handicapped, as they are, in so many ways, they need all the encouragement that can be held out to them to enable them to persevere in their noble though ill-paid and greatly slighted profession.

The day cannot be far distant when every bishop will consider a normal school as essential an institution in his diocese as a seminary for the priesthood. Without a special training in the science of education, our young men and our young women can rarely

---

[1] *The Catholic World*, April, 1890. Art., Normal Schools for Catholics.

become efficient teachers. From the lack of this training great injustice is done to our children. You will not let a carpenter attend to your plumbing, or a blacksmith mend your watch, but you will allow an inexperienced teacher, with no knowledge of method in his teaching, with no clear idea of what a teacher's duties are, with no conception of the onerous charge he assumes, to tinker with the intellect and character of your child. You may remedy the damage done by the unskillful artisan, but what human power can undo the injuries inflicted by an ignorant or incompetent teacher?

Now, one of the most efficient means of guarding against this disaster is the normal school. There the young teacher will learn how to prepare and how to impart his lessons with method ; how to pass from the simple to the complex, from the easy to the difficult ; how to review subject-matters till they are well known and clearly understood; how to awaken and direct the spirit of observation ; how to put questions that will cause the pupil to think. There he will be initiated into the psychology of education ; he will analyze the faculties of the soul ; he will learn how each may best be cultivated, and what subjects are best suited to strengthen and develop each without destroying any of the others ; he will learn how to exercise and improve the memory, how to exercise and improve the judgment and reason, how to exercise and improve taste and sentiment—in a word, every sense and every faculty. He will learn how to combine the various groups and orders of studies so as to produce the maximum result with minimum labor to himself and his pupils. He will learn how to economize mental force and energy, how to keep the child's brain in a state never idle and never fatigued ; he will learn the limitations beyond which a strain should not be placed upon the youthful mind. Then he will learn the discipline belonging to the class-room ; order, punctuality, cleanliness, carrying out the daily regulation with the greatest exactitude, and other such details as constitute an essential part of education. Therein he will study character and how to build it up ; how to take the various dispositions of children ; when to be gentle, when severe, and how to be always firm and uniform and impartial towards his whole class.

Much of this a clever young man or woman can acquire after some years' experience in the schoolroom, by closely observing and following the methods of older teachers ; but while the clever young man and clever young woman are gaining the experience, what is becoming of the generations of children passing under them? Have we ever reckoned the terrible expense at which that experience has been acquired? Have we counted the lives wrecked because the youthful character was ill-understood ; the numbers who abandoned school with a distaste for books and learning which accompanied them through long years, because teachers did not take the pains, or did not know how, to place before them in a clear and attractive manner the first principles of knowledge, and they were obliged to stumble through their lessons with scarcely a single ray of intelligence to light up their befogged minds; the numbers who contracted physical diseases because their teachers knew not how to regulate the air or the temperature of the class-room, or allowed the little chests of younger children to become permanently contracted from stooping over desks or keeping arms folded all day long—have we ever scanned this awful record? Valuable experience this of your untrained teachers! But calculate the holocaust, and then say if normal schools are or are not a pressing want.

M. GABRIEL COMPAYRÉ AS AN HISTORIAN OF PEDAGOGY

M. GABRIEL COMPAYRÉ AS AN HISTO-RIAN OF PEDAGOGY.[1]

I.

M. GABRIEL COMPAYRÉ seems to have given much attention to the subject of pedagogy. He has come to be a recognized authority, even amongst those who do not agree with his views, upon all matters pertaining to education. He has a happy manner of putting things. He writes well. In 1876, he gave out in two volumes a book detailing the doctrines and theories of pedagogy — that is, such doctrines and such theories as it suited him to weave out of the original materials—from the sixteenth century down to the present time. The work was written with an air of judiciousness that won the approval of the French Academy. M. Gréard reported upon it favorably and enthusiastically, and it was crowned. But the judiciousness was only assumed. The small

---

[1] *American Ecclesiastical Review.*

"Histoire Critique des Doctrines de l'Éducation en France." Par Gabriel Compayré. 2 vols. Paris, 1879.

"The History of Pedagogy," by Gabriel Compayré. Translated, with an introduction, notes, and an index, by W. H. Payne. Boston, 1886.

"Les Jésuites Instituteurs de la Jeunesse." Par Père Charles Daniel, S. J., 1880.

"Lehrbuch der Geschichte der Pedagogik." A. Stöckl. Mainz, 1870.

meed of praise sparingly doled out to any man or
woman, system, or institution knowingly Christian,
was wrung from the author because he was conscious
that among his judges were men truly learned and
truly critical, who could not be imposed upon by
grossly palpable misstatements. Withal, palpable
misstatements abound.

The volume which Mr. W. H. Payne has translated is a later work, and certainly no improvement
upon the larger and earlier one. It is simply a condensation of all the bile and virulence and hatred for
everything Catholic therein, but ill concealed beneath
a tone of philosophic moderation. It is the expression of extreme partisanship adapted to the audience
for which it was prepared. No longer speaking to a
dignified body of learned academicians, but addressing students who are taught to hate clericalism in all
its forms; who are in training to profit by the laici-
zation of the schools of France, and supplant religious teachers throughout the land; who are disposed
to swallow any calumny that may be administered to
them, and who are still too young and too ignorant
to unravel the sophistries into which the true and the
false are woven, M. Compayré excels himself in art-
ful misrepresentation. His book is superficial, un-
truthful to history, and shamefully misleading. It is
unfortunate that Professor Payne did not translate
some other manual for students. It is even damag-
ing to his reputation as a professor of pedagogy that
he should have found the book, in aught save the
mere technical form, an ideal book. "It represents
to my mind," he says, "very nearly the ideal of the

treatise that is needed by the teaching profession of this country." [1] Professor Payne has done the teaching profession of America a great wrong in placing in their hands such a tissue of misrepresentation, be it ever so gracefully woven. The teaching profession need not thank him for the boon. A glance at the spirit animating the book will make this clear.

To begin with: M. Compayré is unfair in his mode of presentation. When he would belittle, he closes his eyes to every merit; he accumulates isolated instances and calls them the rule; he unearths usages dead and buried, and blames those of the present for them; he rakes up a scandal here, a tid-bit of gossip there, a random assertion in another place, and upon them grounds some monstrous charge or lays down some general proposition. Where is the sense of fair play in such treatment? Why apply to an institution a different rule of criticism from that we would apply to an individual? Now, he who would know a man thoroughly would not be content with the account his enemies give of him. He would go to his friends as well. Acting otherwise, he would find himself grossly deceived in his conception and estimate of him he would know. Take a man of the most unblemished character. Let envy, or jealousy, or any other petty passion, or the whisperings of those slimy things of humanity, that besmirch men's good names, blind you to every merit he may possess; pry into his daily life, and pick out of it all that is weak and imperfect; dwell upon the divergencies of thought and action that tally not with your own conceptions;

_____
[1] " History of Pedagogy," Translator's Preface, p. vi.

pile together the blunders he may have made in a life-time; attribute to his every action, even that the most indifferent, a sinister motive; read a malicious meaning in his most innocent expressions, and you can finally succeed in convincing yourself and others that he who may be the most genial of friends and the truest of men is a monster unworthy to breathe the same air and bask in the same sunshine with your noble self. You no longer know the man as he lives and moves among men. Even so is it with an institution. And it is for just such treatment of institutions that we attach blame to M. Compayré.

Take the Society of Jesus. Was there ever a re-ligious order more deservedly the pride and glory of the Church? Its members live and move under the discipline of a well-regulated army in face of the enemy. They are equipped for the guidance of every condition of life. We find amongst them men learned in the sciences; men adept in the arts; men trained in the school of spiritual life. They are the body-guard of the interests of Jesus. They are fore-most in all good works. They seek by preference the post of danger. They are faithful sentinels, never caught sleeping, always on the alert to raise the alarm at the slightest note of danger, invariably the first to be attacked by the enemy. The Order is a marvelous embodiment of science and art, zeal and energy, all moulded under one will and guided by one aim. Great in its history, great in its devotedness, great in the great lights which it has given the Church and the world during the past three centuries, it is above all, great in its filial devotion to the Church and the singleness of purpose with which, at all times and under all circumstances, it seeks the greater honor and glory of God. And yet, we have seen the Society of Jesus blackened by men; we have seen it proclaimed in more than one language "that the Jesuits are down-right complete atheists;"[1] we have seen a pope forced to disband the Order and scatter its members to the four quarters of the globe. But we now know that the blackening was the slanderous work of black hate. It was the penalty paid by successful greatness.

Now, how does M. Compayré speak of the Jesuits as educators? He cannot abide them. He does not find in them a single redeeming trait. Every book that speaks in their praise is studiously ignored; every passage in their writings, every piece of gossip about their doings, that tells against them, and that he can lay hold of, is deftly woven into his narrative.

Their method is, in his estimation, false, superficial, laying stress upon forms rather than upon substance. "For the Jesuits," he says, "education is reduced to a superficial culture of the brilliant faculties of the intellect."[2] In their failures and in their successes, they are censured alike. Do they succeed in making college life agreeable to their students by means of sport, fencing, theatricals and other forms of recreation? Be it so; student life in a Jesuit col-

---

[1] The full title of the English version is; "A truth known to very few, viz:—That the Jesuits are downright complete atheists: proved such and condemned for it by two sentences of the famous Faculty of Sorbonne, well known to be the best divines of all the Roman Catholic party; and by the French bishops and Pope Alexander VII." London: T. Dawks, 1689.

[2] "History of Pedagogy," p. 139.

lege is still only prison life with the prison bars gild-
ed.[1]　Do they send out their young men polished,
refined, accomplished?　Thereupon we are told:
"They wish to train amiable gentlemen, accomplished
men of the world; they have no conception of training men."[2]　This sentence has about it an air of epi-
grammatic terseness.

But is it true that, in becoming accomplished,
one loses one's manhood; and if not, is not the expression simply rubbish?　Out of such stuff does M.
Compayré manufacture a history of pedagogy.　A
piece of gossip from Saint Simon is quoted to sustain the charge that in disciplining the students they
were respectors of persons.[3]　Upon a story told of a
young novice who received his mother coldly, this
monstrous assertion is built:　"The ideal of the perfect scholar is to forget his parents."[4]　From the ancient and time-honored rule of all mediæval college
life, that the students be required to converse in
Latin, the inference is drawn that the mother-tongue is
proscribed, and that the teachers of Voltaire, Bossuet
and Molière despise the French language and French
literature.[5]　Because the Jesuits do not teach in the

---

[1] Ibid.

[2] Ibid., p. 145.

[3] Ibid., p. 148.

[4] Ibid., p. 146.

[5] "History of Pedagogy," p. 144.　Among the regulations of the College of Troyes, bearing date of 1436 — that
is, 150 years before the Ratio Studiorum was constructed—
there is a rule insisting upon the speaking of Latin and prefer-
ring even bad Latin to French.　(Boutiot, "Histoire de l'Instruction Publique et Populaire à Troyes," pp. 21, 22.)　We
cannot forbear recalling here that Père Porée, to whom Vol-

poor-schools, therefore they despise the people and seek to keep them in ignorance ; for, according to this philosopher, " the ignorance of the people is the best safeguard of its faith." [1]

The children of the Revolution are indeed hard to please. To-day they tell us we want to keep the people in ignorance. A hundred years ago, they attributed all the ills of France to the fact that we educated too generally. If the University of Paris is brought to ruin, it is due to "the crafty liberality of the Jesuits in teaching the youth." [2] In 1762, the University of Bordeaux, in a memorial addressed to Parliament, gives as one of the signal causes of decadence in attendance "the infinite number of school-masters and heads of boarding-schools." [3] To the same cause the people attributed the falling off in trades and agriculture.

"The country would never flourish," said they, "whilst the rectors of schools remained. If the fields lack strong arms, and the number of mechanics diminishes, and the clan of vagabonds increases, it is because our burghs and villages swarm with schools." [4]

---

taire dedicated his Mérope, and of whom he elsewhere wrote : " His greatest merit was to make his disciples love virtue and letters " (Siècle de Louis XIV., " Ecrivains Français," p. 48). Père Porée taught Rhetoric for thirty years in Clermont College, and among his pupils counted nineteen members of the French Academy (Crétineau-Joly, " Hist. des Jésuites," t. iv., p. 227).

[1] Ibid., p. 155.

[2] " The Jesuits' Catechism, or Examination of their Doctrine," published in French this present year, 1602, and now translated into English. 1602. B. II., chap. iv., p. 87.

[3] Alain," L'Instruction Primaire avant la Révolution," p. 101.

[4] L. Maggiolo, " De la Condition de l'Instruction Primaire et du Maître d'Ecole en Lorraine avant 1789," p. 514.

La Chalotais fears the Revolution will have no chance of success for the tell-tale reason that education is too widespread. He says:

"Are there not too many writers, too many academicians, too many colleges? . . . There were never so many students . . . the people even want to study. . . . The Brothers have succeeded in spoiling everything; they teach children to read and write who should only know how to dig and carry the hod. . . . The well-being of society requires that the knowledge of the people does not extend beyond their occupation."[1]

Another child of the Revolution — Voltaire — thanks La Chalotais for these sentiments, with which he is in full sympathy: " I thank you for proscribing study among the laboring class."[2] And yet, these men are proclaimed the apostles of light, whilst the Jesuits and the Brothers are set down as the abettors of ignorance and paralyzers of brain-force.

In the same spirit and after the same truly original method M. Compayré discovers and reveals to us that the Jesuits disdain history, and especially the history of France. In a paragraph ominously headed, " Disdain of history, of philosophy, and of the sciences in general," we read: "No account is made of history, nor of the modern history of France." Now, this is a serious charge, and we naturally look for sustaining proof. M. Compayré gives his authority, and gives it in all seriousness. It is a piece of hearsay, anonymously quoted: "History," says a Jesuit

---

[1] " Essai d'Éducation Nationale," 1763, pp. 25, 26.

[2] Jules Rolland, " Histoire Littéraire de la Ville d'Albi." 1879. See also the article of M. Brunetière in the *Revue des Deux Monde*, Oct., 1879.

Father, "is the destruction of him who studies it."[1] It matters little to M. Compayré which one of the ten thousand Jesuit Fathers now living, or of the ten times ten thousand that have lived during the past three centuries, made use of the imbecile expression. A Jesuit Father has said so ; therefore all the Jesuits hold by it, and teach their pupils to despise history. Such reasoning needs no comment.

However, we find a charge of the same nature made against the colleges of France generally in the seventeenth century. Louis XIV., through his minister Colbert, complains that the students "learned at most only a little Latin, and were ignorant of geography, history, and nearly all the sciences that avail for business purposes."[2] But so far as the Jesuits are concerned, Père Charles Daniel, in a very instructive little book, has triumphantly refuted the charge. He has shown how Jesuit Fathers—Sirmond, Petau, Labbe, Du Cange, Baluze—have taken the lead in historical studies ;[3] how Jesuit Fathers—Riccioli, Grimaldi, Delisle—advanced geographical and astronomical researches ;[4] how Jesuit Fathers—Daniel, Griffet, Bougeant, Longueval, Berthier—unearthed documents bearing upon the history of France, and laid the foundation of the modern school of historical criticism.[5]

---

[1] "History of Pedagogy," p. 145.

[2] Ch. Jourdain, " Histoire de l'Université de Paris au XVII et au XVIII Siècle." Paris, 1867, p. 239.

[3] "Les Jésuites Instituteurs de la Jeunesse Française," chaps. ii., iii.

[4] Ibid., chaps. iv., v.

[5] Ibid., chaps. x., xi.

And after all this had been written in direct refu-
tation of M. Compayré's statements, M. Compayré
still repeats the same old story, and Professor Payne
has not a word of protest to enter.   But we know the
source whence M. Compayré has imbibed his inspiration.   It is from a work which purports to be a translation of the Constitutions and Declarations of the
Society of Jesus.¹   Both the preface and the appendices are written in a spirit of hostility.   In the former
we are told that these rules are the outcome of pious
zeal on the one hand, which is the inspiration of the
saintly Loyola, and of a thoroughly Machiavellian
policy on the other hand, which is the inspiration of
the plotting Laynez.²   In the appendices are to be
found chapter and page for many of the accusations
quoted both in the smaller and the larger work of M.
Compayré.³   It is a book according to his thinking,
but it is also a book upon which no man with a reputation for historical accuracy could rely, and retain
his reputation.⁴

---

¹ " Les Constitutions des Jésuites avec les Déclarations."
Paris, 1843.

² Ibid., Pref. p. viii.

³ Cf. " Histoire critique," t. i., p. 196, and " Les Constitutions," appendix, in the " Ratio Studiorum," p. 436.   Therein
is also to be found allusion to the gossip of Saint Simon.

⁴ It is phenomenal to note the persistency with which fair-
minded men instinctively rely upon the avowed enemies of the
Jesuits for views and opinions concerning their methods.   We
have before us a short history of pedagogy, modeled after the
French volume of Paroz—"A History of Education," 1887,
from the pen of Professor Painter of Roanoke College—and
the author sketches the Jesuits' principles of organization according to the " Provincial Letters " of Pascal (p. 167).   Herein
he is following Raumer.   Further on (225) the Professor names
Fénelon among the adherents of Jansenism!   And this is the
kind of information our American teachers are given as history.

II.

In proportion as the Jesuits are abused, are the Jansenists of Port Royal praised.[1] We will not stop to inquire how far the praise is merited; or whether, had the Jansenists of Port Royal continued docile children of the Church, they would have Cousins and Sainte-Beuves to eulogize them. Père Daniel has shown how much they borrowed their methods from their Jesuit antagonists. M. Compayré is no less enthusiastic over Luther, whom he represents as a great creator of schools and systems.[2] Far be it from us to deprive Luther of the credit of any good act of his life. He did interest himself greatly in schools. He had a just and an exalted appreciation of the schoolmaster. "Were I not a minister," he said, " I know of no position on earth which I would rather hold."[3] But while Luther respected the schoolmaster, and gave primary education rules that were only a repetition of what Councils had decreed, he introduced into educational matters no new principle. Here is the program of studies for primary schools, which Melanchthon had drawn up, under the eye of Luther, in 1527:

"The master should explain simply and clearly the *Pater*, the Creed, the Ten Commandments, and inculcate the principles of politeness. He should teach reading, writing and singing."[4]

---

[1] " History of Pedagogy," pp. 139 *sqq.*

[2] Ibid., p. 119.

[3] Stöckl," Lehrbuch der Geschichte der Pedagogik," p. 211.

[4] See E. Rendu, " De l'Instruction Populaire dans l'Allemagne du Nord," p. 11.

Luther would have boys attend school only two hours, and girls only one hour a day.

"My idea," he says, "is not to create schools like those we have had, where twenty years were spent in studying Donatus and Alexander without learning anything useful. . . . A boy should pass one or two hours a day at school, and let him the rest of the time give himself to learning some trade in his father's house. . . . So also should girls give an hour a day at school."[1]

All this does not show a very high conception of public primary education. He laid greatest stress upon the Latin or secondary schools.[2] But in all that Luther said or wrote about education, he was only remembering what he had learned in his native town or with his Augustinian masters. He recognized the importance of schools; he attempted to awake interest in them ; but men were too busy with religious controversy, or engaged in wars, to give much heed to his warnings. However, the intellectual activity begotten of the Reformation led both Protestant and Catholic to renewed efforts in behalf of schools. Both parties looked to the schoolroom as the final battle-ground. Both sought to possess themselves of the child and mould its soul into their respective forms of belief. Hence the deep interest evinced in popular education both in Protestant Germany and in Catholic France during the sixteenth century. In

---

[1] "Schrift an die Rathsherren." 1524.

[2] Stöckl., loc. cit., p. 211. For the school-plan of Luther and Melanchthon, see Dr. Henry Barnard's "Memoirs of Teachers and Educators in Germany," pp. 169–172.

This book is largely a translation of Raumer's "History of Pedagogy."

the seventeenth century interest flagged, and in France the primary schools were in a wretched condition when Blessed John Baptist de la Salle came upon the scene and organized his Brotherhood.

And what has M. Gabriel Compayré to say of these educators of the people? He has, indeed, a kind word for La Salle, and seems to appreciate his greatness of soul. Withal he shows but little sympathy for the disciples of La Salle. We recognize the ring of his accent. He speaks by the card. He finds fault with the Brothers and their methods, because to find fault with them is the fashion of the hour. They are in the way. The Jesuits were abused for not teaching the children of the people; the Brothers are abused for teaching them the trades, because, forsooth, such industries take bread from the workingmen's mouths.[1] When the Brothers were confided the normal schools of France, it was called a Machiavellian design. When they established boarding-schools and houses of higher studies, they were called ambitious and designing.

No matter what they do, their motives are impugned and their actions criticised by the party now dominant. Do Brothers, like the late Brother Ogerian, dare cultivate the talents that God gave them, and by their writings conquer for themselves an honorable position in the domain of letters or science? Forthwith they are censured as men who have stepped outside their sphere, as though educators could be too well informed, or professors too advanced in the

---

[1] See Meunier, "Lutte," p. 83. A vile book, which seems to have inspired more than one idea in M. Compayré's works.

knowledge of their subject-matter.[1]   In their historical text-books do they describe the horrors of the
French Revolution in their naked reality?   They are
called unpatriotic.[2]   Do they keep order in school?
At once they are set down as repressing the natural
feelings of children.

M. Compayré finds fault with the silence which
the Brothers cause to be observed in their classes.
How is a teacher to instruct a large class of pupils if
he is not sparing in his own words and does not insist upon silence on their part?   How can children
learn in a class which is a Babel?   All other things
equal, he is surely the best teacher who can command
order, and whose words are few and to the point.

That is the best method by which these conditions
obtain.   We defy M. Compayré to state a better one.
But M. Compayré, like a true philosopher, goes back
of the order and silence, and in doing so makes a
wonderful discovery.

" Is there not," he asks, "in these odd regulations,
something besides the desire for order and good conduct—the revelation of a complete system of pedagogy which is afraid of life and liberty, and which,
under pretext of making the school quiet, deadens
the school, and in the end reduces teachers and pupils to mere machines?"[3]

Unfortunately for M. Compayré, that which he

---

[1] Brother Ogerian died at Manhattan College, in 1869.   He
was greatly esteemed by Agassiz.   He was member of the
Institute of France, officer of the Academy, and affiliated to
many other learned societies.   His chief work is the " Histoire
Naturelle du Jura," in four volumes.

[2] Meunier, loc. cit., p. 24.

[3] " History of Pedagogy," p. 266.

discovers is of his own hiding. Great is the power of a preconceived notion. To him who holds it, if to none others, it explains all things satisfactorily. That religious life is timid ; that it dreads the light ; that it is afraid of life and liberty; that it is palling: here is M. Compayré's preconceived notion, which he has projected from his brain into the order and silence and discipline of the Brothers' class-room. But religious life has none of these fears ; religious men have made great sacrifices in their search after the light ; they have died for truth and liberty. And is activity deadening? Is it deadening to be about one's duty, doing one's task and nothing but one's task? Where does the machine-work enter into a silent and orderly class-room?

Suppose for an instant, that, instead of the order and silence now maintained in the Brothers' schools, there were disorder in every class, no regular plan of studies, no text-books ; that the Brother spoke loud and indistinctly, and did not wait for an answer ; that he boxed the boys' ears right and left ; that he ran about the class like a madman, with no necktie, without a coat, and his long shirt-sleeves hanging down over his loosely waving arms and hands. Suppose this picture given of La Salle or any of his disciples, would M. Compayré find in it aught to admire? Would he have words of commendation for the Brothers? Well ; the picture we have drawn is no caricature ; it is the faithful description of a loving disciple. It is the portrait that Ramsauer has left of his master, Pestalozzi.[1] And yet M. Compayré finds in

[1] See Oscar Browning, " Educational Theories," pp. 156, 157.

Pestalozzi the alpha and omega of educational perfection.

It is true that in the hands of an unscrupulous
teacher, who would take the least possible trouble
with his class; who would not interest himself in the
wants of each pupil; who would therefore not give to
his lessons the thorough and persistent preparation
that they demand, the Simultaneous Method might
become a piece of mere machine-work. But what
evidence or authority has M. Compayré to infer that
the teaching of religious men and women is of this
unscrupulous character? As men and women, they
know, as well as their censor, that it is a duty and
obligation for them to prepare the lessons they give,
well and thoroughly, even though it be the tenth or
the twentieth time that they impart the same lessons.
As religious men and religious women, this duty is
doubly binding. No teacher worthy of his sacred
calling—and there is not in this world among human
callings a more sacred one than that of moulding souls
to higher and better things—will give his pupils to
drink from the stagnant pool when he can control the
running waters of knowledge.

Professor Payne, not content with the amount of
misrepresentation made in the original work, adds his
share. He says:

"The scarcity of teachers and the abundance of
pupils led to the expedient of mutual and simultaneous instruction. Whilst this method is absolutely
bad, it was relatively good."[1]

This is a rather meagre account and a totally false

---

[1] "History of Pedagogy," p. 277.

estimate of one of the greatest discoveries of modern times; for as such do we look upon the Simultaneous Method. It is this method that has made popular primary education a possible thing. It has enabled us to reduce instruction to a science. It has drawn order out of chaos. It is the only method used the world over at the present day. It is the only method Professor Payne himself makes use of in his daily lessons. Even M. Compayré has here been forced to admit its importance. Speaking of its introduction by Blessed de la Salle, he says:

"It was also an important innovation to renounce individual instruction — which was given by the teacher in a low voice, in the midst of a turbulent class, to pupils called up one after another—and to substitute therefor the only method of teaching applicable to public instruction; namely, the Simultaneous Method."[1]

This is a candid admission. M. Compayré considers the simultaneous the only method of teaching applicable to public instruction. M. Compayré is now speaking the language of common sense and sound educational experience. But how shall we characterize the language of Professor Payne, when he calls this same method "absolutely bad"? We shall leave master and man to settle the difference.

III.

We find many other statements to quarrel with in this book of misrepresentation, but we have said enough to show the animus of the author. After all,

---

[1] "Histoire critique des Doctrines de l'Education en France," t. ii., p. 333.

we seem to have abandoned the subject of pedagogy entirely into the hands of our non-Catholic brethren. In Turin, in Rome, in Florence—in all the state universities throughout Italy—in all the leading universities of Germany and France—in Cambridge, England, and the Johns Hopkins, America—we find chairs of pedagogy, and the professors are active, and the work they put forth is, in some respects, admirable. How few—if any—of our Catholic universities have a chair of pedagogy? How few are aware of the vast proportions to which education, as a science, has grown within the past two or three decades?

As a science, education is based upon psychology and moral philosophy. Now, anybody knowing the modern drift of these two subjects can easily infer what distorted pedagogical theories may be constructed upon a psychology without the human soul and an ethics without God. And yet, what are we doing to counteract these irreligious views, applied to the young intellect where they are calculated to effect a most radical change? Will the Buissons and the Compayrés continue to write our histories, and formulate our theories of pedagogy? Children of the Revolution, they find all excellence, all modern progress, all educational reform growing out of that terrible upheaval. Inimical to the Church, they can see nothing good come out of Nazareth.

Aspects of things taken from such a vantage-ground must needs be distorted. History written in such a spirit, becomes woefully misleading. To us Catholics it is a matter of profound regret that the field of pedagogy in the United States should begin

to be cumbered with such briars and thorns.   It is
our own fault.   The past is ours, but we treat it shamefully.   We neglect it ; we let its sacred memory be en-
veloped in a growth of rank weeds, that hide or efface
its noble records ; we permit its deeds to be misrep-
resented, its honor to be stained, its glory to be tar-
nished ; and scarcely—or if at all, in feeble accents—
do we enter protest.   We allow our enemies to
usurp ground that by every right and title should
be ours.

In the whole domain of pedagogy, what Catholic
works in the English language are within 'our reach ?
They are easily named.   There is that admirable
work of Theodosia Drane, a Dominican Nun.   It is
called " Christian Schools and Scholars." [1]   It is charm-
ingly written, and is well calculated to give an exalted
idea of the work of the Church in the education of
Europe.   But it is mainly literary rather than pedagogical.

We have the " Life of Bernard Overberg," trans-
lated from the German of Krabbe, by the humble
Passionist, the Hon. and Rev. George Spencer.[2]
There is a Protestant version prepared by Schubert,
who simply re-wrote Krabbe's book, omitting the
Catholic portions; this has also been translated.
Overberg (1754–1826) was a devoted priest, rector of
the Seminary of Munster, and head of the Normal
School.   He was one of the greatest educators of
his day.   Father Spencer's life is an ennobling vol-

---

[1] Published, in two volumes, by Longmans, Green & Co.,
London.

[2] Derby, Richardson & Son, 1844.

ume, calculated to fire every teacher with love and zeal for the education of youth. It is out of print.

Another work is called "The Spirit and Scope of Education."[1] It is a translation from the German of Dr. Stapf. It is written in the spirit and according to the noble ideal that Overberg held of the teacher's mission. It is highly philosophical in its treatment of the relations of teacher and pupil; its psychological analysis is natural and simple ; above all, it is imbued with a truly Catholic tone. But the book is also out of print.

Rosmini left, in a fragmentary state, the first part of a great work on education. Like everything to which the saintly philosopher of Rovereto put a hand, this work was planned on a scale of vast proportions. Had the author completed his design, we should have a monumental work, showing the evolution of intelligence from infancy to maturity, under a guiding hand, through all grades of education. In the first part of this book, dealing with the child, he anticipated Froebel in many respects, and excelled him in others. This volume has been faithfully translated; for this we may thank a Protestant lady and a Protestant publishing house.[2] We also have an English version of the first part of Dupanloup's work on education. It is called " The Child," [3] and though lacking the depth of Rosmini's work on the same subject, is none the less suggestive reading.

---

[1] Published in Edinburgh by Marsh and Beattie, 1837.

[2] "Rosmini's Method in Education," by Mrs. William Grey. Boston. D. C. Heath & Co. 1887.

[3] Published by the Catholic Publication Society, New York.

We still require a history of methods. Perhaps the one that would give most satisfaction, and would be a valuable acquisition to the library of every Catholic teacher, would be a translation of Stöckl's " Lehrbuch der Geschichte der Pedagogik." Now that Dr. Stöckl is becoming better known to English readers through the elegant translation that Father Finlay of Dublin is giving them of his " History of Philosophy," this other supplementary work should be all the more welcome. Only by means of such works can we make right the falsifyings of slanderous books like those of M. Gabriel Compayré.